PROPHECY'S
END

ALSO BY RICHARD PHILLIPS

The Endarian Prophecy

Mark of Fire
Prophecy's Daughter
Curse of the Chosen
The Shattered Trident
The Time Seer
Prophecy's End

The Rho Agenda

The Second Ship
Immune
Wormhole

The Rho Agenda Inception

Once Dead
Dead Wrong
Dead Shift

The Rho Agenda Assimilation

The Kasari Nexus
The Altreian Enigma
The Meridian Ascent

PROPHECY'S END

THE ENDARIAN PROPHECY
RICHARD PHILLIPS

47N⬤RTH

Text copyright © 2020 by Richard Phillips
All rights reserved.

No part of this book may be reproduced, or stored in a retrieval system, or transmitted in any form or by any means, electronic, mechanical, photocopying, recording, or otherwise, without express written permission of the publisher.

Published by 47North, Seattle

www.apub.com

Amazon, the Amazon logo, and 47North are trademarks of Amazon.com, Inc., or its affiliates.

ISBN-13: 9781542014236
ISBN-10: 1542014239

Cover design by Shasti O'Leary Soudant

Printed in the United States of America

I dedicate this novel to my lovely wife of thirty-nine years, Carol. She has been and continues to be my lifelong inspiration.

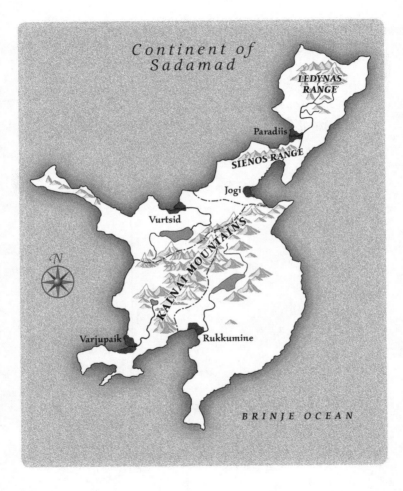

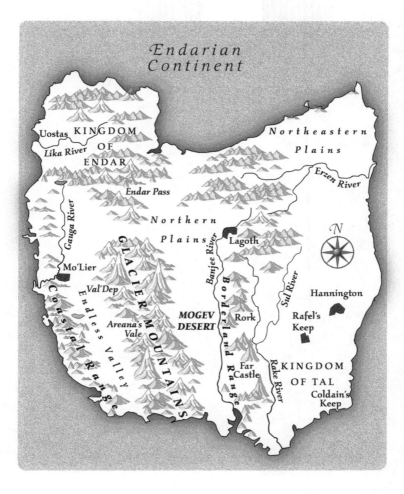

PART I

There are times when one of great ambition must betray those whom he holds most dear if he is to bring the impossible to pass.

—From the *Scroll of Landrel*

1

The spring equinox welcomed Kragan into the bay, ushering in the new year with brilliant sunlight that glinted off the black-sand beach. The fading winter's last squall had washed it clean. He didn't wait for the half dozen longboats to be lowered from the Vurtsid merchant king's command ship. At his summons an air elemental lifted his four-foot-tall body into the air and carried him from the deck of the sea vessel across the harbor.

As his feet settled upon the Endarian coast, Kragan's tawny locks swirled about his face in the brisk sea breeze. He knelt to scoop up sand, letting the fine grains trickle out through his fingers. When Kragan rose to his feet, he turned to look at the longboats, filled with sailors whose strong arms propelled them across the gentle waves toward the spot where he waited.

The mummified fingers of amplification dangled from his necklace to touch the bare skin of his chest, giving an electric thrill. He knew intuitively at this point that magic was of three forms . . . time, life, and mind. And each of these forms had three branches, making nine magics in all.

The ability to contact and control beings from the elemental planes of fire, water, air, and earth was a branch of mind magic at which Kragan excelled.

These olive-skinned seamen didn't serve him out of loyalty. The sailors on the *Poklad* followed Kragan's orders because they feared him. When he had first boarded the ship, their captain had challenged Kragan. The seamen had watched Kragan magically sever the man's arms, legs, and head from his torso, dumping the collection of body parts into the Bay of Paradiis.

But now that Kragan had set foot upon the continent where he would retrieve the final three shards of Landrel's Trident, he needed followers whose loyalty he could rely upon implicitly. It would have been nice if he could continue to use the two hundred crewmen. That wasn't going to happen.

As the first of the boats entered the shallow waters by the shore, men leapt into the bay to pull them up onto the beach. When all six of the vessels were secured ashore, the tenscore sailors formed up before him, trepidation shining in their eyes. Kragan spread his arms wide.

"I offer fortunes beyond your understanding to those who would accompany me on my quest. Any who wish to go to your ship and return to Sadamad, walk back to your longboats. Those of you who will follow me of your own free will, stand in place."

For a handful of breaths, nobody moved. Then all but five of the men turned and hurried back toward the boats that would carry them back to the *Poklad*.

Kragan raised his right hand. Thunder from the clouds that boiled into the sky shook the ground as lightning crawled across the heavens. Kragan's magically amplified voice boomed out above the rumble and made the fleeing men halt, terror freezing them in place.

He stepped forward.

"And so, you reveal your true natures."

His gaze swept across the trembling figures, mentally separating the more muscular of the sailors from those of slighter build. Kragan shoved his cupped hand higher overhead, pulling energy from the storms that had blotted out the sun, summoning chain lightning that branched out to strike the sturdiest of the sailors. When he closed his upraised fist, half of the men lay dead on the sand. Only the weaker half remained.

The corpses of the five who had voluntarily stayed with Kragan lay at his feet. Kragan knelt before these, bowing his head slightly and touching his right hand to his brow.

"Loyal comrades, you shall be the first to rise."

Kragan stood and gazed out over the hundred stunned survivors, summoning the earth elemental Dalg with a thought. Liquefied rock flowed up through the black sand, wrapping the sailors' feet and binding them in place.

Kragan ignored their wailing and pleas for mercy. His left hand slid up to clutch a shard, one of the six mummified fingers that dangled from his necklace. He shifted his concentration from Dalg, summoning the necrotic life magic that coursed through his veins. Dozens of smoky tendrils writhed from his right hand. They crawled through the air to enter the noses of the surviving sailors, pulling forth screams as the men clawed at their own faces.

Ethereal snakes emerged from the sailors' mouths, each targeting a different corpse. The misty tentacles penetrated the bodies, creating a connection between living and dead. Kragan used the channel to siphon life energy until the standing sailors collapsed into limp heaps. All around them, their dead comrades struggled back to life.

Kragan released his grip on the shard that amplified his life magic, letting the smoky channels he'd created dissipate on the salt-laden breeze. Overhead, the sky cleared as swiftly as the dark clouds had gathered.

The sailors who had struggled from the land of the dead climbed to their feet. Their eyes roamed the bodies of their companions whom Kragan had sacrificed. He could see the confusion and anger in the eyes of the newly risen. They understood what he had done. Some of these hardy men of the sea wanted to attack him.

But they couldn't do it. Kragan had restored their bodies and faculties, but the return to life had come at a price. These men generally retained their free will, but his new servants' actions could never contravene Kragan's desires. They were the first recruits of the army he would build to conquer the kingdom of Endar and take the precious artifact that rested within the royal palace.

At the thought of his target, Kragan stroked the six shards from Landrel's shattered trident. His thoughts shifted to the blind witch who Landrel had prophesied would destroy him. Carol Rafel and her assassin husband had come far too close to bringing that ancient foretelling to fruition when Kragan had last invaded Endar.

His thoughts turned to Landrel. Thousands of years had passed since the time seer had found the mummified remains of the masters of each of the three forms of magic. Landrel had cut the thumbs, index fingers, and center fingers from the trio of dead wielders. From these shards he had constructed his trident of magic amplification, a weapon of such power that it would make its possessor a god.

But Landrel had been soft. The Endarian king had feared what he was becoming and had dismantled the trident and encased each of the nine fingers in a separate time stone. Then he had sent his sons and daughters to scatter them across the continents of Endar and Sadamad so that the trident would never be reassembled.

But now Kragan had collected and mastered six of the nine mummified shards. Only three more remained before he remade the trident. With that weapon in his hand, Kragan would be transformed into the true master of the nine magics. And everyone, in every land, would quail before him.

He stared out across the bay to where large waves roiled the surface of the Brinje Ocean. He sensed her presence, far away, yet she was determined in her pursuit.

A slow grin twisted his lips. The next time they met, Kragan would crush the sorceress with magic that not even she could imagine.

2

Merchant Ship **Laskovanie,** *Brinje Ocean*
YOR 416, First Day of the New Year

Lorness Carol Rafel leaned against the railing at the prow of the *Laskovanie*, her white eyes staring sightlessly ahead. Her left hand stroked her wolfish dog's head, sensing the sheer joy the animal felt at her mental and physical touch. With her sorcery she could see through Zaislus's eyes, and for that she was grateful.

Salt spray splashed her face and dampened her shoulder-length brown tresses as the bow of the sailing vessel cut through the white-capped waves. The sky was clear and bright, with the stiff breeze of this first day of spring billowing the sails and producing a sharp popping sound with each change of wind direction.

Arn stood at her side, clad in the formfitting black clothing that the Endarian queen, Elan, had gifted him. Two paces tall, her husband had a rangy build that always seemed coiled to strike. His eyes were brown, as hers had once been, and his curly locks framed an angular face. His black knife, Slaken, was belted to his left hip, and throwing daggers were sheathed along each thigh and in his leather boots. The assassin stood at ease on the heaving deck, his body long familiar with the moods of the ocean.

He glanced at his wife. Carol knew Arn regarded her as beautiful of body, heart, and soul. And still she had chosen to love him, an assassin who had killed hundreds of men, vorgs, and others. Who, as a troubled twelve-year-old orphan, had knifed a minor lord in Hannington's central square for beating a peasant woman. At the time the local magistrate had sentenced Arn to death, but on the day that he was scheduled to hang, Jared Rafel had watched the boy use his last words to curse the law that allowed a lord to beat a woman senseless only because he was of noble birth and she was not. Having uttered his condemnation, Arn stood defiantly as the noose was placed around his neck and drawn tight. Standing in the square that day, Rafel had seen something in the lad that caused him to step forward to intervene. At Rafel's request, King Rodan granted Arn a pardon, but only on the condition that the high lord take the boy into his house and assume responsibility for his behavior.

From the day that he had arrived at Rafel's Keep and been placed under Battle Master Gaar's harsh tutelage, the high lord had informed Arn that the stay of his death sentence remained in effect only at Gaar's pleasure. Seven-year-old Carol had observed Arn's training from afar, developing a fascination for the slender boy with brown eyes that flashed with fury. The battle master had set out to test the depths of Arn's character, rotating him among a trio of trainers in the martial arts, each seemingly determined to break the urchin's will.

Whenever she got a break from her own studies, Carol had slipped away to watch this strange, raging orphan. If he failed to perform to expectation, which was generally the case, his trainer assigned him after-hours duty, lifting heavy stones from one pile to another. Often Arn would stumble to his knees in exhaustion, but he always struggled back to his feet, forcing himself to complete the assigned task no matter how he bled from his falls. Sometimes he would glance up to see Carol watching him, his eyes unreadable. And in those moments she found herself longing to go help him, though she couldn't have lifted even one of the stones.

Over the months that followed, Arn grew taller, with wiry muscles that gave his slender body unnatural strength and quickness. While he became proficient with sword and staff, expertise with a bow eluded him. But put a foot-long knife in his hand and Arn seemed to dance with the gods themselves. Although his trainers continued to press him, their attitudes toward him gradually improved. Gaar took notice, on occasion inviting Rafel to observe the teen's sparring sessions.

With the recognition of Arn's growing prowess came greater privileges, including the right to accompany the high lord on mounted hunts. Over time the lord's interest in his young protégé changed to fondness, and then to a fatherly love like that which Rafel lavished upon Carol and her younger brother, Alan. Rafel took Arn into his house and made him family. But Carol's love for her adopted brother had eventually blossomed into something far greater.

A gust of sea breeze brought Carol back to the present. Four galleons trailed, two to either side of the *Laskovanie*, which formed the tip of the spear that made its way toward Endar. The small fleet carried more than a thousand male and female warriors who had shaved their heads and pledged themselves to the service of Lord Alan Rafel.

Carol shifted her dog's gaze to watch her brother. He stood bare chested, his great crescent-bladed ax slung across his back. Alan oversaw as the two hundred of his Forsworn aboard the ship executed their weapons drills on the main deck, aftcastle, and forecastle. His shaved head and thickly muscled body accounted for part of the aura that surrounded him, instilling terror in his enemies during battle. But it was the fury with which he wielded his ax that had cemented his legend as the Chosen.

"What are you thinking, my love?" Arn asked.

Carol shifted Zaislus to face him. The wind ruffled his curls, revealing the tip of his left ear, which a combatant had sliced to a point.

"Just focused on feeling, letting my mind rest for a change."

As she said it, her right hand moved to the small coin purse at her belt. The contact with the leather pulled forth the image of what lay within. She experienced frustration once again over her failure to discover what form of magic the skeletal shard amplified. Despite her best efforts during all these weeks at sea, she had learned nothing about its function.

Arn's eyes followed her movement before he shifted his gaze back to her face.

"You can't just will what you seek to happen," he said. "You'll discover the artifact's true nature in the course of time."

"Have you had a vision? Has your time-sight shown you that this will happen?"

"No. Not directly. I . . . just have a feeling that this is so."

Carol huffed out a breath, forcing herself not to grind her teeth.

"A feeling?" Carol placed both hands on his cheeks. "I need more than that. I need a clue."

"I'll try again."

"Using your own shard of the trident?"

Arn's jaw tightened and then released. Although her husband had continued to practice his time-sight, he'd been unable to see the most probable future events more than a few days out.

Arn had always displayed an uncommon degree of intuition, especially in a fight. But only in the last year had he learned that he possessed the ability to use the branch of time magic that granted foresight. Carol knew how he dreaded the lurking madness that the shard's amplification of his time-sight threatened to unleash, but her need drove her to push him.

"Kragan has six of the arcane fingers," she said. "We have two, but only yours works. I fear that unless we discover how to unleash my shard's power, we won't survive our next encounter with him. Your visions have hinted as much."

Arn leaned in and kissed her lips. When he pulled back, he nodded.

"I must do this alone."

"What?"

"In the past I used your ability to link our minds as a lifeline to find my way back to the present. I believe that anchor is limiting my ability to reach deeper into the web of futures spinning before us."

The chill of the sea sent a shudder through Carol's body.

"At least let me watch over you. If I think you've lost your way, I'll intervene."

"Not this time."

"Why?"

"Another feeling. If I don't fully commit myself to finding my own way forward and back, I'll fail."

A knot formed in Carol's gut.

"But surely we can—"

Arn reached out to place a gentle finger on her lips.

"Either we fully commit or we don't try. We've already seen that half measures don't work."

Carol looked at him through Zaislus's eyes, seeing in her husband's face a familiar fierce determination.

"When will you make the attempt?"

"At twilight." He paused. "I'd like to share the rest of the day with you."

Carol took his hand in hers and, squeezing it hard, led him back toward the ladder that led down to their cabin. And as she made that walk, she fought the fear that these were the last hours in which she would hold Arn in her arms.

—◊—

Kimber, princess of Endar, half sister of Lorness Carol Rafel, leaned against the railing, not far from where the helmsman worked the whip-staff that moved the tiller. A passing sailor set his hungry eyes upon her, not lowering them as Kim's gaze locked with his. Unlike Alan's Forsworn and the rest of Carol's companions, these hired merchant seamen owed Kim no fealty. And this was just the latest example of their encroachment on her personal space.

The ship lurched atop a swell, and the man staggered. His gaze shifted from her face as he attempted to right himself. Kim channeled a tendril of life magic, pulling just enough of the man's health into herself to make him clasp his stomach and drop to his knees. The contents of his stomach spilled from his mouth onto the deck.

She turned her back on the man, feeling the life energy seeking an outlet. A month ago, she would have had to release it to heal another. No longer. With subtle practice, she had developed the ability to store this extra life inside her body. If she made a small cut in her skin with her knife, that energy would flow into her wound, healing it swiftly.

Of more interest to her, she had discovered that if no wound presented itself, the stolen life energy would gradually burn its way out, enhancing her aura in the meantime. While she maintained this augmented state, all those upon whom Kim focused her talent found themselves drawn to her, unaware that she was the source of such feelings.

She had only recognized this variation of her arcane talent for life-shifting during the long weeks at sea, with nothing to do but think about her magic and experiment. Every person was more than just a beating heart and functioning organs. Each possessed a soul, be it fair or foul. And that essence could be tapped, just like health.

In many respects, soul exchange could be more dangerous than other forms of life-shifting. Kim had only begun to understand the process. It was more of an entanglement of spirit than a tapping. And if she channeled too much, she could find her soul inextricably bound to another.

Her mother's faint voice whispered at the back of her mind.

Those wielders of life magic who find themselves drawn to its necrotic branch are cursed. Wielders of spells that draw the life energy from sentient beings to heal or enhance someone else find themselves seduced by the very magic they channel. It becomes an addiction. That is why I, as queen, have forbidden its use.

Kim thrust aside the unwelcome thought. Lost in the life-glow that filled her with power, she moved to a better vantage point to watch Alan spar against his Forsworn warriors, three at a time. Having laid his crescent-bladed ax aside, he fought barehanded. Whenever he knocked or hurled one of his opponents to the deck, another rose to take the fallen combatant's place.

Alan had long since adapted to the ship's heaving and rolling motion, seeming to enjoy the dance. His torso glistened in the afternoon sunlight. Kim remembered the feel of those powerful arms around her as they had made love weeks ago.

Having defeated his latest challenger, Alan stepped away. Kim watched Kat put her hand on Alan and then sit down to share lunch with him. The two had eyes only for each other. The sound of their banter made its way to where Kim stood.

Alan's rejection of Kim's advances after their initial dalliance had grown from an annoyance into a low-boiling fury in her breast. Her half brother had made his choice. But during the weeks at sea, the seeds of a plan to reverse this error had sprouted in Kim's head.

Feeling the life magic surge within her, seeking a way out that she denied, the princess exhaled. Alan was still there for the taking.

―ᚠ―

Lord Alan Rafel looked up from his latest sparring session with one of the Forsworn on board the *Laskovanie* to see Arn and Carol, hand in hand, descend the steps that led into the forecastle, Carol's wolfish dog leading the way. He had the impression that he was watching two lovers desperately seeking solace in each other's arms before separation.

He felt a gentle hand on his sweat-drenched chest. Kat had stepped silently to his side. Her crystalline-blue eyes studied his face with the intensity of a hawk.

"What troubles you, Chosen?"

Alan released the breath he'd been holding, forcing a smile onto his lips.

"Just a passing fancy."

"It's time for lunch."

Alan glanced up at the sun, hanging in the sky a hand-span past noon. With a nod to his lover, he turned to call down to his warriors. His thousand-plus Forsworn followers firmly believed him to be the Chosen of the Dread Lord who ruled in the land of the dead.

Legend had it that the Chosen was destined to recruit the finest warriors to his side, but was cursed to lose nine of every ten in combat, adding their souls to the Dread Lord's army. Based upon his record in combat over the last two years, even Alan had come to believe the myth.

"Stand down. Take your repast, but be ready when I call you back to work."

"You heard the Chosen," yelled Quincy Long, the lanky swordsman whose wit often lightened Alan's mood. "When I'm done eating, so are you. We shall *not* make the Chosen call us back to our stations."

The sight of a sailor retching over the starboard rail pulled forth a worry that had been growing among the ship's crew over the last several weeks. An unknown illness had gradually spread among many of the *Laskovanie's* crew, seeming to hop from one to another. Although the afflicted seemed to recover rapidly, they repeatedly fell victim to something akin to seasickness, which left them weak and wobbly for a day or more.

What concerned Alan most was that none of the other ships in their small fleet showed any sign of the disease. Neither had any of his

Forsworn on board the *Laskovanie* fallen ill, nor had Carol, Arn, Kim, or Alan. The ship's crew had begun casting accusatory gazes at those who had apparent immunity. Rumors of Alan's curse began circulating among the seafarers.

Alan shook off the worrisome thoughts. He seated himself next to the aftcastle railing, facing Kat as she removed three portions of hardtack from her pack, handing him two of the dried biscuits. She filled two metal cups, then set her water pouch down between them.

Alan dipped the first of the rock-hard biscuits into the water. As he gnawed an end from the crust, Alan let his gaze linger on the lean, dangerous young woman. Like all his Forsworn warriors, she maintained her shaved head as a sign of the life vow she'd pledged to him. Although not classically beautiful, her firm features held an exotic allure.

Kat was the last of the Forsworn who had fought at his side atop the fortress wall of Val'Dep. All the others had fallen in battle, only to be replaced by other hearty souls who had come to believe in the legend of the Chosen and sworn their fealty.

The images of the friends who had fought and died alongside him flashed through Alan's mind. So many ghosts from his past weighted his shoulders with the responsibility for their loss. They haunted his dreams whenever he managed to sleep. He trained harder than anyone else, needing to make himself a better warrior, a better leader.

He looked out across the hundreds of warriors seated in tight groups spread out across the swaying ship's decks. Sailors moved among them, going about their crew duties, while others climbed through the rigging high up on the three masts. One heavily bearded man stood in the watch-basket they called a crow's nest, scanning the horizon through an extended far-glass.

"How far are we from the Endarian coast?" Kat asked between mouthfuls.

"Captain Namornik says that, according to the ancient charts, we still have a couple more weeks at sea."

"My feet ache for dry land. I'd rather sleep on cold stone than sway one more night in one of this ship's hammocks."

This brought a laugh from Alan.

"What little you've slept has been on the bunk in my cabin."

"I find it a bit narrow for two, especially with one as broad of shoulder as you."

"You can always sleep atop me."

"You're lumpy."

"I could sleep on top."

With a dismissive snort, Kat put away her cup and climbed to her feet, brushing crumbs off her leather clothes.

Quincy's stentorian yell sent the Forsworn moving back into their training formations. The efficiency of the collection of bald clansmen, Varjupaik soldiers, and recruits from the defeated armies of Jogi, Paradiis, and Vurtsid made Alan grin. With every passing day, his Forsworn warriors forged themselves into the weapon that he would wield against Kragan.

—⚏—

Prince Galad stood on the forecastle of the *Laskovanie*, his brown skin glistening in the salt spray as the wind whipped his long hair around his shoulders. He watched Kimber, worry furrowing his brow. He recalled her innocence when their mother had sent her to find High Lord Rafel and tell him she was his daughter.

Three decades ago, Jared Rafel, the commander of the army of Tal, had answered Queen Elan's request for aid in the Vorg War. The two had become lovers but had gone their separate ways after their joint victory over the vorgish horde. High Lord Rafel had never learned that he had an Endarian daughter.

Galad had offered to accompany his sister on her quest, but their mother had refused, saying that she needed her commander of the mist warrior brigade in Endar. But his worries for Kimber's safety had proved well founded. Despite the hundred members of the royal guard who had accompanied her on that journey, a large band of slavers had attacked her caravan. Every Endarian guardsman had died trying to defend their princess.

Kimber had been captured and sold at auction to the infamous she-vorg commander Charna. But three men had rescued her from the vorgs. The assassin Arn, the Kanjari horse warrior Ty, and John, the hawk-faced warrior who would become Kimber's husband, had brought her back home to Endar Pass. That journey had transformed Galad's sister into the headstrong woman who'd abandoned palace life and gone with her husband to make a new home in Areana's Vale.

But those changes paled in comparison to the transformation that John's death and the pursuit of Kragan across the Continent of Sadamad had inflicted on Kimber. Galad knew that he was partially to blame for his sister's embrace of the necrotic branch of life magic. He had implored her to use it to funnel the life from their enemies to heal his Endarian time-mist warriors during the battle for Endar Pass.

Despite the queen's disapproval, Kimber had continued to wield her power in the battles in Sadamad. And with each use its hold on her grew stronger. Galad had confronted his sister and expressed his concern, but she had told him to have a care for his own business and stay the deep out of hers.

Galad straightened, stretching out the kink that had started to form at the small of his back. As he continued to study his little sister from across the deck, he realized that she wasn't so different from him.

Her rebellion was much the same as his had been when his mother had pushed him to give up his role as the leader of the time-mist warriors and instead favor his talent as a master time-shaper. He and Kimber shared a stubborn streak that they had inherited from their mother.

Today Galad had seen the way Kimber watched her half brother, Alan. That gaze had been far from sisterly. Then again, Kimber had made it clear that Galad wasn't her boss.

He stared down at the stump that ended his left wrist, the result of trying to channel more time magic than he was capable of controlling. Who was he to preach the dangers of a particular branch of magic?

—⁓—

The gibbous moon rose shortly after nightfall. Arn stood with Carol on the aftcastle, watching the bright stars in the clear sky as a stiff westerly breeze filled the sails. The sound of the waves crashing against the ship's hull built within him a longing to linger here with his love. But what needed to be done could no longer be put off.

The small pouch at his belt seemed to burn through his clothing. Arn knew that this was only his imagination, but the thought of the skeletal shard that rested within filled him with dread.

He released Carol's hand and turned to face her.

"It's time."

Her right palm caressed his cheek as she gazed sightlessly into his face, her milky eyes luminous in the moon glow.

"Can I at least sit watch over you?" she asked.

"I . . . I need to fully commit to doing this on my own. Having a lifeline nearby will weaken my desperation. If I'm to have a chance of achieving a breakthrough with my time-sight, I must do this alone."

Arn leaned into her kiss, feeling her strong arms encircle his neck. Then he stepped back and turned away, feeling Zaislus's eyes bore into his back as he walked to the nearest of the ladders that led from atop the aftcastle down to the main deck.

Arn didn't go to their cabin. He would leave that for Carol. Instead he walked through the hallway that led to the captain's study in the forecastle, the fish-oil lamps casting swaying shadows as he walked by. He lifted one from its hook, opened the door, and stepped inside the room, using the lamp he carried to light another affixed to the small table.

When the yellow flame sputtered to life, he replaced its glass chimney and returned the light he carried to its proper place in the hallway. Then, after shutting the door behind him, Arn seated himself on the chair that was bolted to the floor beside the table. His attention firmly focused on the pouch, he removed it from his belt, loosened the drawstring, and dumped its ancient content on the polished mahogany.

The gnarled long finger lay partially curled, its dancing shadow seeming to crawl toward him. Arn closed his eyes, took a calming breath, and allowed himself to sink into a mental state where his awareness floated, a firefly in a sea of black. Distant images drifted toward him from all directions until they began to resolve into conflicting scenes of near futures that stretched away to the horizons. The visions tugged at his consciousness, each trying to pull him down a different path.

He resisted the urge to explore. Instead he spread his right palm on the smooth wood, allowing it to anchor him to the present. Ever so slowly, he slid his hand forward and clasped the finger in his palm.

The visions that crashed in upon him almost pulled a shriek from his lips.

The present fled before the cacophony. He stepped into thigh-deep water that still carried the chill of early spring, Carol and Zaislus leaping from the longboat alongside him. A thousand men and women splashed ashore, pulling longboats up onto the pale sand of the beach.

Another image washed over Arn. He stood atop a rocky ledge on a cliff face he recognized. The tunnel entrance to Endar Pass lay just ahead, and the Chosen and his followers had halted just before the opening, facing Endarian troops in defensive positions. Not only had the leagues of Forsworn stopped; they reversed course along the trail and marched back out of the gorge the way they had come. What was wrong here?

Shift.

Chief Matron Loraine, the leader of the women warriors of Val'Dep who'd held the mountain fortress against a force of thousands of vorgs, stood atop the city's outer wall in the torchlight. Her normally stoic face twisted in a combination of grief and fury as she stared at the illuminated scene beyond the chasm. Kragan faced hundreds of tied and kneeling horse warriors. Arn's wraithlike form had no substance here but still he shuddered as he recognized the warrior directly in front of Kragan. Larok, the young man who had become khan after his father's death.

Arn moved closer to Loraine so he could look into her eyes. He recognized what was lurking just beneath her gruff exterior.

Dread.

Shift.

Blood ran in rivulets from Alan's bald head, coating his shoulders, chest, and back. His great ax howled through the air, severing the heads and rending the torsos of the horde of vorgs and brigands who stood against him and his Forsworn. Chain lightning skittered across the sky, accompanied by thunder that shook the very ground upon which they fought.

Arn saw himself moving among the combatants, shifting to avoid swords, spears, and maces as he fought to defeat those who struggled to reach the arcane platform of air Carol had erected. His wife stood atop it, arms extended wide, wielding so much magic that a shimmering, translucent bubble rippled with blue fire around her and Zaislus at her side.

Then he saw Kragan, facing her from a similar perch a half league away. The reason behind the grin that stretched the small man's mouth was plain for all to see. His left hand clutched a handful of the shards that had once formed two-thirds of Landrel's Trident. He extended his right hand, fingers spread wide. Ever so slowly, he closed that hand. Sweat trickled down his forehead as the wielder increased the effort he brought to bear.

Arn heard Carol cry out and turned to see her on one knee, desperately clutching at the shard of Landrel's Trident that she possessed. Her pale eyes widened in shock and disappointment. Arn understood. She didn't know how to use the artifact to amplify her magic.

With a pop her shielding collapsed, raining crimson on the Forsworn who fought to defend her.

Arn's anguished moan rasped from his future self's throat.

Shift.

Arn stood between Carol and Kim inside a torchlit tunnel. Along the walls, skulls and bones had been carefully stacked from floor to ceiling. Despite the magic that Carol rained down on the hundreds of attackers, the vorgs forced Arn, his companions, and the Endarian guards who fought alongside them ever deeper into the catacombs. Movement from behind drew Arn's glance. Everywhere he looked, skeletal forms pulled themselves together, flesh re-forming over the corpses as they shambled forward.

Shift.

Time and again, Arn watched as he, Carol, Alan, and their followers fell to Kragan. Each time Arn tried a different maneuver, changing the course of battle but failing to alter the ultimate outcome.

He squeezed the finger in his palm so hard that blood dripped from his fist. The futures roiled out before him, one fading as another took its place in an unending progression that left him breathless. Surely there was a path to stopping Kragan and fulfilling the promise he'd wept onto his parents' graves.

Shift.

The sound of pigs squealing outside the woodcutter's house on the outskirts of Hannington brought five-year-old Arn Tomas Ericson's head up as his father leapt from the dinner table. The inhuman laughter that accompanied the noise stood Arn's hair on end.

"Carl," Arn's mother said, her eyes wide with fear, "what's wrong?"

Arn's father grabbed his woodcutter's ax from its place beside the door. "Marie, bar the door behind me and close the shutters. Do not open them until I tell you."

Without another word, the man stepped out into the night, slamming the door shut. Marie immediately rose, dropping the door's bar into place and rushing to the lone window to close and bar the shutters.

Arn remained frozen, his fork full of mashed potatoes and gravy still halfway between his plate and mouth. His mind struggled to grasp his mother's terror. He wanted to ask her what had made the sounds, but when his father began screaming, Arn knew that he did not want to know.

Then his mother grabbed him by the arms and pulled him to his feet, sending the fork flying from his hand, splattering her blue dress with gravy. Too startled to speak, Arn felt himself being dragged across the room and lifted into the partially filled wood box beside the hearth. As sharp sticks poked his side and back, he opened his mouth to cry out but felt his mother's palm cover his lips.

"Stay silent," she whispered harshly. "Do not make a noise."

She shoved him down and closed the lid. A small shaft of light penetrated through a narrow crack but did little to push back the darkness that enfolded him. A tremor spread from Arn's hands and up his arms until his entire body shook. Outside, he no longer heard his father. There was a sudden blow against the cottage door. He heard the bar crack as the door crashed inward, followed by heavy footsteps.

Arn did not want to look but could not stop himself from pressing his eye to the crack. He blinked to clear the tears that blurred his vision. His mother stood against the far wall, holding a butcher knife, facing two men whose backs were toward Arn. The one on the left wore a black cape that swept to the floor, its hood pulled over his head. The other man was much bigger, with black hair hanging to his shoulders.

Arn's mother suddenly lunged forward, but she froze midstride at a gesture from the hooded man. Red bands of light wrapped her arms and legs, a glowing tendril reaching up to pluck the knife from her right hand.

The hooded one gestured again, and Arn's mother floated up off the floor and back to the wall, as the tendrils spread her arms as if her palms had been impaled.

When the bigger man stepped up beside her, he turned to look back at his companion, and Arn suffered another shock, this one robbing him of his breath. The man was a woman but not like any woman he had ever seen. Her brown eyes looked human, as did her muscled body. But her jaws jutted an inch from her face, and when she opened her mouth, Arn saw teeth more like those of a wolf. His father had told him tales of these beings, the ones he had called vorgs.

She ran a very human-looking tongue over her lips and grinned.

"Well, my lord," she said in the rasping voice that matched the laughter Arn had heard from outside, "do you wish to go first?"

The hooded figure merely shook his head. "Be my guest."

When the vorg turned back toward Arn's mother and opened those jaws wide, Arn could watch no more. Instead he pressed himself away from the crack, again feeling a sharp branch poke him in the back. When his mother began screaming, the echoes formed an invitation to the pits of the deep.

Shift.

Once again, Arn found himself thrown forward. Try as he might, he couldn't find his way to a future where he helped Carol end Kragan's machinations.

"Landrel!" he heard himself call into the seething cauldron of visions.

Arn felt a firm hand clasp his left shoulder and turned to see the head-taller Endarian wielder of the nine magics looking down at him. Arn tried to summon the bitter anger the man deserved but was too wrung out. Exhausted and lost, he merely stared into the mage's dark face, seeing only concern in the depths of his eyes.

A new vision took form, forcing all others aside. Arn stepped from the mist onto the endless grassy plain that swept away in all directions from the two-story house where he'd met Landrel before. A scarlet sunset bathed the western horizon, opening the door for twilight to descend.

Unlike the last time he'd been here, the air was still. No breeze ruffled the ebony hair that draped Landrel's shoulders and back.

Landrel motioned toward Arn's clenched fist. Arn raised his hand, watching as blood oozed between his fingers to run down the corded muscles of his forearm.

"Are you trying to kill yourself?" Landrel asked.

"Why should you care?"

"Bitterness does not suit you."

"In Paradiis, Carol and I had Kragan at our mercy. You helped that foul beast escape with six shards from your trident."

"So it would appear to you."

"Appear? By all the foul gods, I watched you do it."

Again Landrel's eyes shifted to Arn's bloody fist.

"Relax your grip. The artifact you hold responds to subtle nudges. Your rage forces dark paths to the fore. It will immerse you in an endless progression of such futures as you just experienced."

For several moments Arn stared at Landrel. Then, ever so slowly, he opened his hand, palm up. The shard shimmered, the scarlet sunset matching the blood that bathed the finger. A gradual calm crept through Arn's being.

The vision world dissolved around him, leaving Arn sitting at the table, the ancient finger resting in his upturned palm.

3

Kragan let the time-mists he wielded dissipate, leaving him and his hundred followers staring at the distant walled city of Mo'Lier. He paused to allow himself to recover from the effort of expending the time magic that had sped their way from sea to city.

Without the two mummified shards that amplified time magic hanging from his necklace, he couldn't have managed such a feat. He was unlike the Endarian time-shapers in that the arcane manipulation of the rate of passage of hours, days, and weeks wasn't his forte.

The time-mists they channeled were of two types, rychly and pomaly, terms from the long-gone era of Landrel. The passage of time slowed within the lighter pomaly mists and accelerated in the murky rychly mists, each balancing the other. Passing from a slower mist into one within which time moved faster was like fighting your way out of thick mud. The reverse was true as one exited a rychly mist, stepping into a slower zone, pressing oneself into mud instead. If the time difference between mists was too great, passage between them became impossible. Thus any time-shaper who supported mist warriors created complicated flows that contained gentle gradients.

Learning to recognize those gradients took a long time. And because the time-mist warriors preferred to traverse the rychly mists, where time passed more quickly, they aged at an accelerated rate . . . another reason for the scarcity of the special fighters.

He returned his focus to the walled city. Mo'Lier's streets wound up and around the conical hill named after the sprawling temple that topped it. A lake spread out north and a swampy lowland extended to the east of Temple Mount.

Thick clouds hid the midday sun, loosing a slow drizzle that added dreariness to a scene that would have been depressing in bright sunlight. This was home to an order of priests who worshipped the ancient god Krylzygool, which had trapped itself in caverns deep beneath the mountaintop temple. The magic-wielding zealots called themselves the protectors.

The sight of the temple pulled forth the memory of one of the last times Kragan had conversed with High Priest Jorthain.

—m—

Seating himself cross-legged on the ground, Kragan set the fist-size crystal orb half-filled with water down before him. He had long ago distributed duplicates to the most important of his followers spread across the continent. Each of the scrying vases contained water drawn from the same pool beneath Lagoth.

Stilling his mind, Kragan grabbed control of the water elemental Boaa. The fluid crawled up the sides of the crystalline globe, forming a lens mirrored within its twin, which was in the possession of Jorthain. At first Kragan could see nothing, an unusual occurrence that indicated Jorthain must be carrying the orb within his robe's pocket.

"Jorthain!"

The globe transmitted the rumble of Kragan's voice to the water within the vase, and Boaa duplicated the vibration in Jorthain's orb. Kragan saw a sudden light blossom within the globe, along with the image of a hand. Jorthain's skeletal face swam into view.

"What do you desire of me, Lord Kragan?"

He kept his voice calm. "Tell me that your army is finally on the move."

"We march with the arrival of the equinox," said Jorthain. "And as you directed, my protectors will travel with our troops. Spring will clear our path toward Rafel's stronghold."

"What is your final troop strength?"

"Just over thirty thousand."

"Make haste. High Lord Rafel has managed to escape from another such army. If he learns the true size of your force, he will abandon his stronghold and flee north to Endar Pass. You will not allow that to happen."

The scowl on the high priest's face told Kragan that he didn't like the implied threat. At least Jorthain was not so unwise as to mention his displeasure.

Kragan released Boaa, and the water lens flowed back into the bottom of the scrying vase. Once the army of the protectors had Rafel safely bottled in his canyon stronghold, the priests and their forces could throw themselves at Carol Rafel and the rest of the high lord's people at their leisure. And then Kragan could devote his full attention to Endar's destruction.

—⁂—

Kragan rolled his head, letting his neck pop away the stiffness that had settled. Back then, the protectors and their army had proved inadequate for the task. The Rafel witch had broken Jorthain's mind. The will of his army to fight had died with its master.

The priesthood that had remained here in Mo'Lier survived, but they were a fraction of their former might. None of them would recognize his true body, which he now wore. In those days he had clothed himself in the mighty form of the primordial Kaleal. The being with a lion's face and clawed hands stood over seven feet tall. Muscles rippled beneath his bronze skin whenever he moved.

Now Kragan no longer needed to bind himself to the elemental Lord of the Third Deep. Thanks to the six shards that dangled from the chain around his neck, his magical prowess dwarfed any that remained in this world or the next.

Kragan signaled to his hundred and led them across the plain toward the distant city gates. His anticipation of reunion grew. There would be many steps along the way to rebuilding an army capable of capturing the citadel within Endar Pass. This would be the first.

They halted ten paces from the towering city gates. A guard atop the wall called down.

"State your business in Mo'Lier."

Kragan stepped forward.

"Tell your captain that Kragan requests an audience with the high priest of the protectors."

A sneer crept onto the guard's face.

"Then let this Kragan show himself, little one. My captain does not suffer dealing with another's servants."

The rumble that began in the back of Kragan's throat made its way into his voice.

"Last chance. I do not wish to begin my visit to your city with unpleasantness."

"Be on your way."

The guard made a hocking sound, then spat over the parapet, pulling forth laughter from the handful of his fellows who stepped forward to look down from the battlements.

Kragan extended his right hand, binding an air elemental to his will. Kragan lifted the guard from the top of the wall, pulling forth a cry as the man kicked and struggled against the unseen force that held him in its grip, dropping his bow in the process. The shocked onlookers raised their bows but didn't release their arrows for fear of hitting their companion, who floated down to hover in front of Kragan.

The wielder slowly shook his head, watching as the man clutched at his throat, trying to free his breathing. Then Kragan stepped around the struggling guard, opening a clear line of fire to himself.

"I have not yet killed this insolent fool, but my patience wears thin. If you do *not* wish to join your companion, get the captain of the guard. Now."

For several moments indecision froze the captive guard's companions. Then the leftmost of the men moved back out of sight. Kragan glanced over at the purple-faced guard, whose struggles grew steadily weaker. He released some of the pressure on the man's throat, allowing him to gasp in several breaths. Then Kragan settled back to wait.

Suddenly the top of the wall filled with archers, arrows nocked and bowstrings drawn taut as they sighted down on Kragan and his band of followers. A black-bearded officer stepped up into a crenel, a deep scowl wrinkling his forehead.

"I am Captain Klojas. Who are you, and why have you attacked my guardsman?"

Kragan lowered his captive to the ground but kept his invisible magical bonds in place. He spread his arms wide as he addressed the captain.

"My name is Kragan. I made a polite request, but was spat at for my trouble. Despite this one's loutish behavior, I have done your man no harm."

"Should I recognize your name?"

"There are those among your senior protectors who know me well. Jorthain was among them."

"Jorthain is long dead. Bailon is high priest now."

Kragan allowed himself a smirk. The portly Bailon had been party to several scrying communications between Kragan and Jorthain.

"If you send word to Bailon that Kragan requests an audience, all will become clear. In the meantime we shall make camp outside your gates to await the high protector's summons."

"What proof can you give me that you are who you say?"

"Tell your high protector that I demand to convene a Conclave of the Nine. They can summon Krylzygool to determine my identity."

Kragan watched the captain's eyes widen at his suggestion that Bailon summon their shadowy god. Klojas gave an order, and the archers atop the wall released the tension on their bowstrings.

"Let my guard go and I will convey your message to the high protector."

"Done."

Kragan gestured and sent the magically chained guard floating back up to his captain. Releasing the air elemental, he dumped the man atop the battlements. Then Kragan turned and walked back to his hundred.

All things considered, this exchange had gone better than expected.

—⁕—

"A half man claims to be Kragan?" asked Bailon, standing at the window that provided a view over the city that wrapped the hillside below, stroking his closely trimmed gray beard.

"He asks that you convene a Conclave of the Nine and summon Krylzygool to confirm his identity," said Captain Klojas.

The soldier's words chilled Bailon's blood. Anger and confusion roiled his thoughts. How did this stranger know of the ritual?

Rumors of Kragan's death at the hands of the assassin Blade had reached Mo'Lier almost a year ago as the remnants of Kragan's vorgish horde fled southwest from Endar Pass. When Bailon had last seen Kragan, through a scrying device, the wielder had worn the form of a primordial lord.

A new thought wormed its way through Bailon's brain. Kragan was a body hopper who had survived thousands of years by stealing the physical forms of others.

"Return to your post, Captain. I will send a number of my protectors to the south wall to augment your defenses with their magic. Do nothing to provoke the being who waits outside our walls until I decide what to do with him."

"Yes, High Priest."

Bailon watched Klojas turn and exit his chambers. He walked back into his study and tugged on the thick cord that dangled from the ceiling beside his desk. Moments later, the door opened to admit the stern figure of Valden, the priest who served as Bailon's aide. The middle-aged man had a face that resembled a crow's, with a rasping voice that matched his appearance.

"Yes, master?"

"Send six protectors to the south wall. They're to place themselves under Captain Klojas's command until I recall them. Then convene the other eight members of the Conclave of the Nine within my lower chamber. We'll begin the ceremony in an hour."

Without a word the aide strode from the room, closing the door behind him.

When Bailon eventually descended the stairwell leading down into his ceremonial chamber, all the others were already within. The muffled cries that arose from below lent anticipation to the high priest's steps. The occasion of this summoning was perplexing, but he still felt the same familiar palpitations the ceremony always brought. A heady mix of terror and euphoria.

He stepped through the oblong portal at the base of the stairs and emerged behind the altar. The other eight elder priests raised their arms in unison, palms upward, the mouth and eyes of the serpentine band that encircled each one's ring finger turned to face upward with their palms. A soft chant rose and fell in rhythm, timed to pace Bailon's steps up the dais to his place atop the altar.

A rangy man was tied facedown across a great marble ball that formed the altar's center. The stone measured two paces in diameter. Leather straps fastened to hoops of steel embedded in the altar's base bound the stranger's hands and feet. While the sacrifice differed, the ritual would be performed exactly as it had been for centuries.

The high priest reached forward, grabbed the shirtless man's brown hair, and pulled his head back so that Bailon could gaze into his face.

The man appeared to be in his thirties or so, with hazel eyes wide with terror. He moaned through his gag as spasms of fear shook his body. The high priest gazed at him for several seconds before turning to grab the pearl-handled ceremonial dagger from its mounting place on the wall behind the altar.

The chant that filled the chamber rose in volume, with a beat that matched Bailon's thundering heart. The high priest raised the dagger before him, laid across his upstretched palms, revealing the same jewel-eyed serpent entwined in the handle that formed the loops of the priestly rings. Slowly his fingers closed around the handle. Then Bailon stepped forward and slit the man's throat from ear to ear.

Blood arced outward in long spurts, then gushed again in diminishing arcs into the large basin surrounding the round marble stone. Bailon laid the dagger aside on a pedestal, then spread his arms wide before the altar.

"Krylzygool . . . hear me." His deep voice rose above those of the chanting protectors. "Accept this offering most pure and grant us your vision, O ancient one."

The marble stone, now slick with sheets of red on one side, took on a sickly yellow cast.

"Let the pure blood feed your ancient heart. Let the terror of the innocent salve your immortal desires. Let the devotion of your servants stoke your mighty presence."

The stone's color changed to purple, then it pulsed and deepened to scarlet as waves of ecstasy pulled moans from the swaying priests.

"Master, reveal to us now that which we need to see in order to serve you. Show us Kragan's true form, alive or dead."

The stone pulsed as if it had become the beating heart of the god they worshipped. An image coalesced in the air just above the dead body that draped the bloody stone. A petite man stood there, his wild, tawny locks framing a head that seemed too large for his body, as did his hands and feet.

The target of their attention suddenly turned his head to stare directly into Bailon's face and grinned. As impossible as it was, the high priest couldn't doubt what was happening. Kragan was looking back at him through Krylzygool's lens.

Kragan reached up to pull a necklace from beneath his shirt. When he opened his hand, Bailon gasped in awe. There within the small man's large palm lay six skeletal fingers. The knowledge of what he beheld radiated from Krylzygool's mind into Bailon's.

Bailon's shaking legs gave way, dropping him to his knees. Throughout the chamber, the other priests fell to their knees as well. When Kragan's smirk died, he spoke in a voice that boomed from the altar.

"Do not keep me waiting."

The vision faded. As it disappeared, the euphoria their god's presence had infused into the room dissipated.

But the terror lingered.

4

Carol walked beside Arn near the head of Alan's columns of warriors, the entire legion surrounded by the time-mists that Galad wielded to speed their journey toward Endar Pass. They had come ashore on Endar's northwest coast at a place that Carol believed to be a hundred leagues south of the port of Uostas.

Alan signaled the halt, and Galad dismissed the mists to allow everyone to get their bearings. And as the strange half-light of the mist world through which they had been journeying faded away, Carol found herself staring up at the first stars of evening through her dog's eyes. Twilight's deep purple draped the western horizon.

"We make camp here for the night," Alan said. "In the morning we'll cross the Gauga River and begin the last leg of our journey to Endar Pass."

"Good," Carol said. "I'll be happy to see that beautiful fortress on the lake. There's much to discuss with Queen Elan."

"I get the feeling Kim isn't so anxious to see her mother," Arn said.

"Not surprising, considering how harshly Elan treated her as we prepared to depart," Carol said. "I hope the queen has come to terms with Kim's use of necrotic magic. Without it, Endar would have fallen."

"Maybe. Maybe not."

The moonlight reflecting from a nearby stream attracted Carol's attention. Through her mental connection to Zaislus, she could smell the tang of juniper mingled with the scent of deer on the evening breeze.

"I want to go sit in the glade by that stream," she said, pointing down the gentle slope. "I need to meditate."

She saw Arn glance down to where the fingers of her left hand clutched the small pouch on her belt.

"And yes," she said, "I want to try once again to figure out what magic this shard enhances."

"I'll stand watch."

"No need. Alan has his sentries out, and I have Zaislus."

"I'll stay out of your way. I can practice my time-sight while you do your work."

Carol was tempted to argue but sighed and began walking down the hill. Ever since Arn's vision-storm aboard ship, he'd been reluctant to stray too far from her side. His worries were beginning to grate on her nerves.

The glade turned out to be larger than it had appeared from above. Its northern half was draped by the broad limbs of trees sprouting their first spring blossoms. In the gathering gloom, she couldn't make out the colors of the flowers but guessed they were a mix of white and yellow. She picked a spot on the grass beneath the sprawling branches, near a knee-high waterfall, and sat down, letting the sound soothe her. Arn melted away so as not to disturb her.

Carol unfastened the small pouch from her belt but didn't loosen the drawstring that held it closed around the arcane artifact within. Instead she held it cupped in the palms of both hands. Zaislus settled down beside her.

Carol found her dog's gentle touch soothing, but she dropped her mental link to the animal. She took several deep, calming breaths. Her focus shifted from the top of her head into her face, neck, and shoulders. Her consciousness drifted down through her arms, torso, legs, and feet, leaving her in a state of relaxation.

She centered. A vision of herself as a dancing flame formed in the void. Her consciousness expanded, and as it did so, the flame shrank to a distant pinpoint of light. Only then did Carol open her sightless eyes. Ever so slowly, she moved her fingers to loosen the tie at the pouch's mouth. She tipped it up, spilling the skeletal shard into her left hand, then set the supple leather purse aside.

When she had first tried this, she'd expected to feel power course through her body, something as vast in its effect as the visions Arn's artifact bathed him in. But not even a tingle stirred the sensitive nerves of her palm. Carol could feel the sharp tip of the long finger as she clasped her hands around it.

On board the *Laskovanie*, she had tried to gain some sense of which of the nine branches of magic this thing amplified. But it had refused her efforts. Tonight, she would try something different. She whispered the name of the earth elemental Kevir, reaching out with her mind to touch it. She felt the link form, felt Kevir's will test itself against hers, recognizing the being's frustration at the impotence of its efforts.

Normally this was the point when Carol forced whatever elemental she mastered to reach from the ethereal plane where it resided to produce some effect within the physical world. She made no such demand now, content to maintain her connection to the thing, content to merely observe its thoughts and sensations. The entity was angry, afraid. And in the depths of desperation it did something Carol hadn't thought possible.

Kevir departed the elemental plane, followed their mental link, and entered her world.

Carol felt the rocks and earth upon which she was sitting bulge and shift, sending her tumbling through the grass. As she rolled to a stop, she dropped the shard and lost her connection to Kevir. Somewhere nearby, Zaislus snarled. She felt the dog leap across her body to place itself between Carol and whatever Kevir was becoming.

Unable to see, she reached out to touch Zaislus, but the gesture was beyond her grasp. And since she couldn't see or touch Zaislus, she couldn't link to the animal's mind. Suddenly she heard a thud, and Zaislus howled in pain. She heard her dog hit the ground several paces to her right, and his howling immediately ceased.

—⁂—

Arn sat on a boulder twenty paces from Carol, his mind sifting through visions of what might be in the days that sped toward them. Tonight, he didn't tinker with the shard that rested within his belt-pouch. He couldn't afford to lose himself in those depths right now. But maybe he could gather information that would give this legion an advantage in the week ahead.

One particularly vivid dreamscape occupied his mind for the second time. A thousand Forsworn spread out for leagues along the narrow track that wound through the gorge that led to the tunnel that was once again the only southern entrance to Endar Pass. The passages that Kragan had magically bored through the mountains had been buried under massive rockslides the Endarians had triggered.

Arn saw himself, Carol, Alan, and the Forsworn retrace the path they had taken into the gorge to set up camp in the verdant valley beyond. What surprised him was that Kim and Galad weren't with them. Nor had any Endarian emissaries arrived. He had the odd impression that if Carol and Alan were to enter Endar Pass, they would have to fight their way in.

Suddenly Arn's intuition pulled him back to the here and now. He scrambled to his feet, Slaken in one hand, throwing dagger in the other. Arn sprang from the boulder, racing into the moonlit glade where Carol sat beside Zaislus. The ground beneath her heaved upward, sending her and the dog flying.

The thing that clawed its way out of the dirt was as big as a bear, the monstrosity standing erect on two thick legs. Formed of earth and stone, it had no face, but turned toward the spot where Carol lay sprawled. Zaislus leapt toward the creature, the dog's growl deep and guttural, its raised hackles making its head look twice its size.

The thing swatted Zaislus aside, extracting a yelp of pain as the dog flew through the air to land in a crumpled heap. Arn's churning legs carried him to the spot where Carol struggled to rise. Without stopping, Arn swept her into his arms, wheeled away from the monster, and ran back up the hill toward the encampment.

Carol's mind filled his.

"Let me see it."

Arn glanced back over his left shoulder. The rock monster was pursuing them, but what it had in strength, it lacked in speed.

"Stop! Set me down."

A fresh vision-storm echoed her command. Arn slid to a halt, set his wife on her feet, and turned to face the death that lumbered toward them.

—〰—

Through Arn's eyes, Carol watched the earth elemental approach, hearing the crunch of ponderous stone feet. She tried to forge a mental connection to the thing and failed. What was wrong? Then it dawned on her. Although she could forge mental links to living creatures and to beings on the four ethereal planes, she couldn't grab the mind of the elemental who'd somehow made the transition into the physical world.

White-hot fury burned her soul.

"You just killed my dog."

She reached into the elemental planes, commanding beings from the planes of earth, air, fire, and water. Her pursuer stepped upon ground that turned to mud, then hardened to granite as it sank thigh deep in the muck. Carol pulled chain lightning from the sky, the bolts arcing into what she took for the monster's head.

Water fountained from the river, turning into a thick slab of ice as it engulfed the thing's body. The monster shifted its heavy arms, shattering the ice with boulder hands, then hammered the stone that encased its legs. A pillar of flame roared into its space, fanned by a whirlwind that howled through the night louder than the thunder.

Despite the forces she threw against the abomination, it was gradually extracting itself from the earth that trapped its feet.

Carol howled her hate at the thing and hurled forth more elemental minions. Once more the monster weathered the storm. Then, with a growl that sounded like cracking rocks, it rumbled straight toward her.

—∞—

Arn watched the monster tear Carol apart. He saw her take flight, only for the entity to kill Alan and hundreds of his Forsworn. Dozens of images flitted through his mind in an instant. He latched on to the one that gave him hope.

He leaned in close to Carol, grasped her left hand, and yelled.

"Follow me. Now!"

He pulled her across the slope, Carol letting her magical conflagration die out behind her. Arn replayed one of his earlier visions in his mind, sharing it with Carol as they ran. She stumbled, and he barely managed to keep her from falling. When they reached the spot where Carol had been thrown upon summoning the creature, Arn stopped.

"Light," he said.

A globe of light floated into being above him. Arn dropped to his knees once again, replaying the moments when Carol had fallen here, dropping the shard from Landrel's Trident to the ground. The ground trembled beneath the monster's heavy feet as Arn frantically searched through the trampled grass.

Then he saw part of the bony shard sticking out from beneath a leaf. Snatching it up, he pressed it into Carol's hand as the elemental raised its earthen hand to smash them.

—⚉—

Carol squeezed the shard as she lashed out with her mind, solidifying the air between her and the creature to form a shield that shimmered, encasing Arn and Zaislus alongside her. The giant fist crashed into the shield with a sound like the boom of a gong. The shield flashed brilliant white but didn't shatter. Once more, the elemental hammered at the barrier. Again, it held. But she saw thin white cracks spiderweb across its surface.

Arn's visions drifted at the edge of her consciousness, and Carol mentally thanked him for filtering them. She shifted her focus to the finger clutched in her left fist. Carol locked Arn's eyes on the earthen thing and touched its mind, wrapping the elemental's consciousness in a vise grip.

Its body froze, fist uplifted, trembling with an effort that Carol snuffed out. Then the thing lowered its fist and stood still, a few paces in front of her.

Carol reached into the plane of earth, sensing the thousands of elementals that lurked there, and formed another connection. She poured her will into the link. She felt a portal open and, with supreme effort, shoved the monster through.

With a loud pop, the gateway snapped closed.

Carol's legs gave way, but Arn caught her as she fell, lowering her gently to the ground. She found herself gazing down into her own white eyes, seeing the tears that leaked from their corners. Then the world faded away.

—ᴍ—

Kim ran beside Alan toward the spot where the rock creature had disappeared. Fire and lightning left the air smelling of smoke. Kim dropped to her knees beside Carol's prone form and reached out with her life magic to touch her half sister. A gasp of relief escaped her lips.

Arn placed a hand on her shoulder, and Kim turned to face him.

"Carol will be fine," Kim said. "She's just exhausted."

"Thank the gods."

Arn looked to his left and pointed.

"What about Zaislus?"

Then Kim saw the dog's limp body.

"Oh no," she said, rising to her feet and moving to the dog's side.

She ran her hands gently across his body. A low whimper escaped from a muzzle that dripped blood. Several of the dog's ribs had been broken. His internal injuries would be fatal. Kim glanced around at the verdant vegetation lit by the moon's soft glow, then seated herself, cross-legged.

She reached out with her life magic, seeking the essence of nearby animals. But if any animals had been near the glade earlier, the magical combat that had just raged had driven them away. She sighed. She was going to have to do this the hard way.

She could steal the energy of plants, though it was much slower and more difficult than funneling the life from another living creature to heal the dog. As Alan and Arn and some others watched, Kim began funneling the wounds from Zaislus into herself, then draining the nearby grass, bushes, and trees to repair her injuries. She bore the familiar agony of the process without issuing a gasp or a moan. Sweat trickled down her cheeks.

The big dog's breathing became unlabored. The whimpering stopped, and Zaislus rose unsteadily to his feet. Kim continued to repair her own injuries, noting the worry furrowing Arn's brow as he watched her restore her health. Then he stoically led Zaislus to the spot where Carol lay.

When Kim climbed to her feet, she felt Alan gather her into his arms and hold her close.

"Thank you for what you just did for Carol," he whispered.

Kim imagined she could feel Katrin's eyes boring into her back as she returned Alan's embrace, never wanting the moment to end.

5

Kragan strode into the city through gates opened wide in welcome. High Priest Bailon walked forward to meet the master he hadn't recognized. Bailon dropped to one knee and bowed his head, getting dust on his black robes of office.

"Welcome to Mo'Lier, Lord Kragan. My protectors, my city . . . are at your service."

"Let us retire to your temple so that we may discuss this in comfort. Have someone see to accommodations for my company."

The high priest rose to his feet and signaled to his captain, who nodded and stepped out to meet with the commander of Kragan's company.

Bailon led Kragan along the main street, which teemed with oppressed citizens. Vorgs and brigands filled the taverns, even though it was still morning. Raw sewage ran through the gutters that routed the sludge around the hillside toward the lake, producing one of many foul smells that wafted through Mo'Lier's winding alleys and byways.

They followed Freemarket Street, the bustling central avenue, for several hundred paces before turning off onto the paved path that curved up the hill toward the temple that graced its peak. The temple's high walls and spires towered over the city with looming menace.

As they approached the temple, the towering iron double doors swung inward, letting them enter the atrium. Despite hundreds of candles, shadows crawled from the beamed ceiling and lurked behind dozens of statues of dead high priests. Kragan's gaze lingered on the striking likeness of Jorthain, whom Carol Rafel had struck down in the gorge that protected her father's mountain fortress.

Then he followed Bailon up the freestanding spiral staircase, also forged from iron mined from the sacred mount. At the top of the stairs, a set of double doors opened into the high priest's sitting chamber. Bailon, his breath coming in muffled gasps, motioned toward one of two high-backed chairs that angled toward each other before the blazing hearth.

Kragan ignored the priest, moving instead to stand before the flames, spreading his palms to the radiating heat. Regardless of season, this temple of stone and iron perpetually held winter's chill.

"Don't just stand there, Bailon. Sit down."

He heard the other settle his bulk into a chair that creaked under the high priest's weight.

Then Kragan turned toward Bailon. Standing so that his head was at the same height as the seated protector's, he clasped his hands behind his back, watching as small beads of sweat formed on the priest's forehead. Kragan let silence linger, sensing Bailon's discomfort.

"I didn't come here seeking your aid," he said.

Bailon's relief was plain to behold. Kragan's next words wiped it from his face.

"What's the size of your garrison?"

"The size?"

"How many soldiers and guards do you have protecting the city? Include your reserves in the count."

Bailon hesitated, his left hand nervously stroking his chin.

"A little more than two thousand of my soldiers."

"What of the mercenaries I saw in the city?"

"Five hundred vorg scouts. If necessary, I could summon three times that number from the outlands to our south."

"Then do so."

"What? Is a threat coming this way?"

Kragan took a step closer to the seated priest, tapping his steepled fingers together before him.

"No. In the coming days I will be conscripting all of the vorgs and a thousand of your finest soldiers. I will also be taking a dozen of your senior priests. We have a long march ahead of us."

Bailon's face paled.

"But . . . but that will leave Mo'Lier vulnerable to attack."

"Then press your civilians into service and train them."

"Lord Kragan, may I ask what you'll use this fighting force for?"

Kragan raised his right hand, letting glittering energy dance across his upturned palm.

"I intend to take the fight to our enemies."

Then he turned his back on the stunned high priest. He paused at the door that led out of the sitting chamber.

"My loyal supporters will be richly rewarded. Make sure you're among them."

6

Alan stepped out of the dissolving rychly time-mists a hundred paces from the tunnel opening that led through the cliffs into Endar Pass. He held up his fist, signaling for his legion of Forsworn to halt. Subordinate commanders relayed the signal back down the long lines of Alan's warriors. Up ahead, blocking the tunnel entrance, stood a company of Endarian warriors, each wearing their telltale color-shifting uniforms that blended with their background. Although their swords were slung and their bows weren't drawn, there was no mistaking the Endarians' threatening stance.

Alan turned to Arn.

"This is what you foresaw?" he asked.

"Yes."

"Kim. Galad. I think you'd better go talk with your people."

The two Endarian royals merely nodded and began walking toward the spot where their mother's soldiers were blocking access to the pass. Despite Arn having described this very scenario in detail last night, the companions had decided that the prince and princess needed to meet with Queen Elan. For the company to fight its way into Endar Pass was out of the question. Turning away without learning what the queen was thinking made no sense.

Kat stepped up to Alan's side and placed her hand on his arm, pulling him out of his brief reverie. His eyes shifted to the spot she pointed out. Galad and Kim had split up, each locked in stern discussion with a different officer. That made no sense to Alan. Surely there was one officer in charge of the entire company.

The air in front of him shimmered, pulling the scene closer as if he had just raised a far-glass to his eye. Familiar as he had become with Carol's manipulation of elemental magic, he couldn't shake the eerie feeling the effect induced. Although he couldn't hear their voices, the grim expression on Galad's face and the vehemence of Kim's gestures made their unhappiness clear.

Suddenly the Endarian officer talking with Galad turned and issued a command. The formation of soldiers parted, and both Kim and Galad followed the woman through their ranks and disappeared into the mist-filled tunnel beyond. While these events weren't exactly as Arn had described, they were close enough that Alan knew the rest of his brother-in-law's vision would come to pass.

They were going to be stuck here for at least the next few days, waiting for Kim and Galad to return.

Alan turned and issued a command to Tudor, his second in command and the leader of the clansmen who made up the bulk of the Forsworn.

"We cannot camp here, spread out along this narrow road. Ready the Forsworn to reverse course. We'll make camp in the valley outside the gorge."

"Yes, Chosen."

"Shouldn't we ask the Endarians what's going on?" Carol asked.

"You saw how they treated their prince and princess. I doubt they would grant us any such courtesy. We don't want to start a fight with our allies."

Carol looked at Arn. He nodded in agreement.

Alan's sister took a deep breath, stroked her dog's head, then straightened.

"Lead us out of here."

—⁂—

Anger pulsed with each of Kim's heartbeats as she and Galad followed Commander Shaena into the pomaly mists that filled the tunnel leading through the mountain into Endar Pass. Neither the slender woman nor the captain Kim had confronted outside the passage had provided any information about the reason the legion had been denied entrance into the pass.

What was her mother thinking? Even if their mother was still angry at Kim for using necrotic life magic, it made no sense for her to deny Galad's entreaty.

They exited the tunnel to find that sunset had painted the western sky scarlet. Galad enshrouded their path toward the white-walled city in the lake in the accelerating rychly mists, dismissing the fog only as they approached the ivory bridge springing from the lake's south shore. Bathed in the sky's red glow, the citadel's white walls seemed to bleed.

The once-lovely forest that covered the shore and stretched all the way to the mountains that surrounded the crater lake was dead and brittle, as if it had been consumed by a forest fire. The sight kicked Kim in the gut, a monument to what she and other Endarian wielders of life magic had done to their beloved home. In her efforts to funnel life energy from the forest to heal the warriors who had battled Kragan's horde, she hadn't only killed the plants but had emptied the soil of the tiny lives that made it fertile.

When she stepped between the two ceremonial guards onto the arching span, Kim received another shock. The high city walls were sparsely manned, as if no danger threatened the capital.

"Where are all the soldiers?" she asked.

Commander Shaena didn't break stride.

"All will be made clear when you meet with the High Council."

Kim noted the commander's failure to use the honorific *Princess*.

"Prince Galad and I desire to see the queen first."

Shaena didn't respond. When they passed between two more gate guards, the guards slapped their right fists to their chests in salute, as had the pair at the bridge. But Kim had the odd sensation that the military courtesy was directed solely at the commander instead of the prince and princess. What in the deep was going on? And why didn't Galad rebuke the officer who escorted them?

She glanced up at her brother's face, noting the tightness in his jaw.

Once through the gates, Kim halted. The gardens she had left as dead as the forest had been restored to their lush glory. The time magic that must have been wielded here wouldn't have come without significant cost. For the soil to heal and for new flowers, hedges, and trees to grow would have taken two centuries. The time-shapers who had channeled the mists and the gardeners who had worked alongside them would have grown old within the fogs.

Worry formed a knot in Kim's throat. Her mother would never have allowed time-wielders to sacrifice themselves for such nonessential tasks. Neither would she have relaxed the Endarian military readiness knowing that Kragan still lived.

They passed more guards as they entered the palace, but Commander Shaena didn't lead them to the throne room. Nor did she take them to the queen's rooms. Instead she directed them down the hall that led to the High Council chamber.

When Kim entered the room, she noticed the queen wasn't present. A loose circle of thirteen chairs faced the center. High Councillor

Kelond sat in the queen's place at the far end of the room with High Councillor Sersos seated at his right. All the chairs were filled, several with councillors Kim didn't know.

A score of armed guardsmen were arrayed behind the councillors, hands gripping the hilts of their swords while the tips of their weapons rested on the stone floor. Commander Shaena directed Galad and Kim into the center of the ring. In contrast to the fury that seethed within her breast, Kim felt a chill work its way up her spine.

"Where's our mother?" Galad asked.

His voice carried a hard edge, and Kim noted that his hand had clenched into a fist, tiny tendrils of time magic curling around it like white and gray smoke. Kim felt the necrotic call of her own arcane talent but held it in check.

Kelond spoke, his voice stern and commanding.

"Elan is queen no more. The High Council has made me king in her place."

"*We* are part of this council!" Kim yelled. "Any such decision made during our absence is illegitimate."

"We've had no word of you in months. The counsel had no choice but to presume you both dead. Your seats on this counsel have been filled by two others."

"Now that we've returned," Galad said, "we'll resume the seats you erroneously concluded were vacant."

Kelond stood, the middle-aged warrior's face grim.

"No, you will not. Your mother refused to allow our life-shifters to use their magic against Kragan's foul horde to heal our warriors. In so doing, Elan forced them to funnel the life from our once-verdant forest into the wounded. You've seen the resulting wasteland that lies just beyond our bridge. This council stood ready to depose your mother over this issue prior to the battle with Kragan that imposed such devastation. After you departed, the new majority had its say. We have stripped Elan of her title and you of yours. You're no longer entitled to seats on this council."

"Seats on this council are earned, not given based upon titles," said Galad. "I earned mine leading mist warriors in battle against our enemies. My sister earned hers through arcane prowess and by way of all the Endarian lives she has saved."

"I do not argue that, Galad. Nevertheless, this council has moved on."

"Where's our mother?" asked Kim.

"As king, I had her placed under house arrest in the north wing of the palace."

"You did what?" Galad's question came out as a snarl.

He unsheathed his sword in a movement faster than the eye could follow. All around the circle of councillors, the guards raised their swords and stepped into the circle.

Kim barely managed to halt the tendrils of life magic crawling from her fingertips toward Kelond as he took two steps backward.

Devan, a councillor whose long white hair framed her ebony face, stepped into the center of the circle alongside Kim.

"My king," she said. "Please put an end to this. Of course Galad and Kimber are shocked by the situation. Let us all take a step back, lest there be bloodshed in the High Council chamber."

For several moments silence draped the room. When Kelond spoke, his voice held a forced calm.

"Guards, return to rest. Galad, lay down your sword."

Kim's thoughts seemed to fog as she struggled to come to terms with what had happened in their absence. She didn't recognize the kingdom to which she'd returned.

She watched Galad exhale, then sheathe his sword. As he did so, the guards moved back to their original positions. The king sat down, and the other councillors who had left their seats followed his example.

"Please understand me," King Kelond said, his voice registering regret. "I didn't want to do this to your mother. After the council deposed her, she wouldn't accept the outcome of the vote. Elan began speaking publicly against the High Council and her king.

"Twice I warned her what would happen if she didn't cease fomenting insurrection. But Elan is stubborn. She chose incarceration over compliance. She can change her situation with a word of contrition."

Kim heard the truth in his language. Nobody had ever accused Queen Elan of being weak willed.

"Now, I'd like to hear your report on your mission to eliminate Kragan," said Kelond.

"We'll brief you after Kimber and I visit our mother."

A scowl briefly marked the king's face, and Kim feared that he would refuse. Then he gave a single nod.

"Commander Shaena, escort the former prince and princess to their mother's cell. Give them ten minutes of privacy. Then bring them back to this chamber."

"Ten minutes is wholly unacceptable," Galad said. "We haven't seen our mother in months and wish to have a proper visit. An hour."

"A reasonable request," High Councillor Devan said.

King Kelond scowled again but nodded.

"One hour, then."

Inclining her head, Shaena turned and led the siblings out through the door and into the palace depths.

—⁂—

Commander Shaena led the two former royals up a spiral stairway and down the long hall to the palace wing where the High Council and important guests were quartered. Shaena paused before the fourth door on the left, nodded to the guards positioned on each side, and rapped twice. His mother's voice sounded as firm and strong as Galad remembered it.

"Enter."

Elan sat on a blue couch, her gem-studded emerald dress spinning glints of reflected light across the room as she shifted her body to face her children. Her eyes widened as they darted from Shaena to Galad and Kimber. The former queen rose to her feet, beaming. She spread her arms, and Galad watched Kimber step forward to meet her mother's hug.

Elan released Kimber and turned to embrace Galad.

"Come sit with me," Elan said, motioning toward the couch and the comfortable chair that faced it at an oblique angle. "I would hear of your travels and mission."

The formality of his mother's greeting didn't surprise Galad. She had always maintained a royal bearing, even with her children. Kimber seated herself beside her mother while Galad took the chair.

"An hour," Shaena said, and then closed the door behind her.

"Why don't you grant Kelond his small victory and walk free again?" Galad asked.

Elan's jaw clenched.

"Walk free, you say? The so-called king would rob me of my voice. I will die before I submit to that."

"My father wouldn't have wanted this," Kim said.

"High Lord Rafel died fighting for this kingdom. For me to bow down and surrender my principles would betray your father's sacrifice."

"Let me bring an appeal for reconsideration of your imprisonment before the High Council," Galad said. "You have supporters there still."

Elan frowned.

"Ah, my impetuous son. My enemies are in ascendance. The High Council is stacked against us."

"Mother," Galad said, "we've returned to find you imprisoned for exercising your right to free speech. Kelond sits upon your throne and, from what I've observed, is making decisions based upon emotion instead of reason. My sister and I are clearly unwelcome in our city. How has the kingdom we love changed so much in such a short period of time?"

"You've studied our history. Thousands of years ago, when King Landrel was deposed and forced to flee these lands, our kingdom changed course in a day. Now time has come full circle. I dread what this change portends for our kingdom."

When Galad began to argue, Elan raised her hand, cutting off further discussion of the matter.

"Tell me of your journey."

For the remainder of the hour, Kim and Galad told Elan of their pursuit of Kragan across the Continent of Sadamad, culminating with the wielder's escape from the city of Paradiis with six of the nine shards of Landrel's Trident.

The sound of booted feet coming down the hall was followed by a double knock on the door. Commander Shaena entered without waiting for an invitation.

"It's time to return to the High Council."

Galad rose to his full height of six and a half feet.

"Mother," he said, "is there nothing else we can do for you?"

Elan paused for two heartbeats. When she spoke, he heard iron in her voice.

"Find Kragan and kill him."

7

Kragan stood on the hillside above the valley that sheltered the twenty-five hundred soldiers and vorg warriors he'd led from Mo'Lier. His hundred personal guards, the Resurrected, were arrayed before him in combat formation. Unlike the conscripts and mercenaries who formed the bulk of his new legion, these people were tied to him with unbreakable arcane bonds. Now Kragan intended to expand his elite guard.

The vorg scouts had reported a horse warrior patrol from Val'Dep moving through the hills less than a league east of where Kragan now stood. Perfect. The riders numbered sixteen, not enough to provide a significant boost to Kragan's force, but plenty to serve the wielder's purpose.

He grasped the artifacts that dangled from his neck and pulled forth the air elemental Nematomas. Long before he had acquired the six shards, he had used this being to cloak himself in invisibility. Now Kragan could channel enough magic to mask his Resurrected. He issued his mental command, sending these special warriors forward at a double-quick march.

It didn't take long to reach a spot in the adjacent canyon that formed an excellent place for an ambush. Cliffs closed in on each side, funneling any that approached from the northeast into an opening where only three could ride abreast. All he needed to do now was bait the trap.

Kragan uncloaked a half dozen of his soldiers and sent them walking through the opening and out into the meadow beyond. From the perch where he intended to wield fresh magic, he watched the six walk a few dozen paces before the first of the distant horse warriors rounded the bend and spotted them.

One of the mounted scouts put two fingers to his lips and emitted a loud whistle. The rest of the horsemen rounded the bend, unlimbering axes or bows and spurring their horses into a trot.

Kragan's six soldiers turned and ran back the way they had come as the horses bore down on them. The leader of the riders yelled a single command at the fleeing soldiers.

"Halt and live."

When the fugitives didn't obey the order, the commander brought his patrol from trot to gallop. As they reached the narrow opening, Kragan cast a spell that caused the ground to ripple beneath the running horses. The lead stallions fell and rolled, tripping those that followed them and sending warriors flying.

The final six of the Val'Dep warriors managed to bring their mounts to a sliding stop, but before they could reverse course, Kragan wrapped their bodies in shimmering red ribbons, lifted them into the air, and pinned them against the face of the opposite cliff.

He released Nematomas, revealing himself and his followers. The Resurrected leapt from their ambush positions, putting to the sword all the fallen men and injured horses. Kragan's soldiers quickly corralled the rest of the mounts and led them away.

Kragan walked down from his perch, gave an order, and watched as his men laid the bodies of the ten dead horse warriors side by side on the ground where he could inspect them. The wielder walked down the line, carefully examining each of the fallen. He selected six, signaling for the others to be tossed aside.

He shifted his gaze back to the six living warriors of Val'Dep, lowering them slowly to the ground but not releasing the magical bonds that secured their limbs. Like those of their dead compatriots, their tresses and beards were tightly braided. Defiance shone in their eyes as they looked down upon him.

"Kill us," said the warrior in the center, his voice dripping with derision. "We'll join our kin in the land of the dead, our honor unbroken."

Once again, Kragan clutched the mummified shards in his left palm, sending forth a half dozen smoky tendrils that flowed into the prisoners. Kragan released the bonds, letting the men drop to the ground in violent convulsions.

The miasmas crawled from their bodies to plunge into the corpses arrayed opposite them. And as life essence left the living to reanimate the dead, Kragan stepped forward to look down at the newly reborn.

"Welcome back, my children."

—◊—

Khan Larok sat upon his throne, barely able to contain his anger, having just been informed of the return of one of the scouts he had sent out in the morning. Only one member of the patrol had returned to Val'Dep. The survivor was headed to the throne room to brief the khan.

When Mocna, the captain of the khan's royal guards, opened the oaken doors, the sight of the warrior who accompanied him only stoked Larok's rage.

The man approached the throne, dropped to one knee, and bowed his head to Larok. Dried blood matted his blond braids and caked his chain mail shirt.

"Rise, Kladivo," Larok said, "and tell me what happened."

The scout stood, his gray eyes locking with the khan's.

"We were conducting a standard patrol three leagues southeast when we were ambushed by a large contingent of vorgs."

"How many?"

"Two . . . maybe three hundred. And they had a she-vorg magic wielder with them."

"Vorgs," the khan said, pounding the right arm of his throne. "Inside my lands?"

"Yes, my khan. We lost fifteen warriors in the first few minutes of combat. Only I managed to escape the valley to carry this foul news to your ears."

Larok rose from his throne.

"Captain Mocna, I want a thousand riders assembled outside the gates by midnight. We will ride by moonlight. At dawn we will ride down these intruders. I want their heads on pikes along our southwestern border before the next sunset."

The captain spun on his heel and strode from the room. Larok shifted his gaze back to the scout.

"You must rest, Kladivo. Tomorrow morning you'll guide us to the spot where this attack happened. Together we shall avenge our fallen brothers."

—ɷ—

Even Kragan lacked the power to conceal the twenty-five hundred soldiers who marched under his command. He didn't need to. Instead he sent an advance guard of three hundred vorgs into the valley where Kragan's Resurrected had ambushed the horse warriors. Once there, they would post sentries and make camp.

Kragan gave Droga, the vorgish commander of the three hundred, one of the water-filled crystal scrying globes. Kragan kept that orb's twin, which would allow him to speak with Droga from afar.

Kragan remained with the rest of his legion. He would spend the night in meditative preparation for what would be a challenging day tomorrow. Not that any magic wielder from Val'Dep might pose a threat to him. Rather it was another arcane task that would test the limits of Kragan's power.

He couldn't be certain how Val'Dep's khan would react to the attack upon his patrol, but based upon the aggressive nature of the horse warriors, Kragan had confidence in his plan. After all, he had flung a gauntlet in the khan's face. Based upon the information the six resurrected horse warriors had given Kragan, Khan Larok would respond to the challenge with violence. Kragan had dangled an encampment of three hundred vorgs as bait. Dawn would tell the tale.

He ducked through the leather tent flap, summoned a magical light, and sat down cross-legged on the rug. He set the crystal orb in front of him. When the khan and his warriors approached the vorg camp, Commander Droga would use this device's twin to contact Kragan. Since he didn't know the time that the khan's attack would occur, Kragan had ordered his legion to remain in formation, ready to march at a moment's notice.

Nobody would sleep tonight.

—ɯ—

The crystal orb lit up just before dawn, as first a hand and then Droga's face swam into view, the vorg's extended jaws revealing glistening fangs.

"Lord Kragan, they come."

"How many?"

"More than three times our number. We've taken up defensive positions along the western ridge."

"Good. Hold your ground and force the horse warriors to fully commit to the attack."

"As you command."

Kragan lifted the water-filled sphere and placed it in the pouch that hung from his belt. He arose and walked out of his tent. It would remain in place until he returned.

Then he summoned the time-mists. The deep-gray rychly fog flowed around him and engulfed his legion, extending to the northwest, while a white pomaly mist formed to the west of the camp. He uttered the command that set his soldiers marching forward.

Kragan swung wide, passing by the valley where the khan battled the outnumbered vorg detachment. For several hours they marched within the mists while an hour passed in the normal world. If his force had consisted of trained mist warriors, which only the Endarians had, Kragan would have attacked the khan's forces from within the fogs. But his force possessed no such skills. So he maneuvered his legion until he judged they were between the khan's thousand and the city of Val'Dep. Then he dispelled the mists.

Kragan had hoped to emerge close enough to the horse warriors that his charge would surprise them from behind. Unfortunately, the brilliant dawn revealed the battle raging almost a half league to the southwest, a distance that would take his foot soldiers fifteen minutes to cover at a double-quick march.

It was only moments before the khan's mounted brigade saw them, wheeled their mounts, and charged. The warriors' braids blew out behind them as they raced toward Kragan's forces, bathed in the bright light of the new day.

Kragan issued a command that Bator, the legion's commander, relayed to his subordinates. More than two thousand soldiers spread out in defensive ranks across the valley, pikes bristling across the front lines, archers arrayed behind them.

An air elemental lifted Kragan twenty paces into the air, then solidified an invisible platform for him to stand upon. The charging horsemen raced forward in a long column of three riders abreast, led by a man in resplendent white armor. Their khan. With a practiced motion, the khan hooked his ax through a strap on the saddle and unslung his bow. A thousand riders mirrored him.

The thunder of approaching hooves reached his ears, a fitting accompaniment to the magnificence of these warriors throwing themselves into a charge. Then he spotted something very different. A bald, white-bearded rider in blue robes trailed the running horses, bringing his black horse to a halt a thousand paces away. The beefy, diminutive fellow dismounted, then rose into the air to match Kragan, arms outstretched to the heavens.

Kragan felt his hair billow around his head as an electric charge surged around him. Lightning forked down from the blue sky, but Kragan deflected it into the ground a dozen feet short of his lofty perch. Thunder boomed as the bolt set the knee-high grass ablaze.

So the khan had brought his own wielder. Good.

The wind howled from behind Kragan, fanning the flames into a wall of fire and driving it toward the rear of his legion.

Ah, he thought. *This wielder uses an indirect attack.*

Kragan pulled the moisture from the air, drawing rain from the clear sky to quench the flames that threatened his legion.

Two dozen paces in front of the pikemen, the khan fired three arrows in rapid succession, then turned his palomino stallion away. The next rank of riders executed the same maneuver, turning their mounts parallel to the enemy lines when they hit the khan's mark. Their arrows arced out like water from a pipe. As the warriors wheeled away, the endless stream of arrows punched a hole in the lines of pikemen.

It was time to put an end to this.

Kragan reached out toward the blue-robed wielder, his fingers curled into claws, and squeezed. The distant wielder drew in his arms, shielding himself against the attack. Kragan felt the pressure against his palm, resisting his effort to close his fist. And the air around his opponent shimmered into a white globe.

Kragan performed a separate summoning. Black and red worms crawled into the sky from the ground beneath the blue wielder, squirming over the surface of the white orb. Inch by inch, they burrowed inward. A red worm was the first to penetrate the mage's defenses, and when it slithered through its tiny hole, the orb changed from white to transparent. Cracks webbed across its surface.

Kragan's right hand snapped closed. From the air where the enemy wielder had stood, a shower of red rained down to the ground.

He shifted his gaze back to the khan. When the last threesome of riders launched its arrows into the wall of pikemen and wheeled away, the horsemen re-formed into tight ranks, two dozen riders abreast. Swapping out bows for battle axes, they charged the weak point in the enemy lines that their arrow swarm had created.

Still Kragan's archers held their fire, just as their master had commanded. Kragan needed the horsemen bunched, just as they would be when they hit his legion's front lines. His need to capture the bulk of the warriors alive left him willing to accept the inevitable casualties among his own forces.

The khan and his riders smashed through the ranks of the enemy, leaning over their horses' necks to slash aside the pikes angled toward their mounts. Horses fell, trampled by the onslaught that followed. The center of Kragan's legion buckled. But the charge slowed to a melee.

Kragan grasped the skeletal shards in his left hand and locked a dozen earth elementals to his will. Hundreds of tendrils of liquid stone squirmed up from the ground, changing in density from mud to solidify around the horses, locking their legs and bodies in place. Amidst the shrieks from the panicked mounts, the riders lashed about with axes, only to find their hands and arms ensnared by the flowstone.

With the last of the khan's riders imprisoned, Kragan released his hold on the elementals and lowered himself to the ground. He took a step forward, staggered, and almost fell. He released his grip on the six shards, only then realizing that they had grown cold enough to frost over.

Someone cheered, and two thousand voices joined in. The sound reached a crescendo that echoed from the surrounding hills. But Kragan didn't celebrate. Crushing fatigue draped his shoulders like a damp cloak. As he looked at the terrified eyes of the animals and men he had cemented in place, Kragan knew the day's work was only half-done.

Kragan amplified his voice so that every member of his legion could hear his command.

"Disarm the horsemen, but do not injure them further."

When his soldiers had accomplished their task, he issued a mental order to his Resurrected.

With me. Bind the horsemen as I release them.

It took two hours to gather the captured warriors from Val'Dep, their hands tied behind their backs and feet hobbled so they could take only short strides.

Once more his voice boomed across the valley.

"When I release their mounts, stand aside. Let them go home."

He grasped the shards and changed the stone into mud that sloughed from the horses' legs and bodies. The panicked animals stampeded from the valley, running back out the way they had come.

Kragan turned to Commander Bator.

"Give the legion an hour's rest, then ready them for the march. I want to reach Val'Dep before midnight."

8

"Chief Matron, you're needed at the outer wall."

Loraine turned to see the look of horror on the face of her aide, Sarah, who was generally quite sturdy.

"What's the matter?"

"You need to see for yourself."

Loraine followed Sarah out of the city. They emerged onto the broad parade ground that separated Val'Dep from its great outer wall.

As she approached the sod ramp that led to the top of the wall, Loraine's eyes were drawn to the armored women manning the battlements, replacements for the male warriors who had ridden out with the khan. Many of the women had their faces in their hands, sobbing.

Gods, what had happened?

Loraine hiked her long skirt up above her knees and sprinted to the top of the ramp. When she stepped out onto the top of the broad granite wall, the oppressive sense of calamity almost brought her to a stop. She took a deep breath, girded herself for the sight that awaited, and walked to the forward battlements.

A female guardsman stepped aside, letting Loraine look out through a crenel. Her first glance robbed her of breath. Hundreds of saddled horses milled about the narrow valley floor on the far side of the chasm that blocked access to the wall. Where were their riders?

Even if they had all fallen in battle, most of the horses would have been killed along with the warriors who had ridden them. The khan and his men were just gone. Chills raised the gooseflesh on her arms and neck. Whoever had done this had intentionally let the horses return. Perhaps as a message that said, "You're next."

The khan had left the chief matron in charge of Val'Dep when he departed. Since he was most unlikely to return, she needed to take action right now.

Loraine's mind snapped back to when the last khan had left the fortress city in her charge. Now, as then, she had a few thousand women, children, old men, and boys at her disposal.

She barked out a command.

"Lower both ramps. Let the horses back in."

The two ten-pace-wide cantilevered ramps slowly swung outward from left and right to touch down on the far side of the chasm. A stallion whinnied and galloped up and over the wall, followed by the others. The sound of their hooves on the thick wood planking echoed from the eastern and western cliffs against which the fortifications were anchored. The sound of the waterfall that plummeted down into the chasm on the eastern wall accompanied the thunder.

"Sarah. Send runners back to the city. Tell them to open the armory and summon all able-bodied women, men, and teens to arms. I need them on the wall within the hour."

The woman turned and rushed off to do Loraine's bidding.

Loraine shoved aside the depression that tried to sap her strength. As the last of the horses rushed over the wall, down the sod ramp, and out onto the parade ground beyond, the chief matron raised her voice so that all atop the battlements could hear.

"Soldiers. Battle ready. Now!"

Her words snapped all the guards back to attention and put an end to the sobs and wails. Hefting their bows, the women resumed their stations.

Then the chief matron turned and strode down the ramp toward her city. It was time to armor up.

—⁂—

Night fell as Kragan marched within sight of Val'Dep. He led his legion forward, his Resurrected personal guards forcing the captured horse warriors to follow him.

Kragan brought his legion to a halt at a spot just beyond the range of the catapults arrayed atop the mighty wall. Dozens of torches lit the extensive battlements.

He sensed the thousands of vorgs and men who had died on the battlefield in the not-too-distant past. Only a few had escaped to tell the tale. The high priest of the protectors had told Kragan how the army of Tal had fallen upon the protectors' horde from behind, putting them to the sword right where he and his legion now stood. The Talian soldiers had piled the bodies here and burned them.

Val'Dep's khan and his brigade of horse warriors were Kragan's prisoners. The horsemen he had killed and brought back to life had informed him that the people left in the fortress city were mostly women, children, and the elderly. The stinking mound of flesh that had been their lone wielder lay rotting in a valley several leagues to the southwest.

The people who cowered behind the wall and in the fortress city beyond posed no threat, trapped inside their own battlements. He looked forward to letting them watch the show.

Kragan conjured a ball of light to hover a dozen paces above his head, its bright glow illuminating the hundreds of bound horsemen whom Kragan's Resurrected warriors forced to kneel before him. Then his men tied the khan's warriors' hands to their ankles such that they could not rise.

Kragan seated himself, crossed his legs, and removed his necklace to clutch its shards in his left hand. He took a deep breath, held it for several moments, then slowly exhaled and dropped into deep meditation. Because the ashes and other remains of those who'd died on this battlefield were so scattered, the coming resurrection would be the most difficult he'd yet tried. The price was still a life for a life, but the call upon his power to reassemble the corpses would mean he could handle only a few at a time.

He summoned earth elementals to bring the charred bones to the surface and air elementals to gather the ashes. The ground rumbled and the wind moaned through the crenels atop the great wall. Tightening his focus, Kragan lifted his eyes and selected seven of the nearest kneeling horsemen. Smoky strands of life magic seeped into the warriors. They shrieked and convulsed, flopping down upon the ground.

The arcane mist boiled from their bodies and spread out to engulf bones and ash, pulling the remains together into seven individual piles. Kragan intensified his casting, transferring the life energy from the dying into those about to arise.

He let the women and boys atop Val'Dep's wall watch the flesh rot from the bodies of the dying as the seven piles of bones assembled into skeletons. Skin sprouted, crawling across the corpses. Internal organs and blood-filled veins formed beneath the flesh. The howls of agony from the resuscitating vorgs rose even louder than the cries of the dying.

When the rebirth ended, the cacophony stopped, cloaking the night in the silence of a tomb. Seven naked male and female vorgs stood a dozen paces in front of Kragan. The extended muzzles on their vaguely human faces opened in unison to utter the words the wielder willed them to say.

"Hail Lord Kragan."

From where he sat, Kragan nodded. He released them to scavenge the clothes and armor from the desiccated corpses of the fallen horsemen. Then he turned his attention inward to assess how much the effort had drained him.

A grin crept onto his face. His strength had barely diminished. It was time to go bigger.

But this time, when he focused his magic, a strangeness drew his attention, the like of which he had never felt. He felt his mind drawn to the ashes of a corpse that lay scattered beyond the wall that blocked the way to the city of Val'Dep. Kragan summoned more power, feeling one of the shards in his left palm grow cold in his grip. A vision formed in his mind's eye.

—⁊⁊—

His spirit floated outward from his body to soar over the battlements. Moonlight bathed the vast parade ground beyond the wall. An ivory throne sat atop the pyramidal dais rising from the arena's center. But he found himself drawn to the scattered bits of ash that glittered with the remnants of ancient power. What was this?

Suddenly daylight swept away the night. Twin wooden pyres had replaced the throne atop the pyramid. A thousand ghostly horsemen galloped from the city to slide to a halt in a great circle at the base of the dais. A pair of riders bearing burning torches jumped from their mounts and raced up the steps to the top of the dais. Together they lit the wood piled at the base of the two funeral pyres.

A gust swept through the canyon, whipping taut the flags atop the city towers. The wind raced south, fanning the fire under one of the scaffolds into a roaring blaze but snuffing out the fire beneath the other. As the burning funeral pyre turned to ash, darkness descended. Storm clouds buoyed up across both rims of the canyon. Lightning skittered through the sky. The heavens unleashed torrential rain, as if at the thunder's summons.

Three separate bolts arced downward to blast the wood piled at the base of the remaining pyre. Thunder shook the earth, and a monstrous blaze consumed the scaffold, atop which a body lay. Clouds roiled overhead and wind shrieked around the fire, sending up a funnel of flame and ash.

The downpour ended as abruptly as it had begun. The silence that cloaked the valley seemed louder than the turmoil of the supernatural storm. The top of the dais stood empty, swept clean by the fury of the winds and rain.

A palomino stallion appeared atop the canyon, rearing high and pawing the air, sending forth a lonesome, piercing whinny.

As its echo died, a thousand horse warriors yelled out a name.

"Dar Khan!"

—◊—

Kragan found himself back in his body, breathing heavily. The presence that he had touched had sent him the vision. He was sure of it. Someone of immense power had lain atop that second funeral pyre. Whoever Dar Khan had been, Kragan wanted him.

A life for a life.

Once again, Kragan gathered his magic, sending elementals to collect the burned fragments that remained of the body he sensed beyond Val'Dep's outer wall. The wind stirred and eddied. Ever so slowly, a pile of ash and bone fragments accumulated before him. And as the pieces of the corpse built up, so did Kragan's anticipation.

He looked at the khan of the horse warriors, who stared at him with eyes filled with hate. To this man's credit he didn't yelp when the necrotic magic flowed into his body to extract his life essence. The monarch toppled over to writhe silently on the ground. Then the smoke flowed from him to engulf the remnants of the mighty corpse.

It was time to pluck another soul from the land of the dead.

—m—

The Dread Lord sat upon his black throne in the land of the dead, contemplating the recent spate of souls that had been stolen from his realm, when a sudden compulsion assaulted him. He understood what was happening. Some fool was attempting to summon him as well.

The Dread Lord stood, his blond mane draping his muscular shoulders, his blue eyes flashing. He grabbed the misty tendril that tried to bind him to another's will and jerked it from his neck. Then, taking the rope of magic in both hands, he tore the foul thing asunder.

—m—

When Kragan's hold on the underworld spirit broke, a spike of agony hammered into his brain and he slumped to the ground, releasing his grip on the arcane shards. For several moments he lay there, clutching his head in both hands. His fury soon quenched the pain.

He opened his eyes to see that his magical light had departed. Kragan forced himself back to a seated position and reached down to retrieve the precious necklace, this time clutching it in both hands. When he conjured a new light orb, he saw the khan's hog-tied body staring lifelessly back at him.

Then he understood. To resurrect the being he wanted would require a much greater sacrifice than one man, even if that man had been the khan of the horse warriors. Kragan focused his will, pulling more life magic through one of the shards of amplification than he had ever attempted, sending tentacles into the bodies of the hundreds of bound horsemen. Their screeches split the night as those cords exploded from the dying men and into the pile of ash and bone.

That magical assault met resistance. For several moments Kragan's effort faltered. But he chained the soul of the man with the force of a thousand lives. With a mighty effort, Kragan pulled the being from the land of the dead. The pile of ash and bone heaved, then slowly coalesced into a skeletal body. Flesh flowed over bones, eyes formed in empty sockets, lips covered teeth, and shoulder-length tresses whipped in the stiff breeze.

The man rose to his full height. His lean, muscular form stood a head taller than any of Kragan's Resurrected guards.

"So you are the one these people called Dar Khan."

The naked warrior looked up toward the stunned figures who had observed the ritual from atop the great wall. With a voice that rumbled from his throat, the man spoke.

"My name is Ty."

—⚬—

Chief Matron Loraine stared at the illuminated scene that unfolded beyond the great wall. She and the thousands of women, old men, and boys who defended the wall watched in horror as the small wielder sacrificed seven Val'Dep warriors to raise vorgs from the dead.

But what rendered her breathless was the spell that rotted hundreds of captive horsemen alive, all to raise a man. Naked, the warrior towered over the wielder, a scowl tightening his countenance. She knew this man. She had watched as his body had been consumed in a funeral pyre atop the pyramid dais at the center of the training ground behind her. A whisper escaped her lips.

"Dar Khan."

Stunned, she stood frozen in place. Two hundred paces from the battlements, the wicked mage turned to face her. The broad grin on his face put ice in her veins. She had no casters of magic within Val'Dep, and the wielder knew it. Despite the catapults, ballistae, archers, and warriors at her disposal, the city was defenseless against sorcery. And from what she had seen, even if the khan had left his wielder behind, Val'Dep's defenders would still be overmatched.

Loraine turned and walked the length of the wall, infusing into her voice a calm confidence that she didn't feel as she spoke words of encouragement to the city defenders awaiting the hell that they all knew was coming.

"Fire!" Loraine yelled.

Torchbearers all along the battlements waved their firebrands in the signal that launched every one of the dozen catapults, hurling their baskets of stones across the chasm. Hundreds of archers loosed arrows as fast as they could nock and pull.

The enemy wielder didn't leave her waiting for long. Clutching something she couldn't make out against his chest with his left hand, he raised his right hand to the sky. Electrical energy arced around him. Lightning skittered across the sky, concentrating into a spot directly above the wall upon which she stood.

When the clouds released the storm's might, the bolts crackled down by the dozens onto the battlements.

The enemy return fire rained down upon the wall, killing and maiming defenders and pulling forth agonized shrieks. A boy, barely fourteen, took an arrow in the throat two paces from Loraine. The lad dropped his bow, staggered forward, eyes wide in terror, then plummeted through the crenel and into the depths.

Loraine picked up the bow, grabbed a quiver from another woman's corpse, and began firing into the horde. A river of flame flowed from the enemy wielder's outstretched hand, forcing her to duck behind the nearest merlon. The heat from the fires blistered her skin.

When the torrent of flame died out, Loraine moved back into the crenel and resumed firing, taking careful aim at the distant mage. She pulled the string against her cheek, feeling the sharp pressure against her two fingers, then released it with a sharp twang. Her bolt flew straight and true, illuminated by the dancing remnants of fire. But, two paces from her target, something deflected it.

Then the wielder raised his hand, palm up, sending hundreds of vorgs spilling up onto the battlements as if they had been poured from a fountain. Loraine dropped the bow, pulled the long knife from its sheath, and buried its blade deep in the stomach of the nearest enemy as he struggled to regain his feet.

When she turned to meet one of the dying one's comrades, the she-vorg hammered her shield into Loraine. The blow lifted the chief matron from her feet. Loraine felt herself hurled into a turret. Her head hit stone and brilliant sparks flashed before her eyes. A sea of black consumed her.

It seemed as if she lost consciousness for only a moment before she was able to open her eyes once again. Her body lay wedged into a crenel so that her arms were pinned to her sides. Her head and shoulders dangled over the wall and she found herself staring straight down into the chasm. The left side of her body seethed in torment from the burns that extended up her neck and face.

For several moments she almost allowed herself to fall back into unconscious bliss. But she had to know what was happening to her people. Unable to see from her left eye, she managed to turn her head so that she could look along the wall. What she saw filled her with loathing.

Moonlight cast a pale illumination on the two great ramps that had been lowered across the gorge that protected Val'Dep. Vorg warriors herded hundreds of women, children, and the aged down the ramps into the valley beyond. The sound of their terrified wails pulled tears from Loraine's good eye. She angrily blinked them away, shifting so that she could see where her people were being taken.

What she saw doused her anger with horror. The entire population of her city was being gathered into a mass, crowded together so tightly they could barely move, cattle gathered for the slaughter. When the last citizens were pushed in with the thousands of their countrymen, Kragan walked forward, halting two dozen paces from the terrified assemblage.

Suddenly he rose high into the air. When he extended his right arm toward the people of Val'Dep, their wails turned to screams that built to a deafening crescendo. Loraine wanted to close her eye but couldn't tear herself away from the scene that unfolded.

The people crumpled atop each other, their bodies withering away. All around them, corpses assembled themselves, contorting in their own special agony as flesh and bone reknitted.

Loraine's stomach emptied itself down the wall, but no one could hear her violent heaves. When she was done, she finally surrendered to the slumber that ached to claim her.

PART II

Ash to flesh, flesh to flame. All things must hang in the balance. For only at that nexus may I tip the scale of destiny.

—From the *Scroll of Landrel*

9

"Two days and still no word," Alan said. "How much longer must we wait before we take action?"

Carol shared her brother's frustration, but Arn's visions held them all within the broad valley, six leagues from Endar Pass. The sound of approaching footsteps pulled her dog's gaze to Quincy Long. The hint of a mischievous grin tweaked the corners of his mouth.

"Ah, Chosen," he said. "So this is where you've been hiding."

"Hiding? I've been standing right here with Carol and Arn for the last hour."

"Yes. But why would I expect to find you at your headquarters?"

"Where else would I be?"

"With twilight approaching, I figured you'd have slipped into the woods with Kat on your arm."

Carol heard a chuckle escape Arn's lips as wrinkles creased Alan's brow and his cheeks reddened.

"If you have anything important to tell me," Alan said, "then say it."

Quincy leaned down to ruffle Zaislus's fur, shooting a quick wink into the canine eyes through which Carol observed him. When he straightened his lanky body, he shifted his gaze to Alan.

"It's just as Arn's recent dream foretold. Our scouts report a tendril of fog rapidly approaching from the direction of Endar Pass."

Sudden excitement sped Carol's heart. Galad and Kim.

"Show me," Alan said.

When Quincy turned and led Alan toward the ridge that formed the northeastern lookout for the campsite, Carol, Arn, and Zaislus fell in behind them. They reached the ridge crest and stepped up beside the two Forsworn lookouts. Carol directed her gaze to where the nearest of the men pointed. A league farther up the valley, the mists boiled forward faster than any clipper ship on the high seas.

The mists swept over them, revealing Kim and Galad striding toward her. Carol rushed to fling her arms around her sister, a hug that Kim returned. Then Arn wrapped them both in his arms. For several moments they just stood there, saying nothing. Then Kim stepped back, wiping her eyes.

The look on Kim's face was as grim as that on Galad's. Carol inhaled deeply, then asked for the news she'd been dreading.

"I take it that your welcome home wasn't a warm one."

Kim shook her head. "In our absence, the High Council deposed our mother. She's imprisoned in the royal palace, queen no more."

"What?"

"Our mother refused to comply with the High Council's orders not to incite dissent within the population. She made her choice," Kim said.

"How did the council react to your news of Kragan's return?" Arn asked.

"We managed to convince them to bring the kingdom back to a war footing," Galad said. "But the king made it clear that he regards Kimber and myself as potential enemies of the state. He offered us the choice of banishment or joining our mother under house arrest."

"Even the knowledge that Kragan now possesses six of the nine shards of Landrel's Trident couldn't change Kelond's mind," Kim said.

"Which makes no sense," Carol said. "Were it not for our talents and the assistance of my father's legion, Endar would have fallen to Kragan last year."

"The king fears that, should he allow you and the Chosen's Forsworn back into Endar Pass, you would help Galad and me restore our mother to power."

"Well," Alan said, "that leaves us with one option. We need to make haste to Areana's Vale, where Carol can take her place as high lorness, commander of Rafel's legion and the army of Tal. With that twenty thousand added to my Forsworn, we can crush Kragan before he can raise an army of his own."

"Perhaps even Val'Dep will support us with some of their horse warriors," Arn said.

"What does your time-sight tell you?"

"Nothing is clear. But my dreams of Val'Dep leave me uneasy."

"Ah," Quincy said, "no change then. Worst case, we gather Carol's army and chase the murderous bastard down. That overly large head of his would grace a pike nicely."

This last remark brought a grin to Carol. Thank the gods for the rogue's merciless wit. She lifted her face to the warmth of the midmorning sun. One advantage of her blindness was the way the direct sunlight soothed her sightless eyes. Shifting her dog's gaze to Alan, she rubbed her hands together.

"Ready your Forsworn for the march through Galad's time-mists. We shall hasten to the vale. I long to be reunited with our people."

10

Arn stepped out of the dissipating time-mists into the brightness of the morning sun.

"Gods, how I've longed for this sight, for these smells," Carol said as she placed a hand on his left arm.

Now that they'd left the towering trees of the Great Forest in their wake, Arn's eyes locked on the distant cliffs through which the gorge that formed the only entrance to Areana's Vale carved a narrow rift. The sight tightened his throat with anticipation and a sense of dread. For a moment he was tempted to reach for the pouch where his shard of Landrel's Trident rested.

But there had been no time to practice his nascent skill in wielding his amplified time-sight, so hurried had been their journey south from Endar Pass. Now wasn't the time to dampen Carol's mood with his maddening dreams of what might lie ahead.

"I recommend that Alan have his Forsworn make their camp here," Arn said. "I don't think we should march a thousand foreign warriors into the gorge without an introduction."

"I agree," Alan said.

Carol nodded, petting Zaislus's head as she considered this.

"We'll only take those with whom Hanibal is familiar. Alan, Quincy, Kat, Kim, and Galad will accompany Arn and me. Let's approach the gorge in an unhurried fashion, without using the time-mists. I want Hanibal's ranger patrols to recognize us from afar."

"Okay," Alan said. "I'll have Tudor get the Forsworn started setting up camp."

Within minutes Alan rejoined the small group, and they strode toward the distant gorge. Halfway to their objective, three riders approached. Jaradin Scot was in the lead. When they pulled their mounts to a halt, the one-eyed ranger leapt from the saddle. His broad grin suddenly faded from his scarred face as he looked at Carol.

"Lorness! What's happened to your eyes?"

The question pulled forth the memory that filled Arn with guilt. Because he'd tried to deny his time-sight, he had failed to foresee the attack from Kragan that had aged Carol's eyes and blinded her. Had he embraced his ability, he would have killed Charna, the she-vorg through whom Kragan had funneled his time magic.

"That's a story too long to be told right now." Carol stepped forward and hugged Jaradin, the ranger whose mind she had rescued from an imprisoned body not his own. Arn watched the man heartily return the embrace. When Carol released Jaradin, Arn gripped forearms with his friend. After greetings had been exchanged all around, the ranger's face clouded.

"There are things you must know before I take you to Areana's Vale."

"Go on," Carol said.

"There's no easy way to say this, so I'll be blunt. Hanibal has named Areana's Vale the new capital of the kingdom of Tal. He has proclaimed himself its new king."

Arn's dread had found its source.

"What?" Alan's outrage matched the icy fury that clenched Arn's jaw.

Carol placed one hand on her husband's arm while she gripped her brother's with the other.

"Calm down," she said, her voice steady. "Let's hear Jaradin out."

"After Hanibal led Rafel's legion and the army of Tal back to Areana's Vale, he formed an expeditionary force of two thousand soldiers and named Derek its commander."

"Your brother?"

"Yes. Hanibal gave Derek the mission of returning to Tal to recruit any soldiers that Kragan hadn't killed or pressed into his service. Derek was also to discover if any of the kingdom's wielders still lived and bring them, the soldiers, and any civilians who wanted to travel with him back to Areana's Vale."

"I take it that Derek succeeded," Arn said.

"Beyond Hanibal's wildest expectations. Derek's expedition returned six weeks ago, bringing six magic wielders, four thousand soldiers, and a wagon train carrying supplies and more than ten thousand Talian civilians. And on his way back, he established outposts at key points along the route."

"Derek created a road through the desert?" Carol asked.

"No. He skirted the coast south of the Mogev Desert, then crossed the Rake River and turned northeast into Tal. But what we didn't realize was that Hanibal filled the expeditionary force with the soldiers who were most loyal to Carol and Alan."

"Devious bastard," Arn said.

"With most of Carol's loyalists out of the way," Jaradin said, "too few of those who opposed Hanibal's proclamation remained in the vale to prevent his ascension to the throne."

"I feel the need for a private conversation with this new king," Arn replied.

"You'll have to beat me to him," Alan said.

Carol raised both hands, motioning for the two to be quiet. Arn clenched his teeth but heard a low growl from Alan.

"How did our people react to Hanibal's usurpation?" Carol asked, her voice carrying an undertone of forced calm.

Jaradin shrugged.

"There was some initial grumbling, but Hanibal has always been popular among the soldiers. When Derek returned with thousands of refugees from Tal, the mission's success increased the people's regard for their king. Right now, the newcomers are building three towns in the western part of the vale. With spring planting complete, the people are at peace and happy."

Carol paused for several moments, her white eyes unblinking. As her silence dragged on, Zaislus moved to place his head beneath her left hand. The action forced Arn to notice his own left hand clenching Slaken's ivory haft.

"I think it is time for you to escort us into the vale," Carol said.

"Would you like to ride? You can have my mount."

"Thank you, but no. Please lead on."

Jaradin swung up into the saddle and turned his mount away. When the rangers were beyond earshot, Carol turned to the others, keeping her voice low.

"Let's wait until we talk with Hanibal before jumping to any conclusions about his intentions."

"His objectives seem pretty obvious to me," Arn said.

"And me," Alan said.

"It's the same situation Galad and I faced in Endar Pass," Kim said. "Our entire world has gone crazy."

"I'm not going to stand for Hanibal's betrayal," Alan said. "As far as I'm concerned, he's dead."

Arn nodded in agreement. "Something like that is best left to me. But I agree with Carol. We can assess the situation once we meet with Hanibal."

"Alan," Carol said, "I want you to take Galad, Kim, and the others back to your Forsworn. Arn and I will accompany the rangers to the vale. Should we fail to return within a week, I leave whatever actions you take to your discretion."

Arn watched Alan's frown deepen, but then he inclined his head and hugged his sister, who kissed his cheek. When Alan released her, he clasped Arn's wrist.

"I trust you to keep her safe."

"Have no doubt."

Then Alan and the others stepped into the time-mists that Galad summoned to take them back to the Forsworn encampment. Arn, Carol, and her dog turned and followed the rangers toward the distant gorge that led to their mountain home.

Arn tamped down the fury that weaponized him, storing it deep inside for a time when he might unleash it.

11

Glacier Mountains
YOR 416, Mid-Spring

It had taken ten days for Kragan's six thousand Resurrected vorg and human warriors to reach the high pass through the Glacier Mountains, thirty leagues northeast of Val'Dep. Part of the cause for the delay had been the need to gather supplies for the long trip that lay ahead of them. The horde had raided the vast stores within the city of the horse warriors for armor and weapons. The rest of the supplies from the city's stores had been packed onto hundreds of wagons.

But Kragan's real frustration lay in his discovery that despite his use of the shards of magic amplification, he didn't possess the talent of an Endarian master time-shaper. He simply didn't have the power to wield enough time-mist to encompass an army of this size. So the march had been a slog, limited to the pace at which the teams of horses could pull the supply wagons.

He signaled to Ty, the recently appointed commander of Kragan's legions. He watched the shirtless horse warrior trot toward him, riding bareback atop a magnificent stallion, guiding the animal with only the pressure of his legs. Every time Kragan looked at his bronze-skinned commander with the battle ax slung across his back, a sense of envy hovered at the edge of his thoughts. This resurrected lord of the underworld looked every bit the god of war.

Ty brought the animal to a halt and dismounted with the fluidity that graced his every movement. When he stepped forward, Kragan could feel the challenge radiating from the man. The warrior's tremendous will continually strained against the binding of the spell that had summoned him to Kragan's service. It was a constant itch in Kragan's mind, siphoning off some of the wielder's magic.

"Your orders?"

Kragan noted the lack of an honorific in the question but chose to ignore the slight. He could force this one to kneel before him, but the more he violated the man's self-image, the harder Ty fought him. And the wielder had more than enough on his mind.

"Once we emerge on the east side of this pass, I want you to set up an encampment at the edge of the Northern Plains. There you will await my return."

"Where will you be?"

"I'm going to gather reinforcements. Be prepared to incorporate them into our army."

Ty turned and leapt onto the stallion's back. With a nudge of his left leg, the barbarian whirled his mount and galloped away, the animal's hooves spraying Kragan with dust and gravel.

Not for the first time, the thought occurred to Kragan that Ty's resurrection might not have been worth the trouble the man caused him.

Shrugging off his annoyance, Kragan summoned the balancing time-mists to engulf him. Something far more important than slogging across the Northern Plains awaited him many leagues to the southeast, across the Mogev Desert.

12

Carol walked beside Arn with her left hand caressing the black fur on Zaislus's head. The magic of her connection to the dog's mind didn't limit itself to his eyesight. She savored the scent of pines and nearby animals on the clean mountain air. She could hear the worried conversation among the rangers who led them into the mouth of the gorge that led to Areana's Vale.

The group burst out of the trees as they reached the floor of the canyon. Directly to the east, a swift-moving stream roared through a narrow opening between granite walls that rose straight upward to touch the sky, blocking Carol's view of what might lie beyond the constricted opening. Jaradin headed toward the gap in the cliffs, followed closely by the others.

The burbling river that had cut the chasm through the cliffs that towered on her left and right carried a peaceful murmur that belied her current situation. The floor of the canyon wound its way between the magnificent cliffs for several leagues, the rushing mountain water switching back and forth across its width in a series of rapids broken briefly by stretches of relative calm.

She came to the place where the lower of High Lord Rafel's three forts had once stood. During her absence Hanibal's people had cleared all remnants of the burned walls and buildings away, leaving the path ahead pristine. Hanibal's people? Why had that thought wormed its way into her head? The soldiers and townsfolk of Areana's Vale were *her* people. She barely noticed the towering thunderheads building in the sky behind her as her feet carried her ever closer to the confrontation with the regent who had named himself king.

Up ahead, two of the rangers spurred their horses into a trot, leaving Jaradin to escort Carol and Arn back to their mountain home. When they passed through the spot where the middle fort had stood, Carol was shocked that its ruins had been removed and that there had been no attempt to rebuild it. But the sight of the last of the three fortresses that blocked entry into the lengthy valley that opened at the eastern end of the gorge assuaged her worries about Hanibal's defenses.

The partially burned upper fort had been rebuilt, the high outer wall made of stone instead of timber. Archers manning the battlements watched the group's approach, and a squad of ten soldiers awaited them on the drawbridge that had been lowered to connect the riverbanks. The surface of the roiling waters swelled by spring snowmelt lay only two paces below the bridge.

Jaradin dismounted and handed the reins of his horse to a soldier, who led it into the fort. Derek Scot stepped forward to greet Carol and Arn, his black bear at his heels. Carol heard Zaislus's low growl and placed her hand upon his head while she mentally soothed him.

Jaradin's brother stared into her unseeing eyes, concern in his gaze.

"High Lorness," he said, "Jaradin told me of your affliction. The sight of your wounds saddens me."

Carol reached out to place her right hand on the ranger's arm and beamed.

"You and Jaradin have long called me Carol, my friend. I would prefer that you both continue to do so. As for my damaged eyes, I retain my sight through other means."

Derek's eyes shifted down to her dog, and he nodded in understanding. A slow smile formed on his lips as he glanced at Arn.

"I see that two wolves now escort you."

Arn looked at the black bear that halted beside the ranger. The beast had grown to maturity since Arn had last seen it, perhaps weighing as much as a half dozen warriors.

"Lonesome has sprouted since last we saw him," Arn said.

"A lot can happen in a year."

"So we've heard," Carol said. "Will Hanibal see us now?"

"The king sent me to serve as escort. He wishes to allow you a couple days' rest and to visit the towns spread out along both branches of the vale, that you might see what our people have accomplished during your absence. He wants you to visit with the people and determine for yourself their level of satisfaction with his rule."

"Does he?" *Shrewd,* she thought. "It sounds like he's reluctant to meet with me."

With a shrug, Derek turned toward the fortress that blocked the narrow chasm from the sheer cliffs on the south to the raging rapids that cascaded along the gorge's northern face. Once past the fort, the river turned sharply, crossing the passage in front of Carol and blocking the way forward.

She followed Derek onto the lowered drawbridge that spanned the raging waters, providing access to the fort. As she approached the opening that lay ahead, Carol noted that the stone battlements were two strides thicker than the log walls she remembered.

As Carol followed Derek into a broad courtyard, she felt the eyes of the soldiers who'd stopped what they were doing to stare at her and the assassin they knew as Blade. Her mind reached out to touch these people so lightly that they weren't aware of her caress. The act was just enough for her to sense their emotional state.

Some exuded shock at the sight of her pearlescent eyes. From others she felt hope. But varying degrees of fear underlay the thoughts of most of the fighters. As painful as that knowledge was for Carol, it didn't surprise her. When she had almost allowed her magic to destroy her mind, most of the people who'd once loved the lorness had come to fear her.

Carol shifted Zaislus's gaze to her husband's face. Arn had rescued her from the drug-induced delirium into which High Priest Jason and his subordinates had placed her. He had spirited her away to Misty Hollow and worked with her through the long winter to master the magic that threatened her with madness.

The display of arcane power she had unleashed upon her return had wrung respect from her people but had only enhanced the fear with which many of them regarded her. Even though they'd watched her defend Areana's Vale from the protector army and its hundreds of wielders, their trepidation remained.

Carol walked out the back gate of the fortress. The familiar verdant valley widened out before her, grassy meadows amidst groves of towering pines. What brought the tightness to her throat, however, was her view of the sheer cliffs that formed the sides of the lowland. Those walls rose thousands of paces, turning the wide valley into an unassailable fortress for as far as Zaislus's eyes could see.

The mountain walls looked as if they'd been hewn by a god bored with the normal order of things. From high up on the walls, streams leapt outward to plunge toward the grassland below, spreading like the train of an Endarian queen's gown. All the streams flowed into the watercourse that cut its path through the valley's center, exiting through the narrow gorge from which Carol and Arn had just emerged.

One particularly spectacular waterfall cascaded from the summit before smashing onto the rocks below, only to plunge over another ledge farther down. A misty plume obscured large portions of the canyon. She was home at last. Tears flooded her eyes, streaming down her cheeks and dripping from her chin. Arn gripped her hand, squeezing her palm with a passion that said he shared her feelings.

As she hungrily consumed the views of the magnificent rock walls that ancient glaciers had carved through these mountains, an unexpected sight focused her stare. Atop a ledge a hundred feet above the valley floor, a new stone fortress was under construction, protected from above by an outcropping on the sheer face of the north wall. A winding road, just wide enough for ox-drawn wagons, led up to the gates of the walled-off cavern entrance.

"What's that?" Arn asked, voicing her words before she could utter them.

"Ah," said Derek. "Our king's new castle. Hanibal's throne room, quarters, and council chambers are already complete behind those battlements."

Carol scowled up at the brutish edifice.

"I see he wasted no time in ensconcing himself as ruler here."

"Not just here," Derek said. "Over all of Tal. By recruiting the bulk of Tal's surviving military, he's accomplished his goal. He merely needs to consolidate those holdings over time."

"Time is exactly what he doesn't have," Carol said, letting the heat she felt creep into her voice. "We must speak with Hanibal now."

"Why?"

"Kragan is back."

13

Kim loved the giant conifers of the Great Forest. Having wandered a few hundred paces south of the extensive campsite, she seated herself and leaned back against the rough trunk of the nearest of the arboreal monsters, savoring the pungent fragrance, so heavy on the air that she could taste it. Tudor had chosen to make camp here due to the excellent concealment the towering trees provided and the abundance of game.

She looked up into the branches that blocked out the sky, thinking about the thousands of years this tree had lived. It had stood here when Landrel was Endar's king. It was even older than Kragan. Kim would die before she hurt one of these ancient wonders of nature. If she could simply meld with this tree, she would.

She imagined leaving all the pain and terrors of this world behind for a respite from the grief she felt over John's death. To enjoy the warm energy of the sun's rays, to partake of the earth's nourishment, to drink from the abundant flows of water, to share her existence with a towering community of neighbors . . . that would be wonderful.

"Ah, so here you are."

Alan's voice startled her out of her reverie.

Kim's eyes took in the man who stood above her, the so-called Chosen, wielding an aura that felt like destiny incarnate.

She reached up and took his hand, allowing him to pull her to her feet. At six feet tall, he matched her in height. As her eyes met his, Kim channeled some of the life from nearby shrubbery into her body. The tingle of the transfer filled her with caged energy that sought an outlet through her own aura.

Though Alan fought to hide his feelings, she detected the catch in his breath. She held on to that feeling for a handful of heartbeats before releasing her tap on the plant's life force. As she did, she allowed her aura to return to normal.

This was not the time or place for blunt-force seduction. She dared not make direct use of her unusual talent for life magic to tether his soul to hers. All magic had a cost. Such a binding affected the spell caster as much as the target. Despite the attraction she felt toward Alan, Kim still valued her freedom. Right now, she just wanted to resurrect the seed of the desire that had previously bloomed within his heart, hoping it could fill the hole the loss of her husband had left.

"How did you find me?" she asked.

"The sentries told me you had gone this way."

Kim studied his face, seeking some sign of his true motivation.

"Why did you seek me out?"

"I need you for a leaders' meeting. Galad and Tudor await us at my headquarters."

Kim tilted her head slightly.

"Yes, but why did *you* come to fetch me rather than sending Galad?"

"I thought a walk in the woods would clear my head in advance of the decisions that confront me."

"And that was your only reason?"

Alan paused for a moment, never taking his eyes from hers.

"Truthfully, I value your company and your insights. I want to hear your opinion of my thoughts before the group discussion."

The revelation that he placed such value on her judgment filled her with a warm glow.

"I'm listening."

Alan's fists clenched at his sides, knotting the muscles in his forearms.

"I should have gone with Carol instead of letting her put herself at the mercy of a traitor."

"Our sister can take care of herself. And Arn is with her."

Alan turned to gaze through the forest in the direction of Areana's Vale.

"I don't doubt either of their capabilities. But Carol has a weakness for our people. I don't think she can bring herself to hurt them."

"Maybe," Kim said. "But Blade has no such qualms. I wouldn't care to be Hanibal if Arn perceives a threat to Carol."

Alan took a deep breath. Kim watched as he forced himself to relax. He nodded toward the camp and turned to walk. Kim matched him stride for stride.

"I'm contemplating marching my Forsworn toward the vale."

This revelation caught Kim by surprise. She'd never known Alan to act against Carol's wishes. After all, High Lord Rafel had directed that their sister would assume leadership after his death. By all rights Carol was high lorness, despite any proclamation that Hanibal had made.

"Hanibal has thirty thousand soldiers under his command. Do you really think it's a good idea to take such a threatening posture while Carol and Arn are within his gates?"

"I don't intend to enter the gorge. I would merely set up camp outside it."

"What would that accomplish?"

"It would let our supporters within Hanibal's ranks know that I've returned with ten times as many Forsworn as when we left for Sadamad."

Kim walked beside him in silent contemplation. As dangerous as Alan's plan felt to her, she had no doubt that such a display would reinforce the legend of the Chosen among the thousands of soldiers who'd fought alongside him during the battle for Endar Pass.

"No thoughts?" Alan asked.

"Carol isn't going to be happy with you."

Alan stopped a dozen paces short of the sentries and turned to face her.

"I was asking what you think."

The words that came to Kim's lips surprised her.

"It's a bold move. But I think I like it."

Alan grinned, then turned and escorted her into the camp. As she strode alongside him, Kim found herself regretting the minor amount of magic she had used on her half brother only minutes earlier. She vowed that if she was going to win his affection, she would earn it honestly.

14

With Carol at his side, Arn watched as Derek halted where the road began its winding ascent toward the stone fortress on the ledge above. The ranger issued a command that sent the black bear to seat itself beneath a pine. Then Derek led the couple and Zaislus toward the meeting he'd arranged with Hanibal.

When they reached the gates that opened into the courtyard beyond the outer wall, they passed between two ranks of guards, twenty-four in all. Arn recognized some. The courtyard bustled with activity as hundreds of men bent their backs at the varied tasks associated with the ongoing construction of the castle.

It was unlike any fortress Arn had ever seen. The solid rock of the overhang limited the height of any structure to sixty feet. The outer wall was a half dozen paces thick. Steps led to the walkway, where more guards roamed the battlements. Whereas the tops of the castle and fortress walls were crenelated to give archers protection, this wall rose to connect with the solid rock that formed the broad cavern's jutting ceiling. The crenels thus looked more like slotted windows. Other openings in the top of the wall were clearly intended as spouts to discharge boiling oil down onto attackers. Except for a pool of sunlight at the entrance gates, shadows reigned behind the protective barrier.

Arn noted the flaming torches in regularly placed brackets that lined the walls around the courtyard. A small stream cut a path along the west side of the cavern and out through an iron-barred opening in the west wall, forming one of the many waterfalls that were a prime feature of the cliff-lined valley Carol had named Areana's Vale.

"Gods," she said. "I thought Kaleal's lair was the most dismal place I'd ever entered."

Arn sniffed. The odor of smoke from the torches hung heavily in the cavern.

"The air in here could use some freshening."

"The guards and builders say you get used to it," Derek said.

Carol wrinkled her nose. "It makes you want to get back out into the open."

From the way Zaislus sneezed, Arn knew that Carol was experiencing the true intensity of the scent through her mental connection with her dog.

"Let's go see Hanibal," Arn said.

Derek grabbed a torch from the wall and led them around a partially completed building that Arn judged to be a large barracks. Beyond that, a winding street led deeper into the cavern between a variety of nondescript structures. With each step, the ambient light receded behind them. Here the cavern ceiling lowered to half its height at the outer wall.

Shortly after he had arrived in Areana's Vale in the company of John, Kim, and Ty, Arn had explored this horizontal crevice in the face of the massive cliff that towered three thousand feet above the valley floor. The cave penetrated the rock wall for a couple of hundred paces, ending at the source of the stream that plummeted through the entrance that Hanibal had walled off.

Around one last bend, the light of a dozen torches lit the top of the wall of a secondary fortification. Another group of guards that Arn didn't recognize stood at attention outside the iron-banded oak door that opened between them. Their eyes swept over him to lock on Carol and her waist-high dog.

Derek paid the guards no mind, leading Carol and Arn through the portal and across a wide hall that was clearly a meeting room. When they reached the closed double doors on the far side of the chamber, Derek gave it two sharp raps with his closed fist.

"Enter."

Arn recognized the voice that answered that knock. Hanibal.

Derek shoved the doors open, and they stepped into the torchlit throne room of the self-proclaimed king of Tal. Seated upon a throne carved from the reddish wood of one of the trees from the Great Forest, Hanibal leaned back, his flame-red locks and beard cascading over his leather armor. Since Arn had last seen him, Hanibal had added weight to his lithe form, most of it muscle.

High Priest Jason stood on Hanibal's left, the old man's right hand, minus the ring finger that Arn had cut from it, clutching his staff. Lektuvu, the petite female wielder with a spiked blonde mane, stood at Hanibal's right, resplendent in her billowing silver robe. A fire blazed within the large hearth on the back wall, its smoke rising through a chimney that disappeared into the log ceiling.

Except for the bear hides spread out before the throne, the rest of the room was barren. The fact that no guards had entered the room before Derek closed the doors spoke volumes. Hanibal didn't fear Carol and Arn. From the pleasant smile on his face and the way he spread his arms wide, the man was truly pleased to see them.

"Ah, I'm happy that you've survived your quest and returned to your homeland. I was sorry to hear of the extent of your injuries, High Lorness, but you seem to be bearing your burden well."

Carol halted before the throne with Arn and Zaislus at her side. Neither she nor her husband made any attempt to bow.

"I left you as my entrusted regent, to rule in my absence," Carol said quickly, her words tight. "Yet I return to discover that you've named yourself sovereign, not only of Areana's Vale, but over the remnants of the entire kingdom of Tal."

Arn noticed his hand straying to Slaken's haft and embraced the calm that crept over him.

"I merely did what I thought best to ensure the long-term safety and well-being of our people," Hanibal replied. "The title *regent* doesn't come close to inspiring the confidence that having a king brings to the people. That title helped me rescue thousands of soldiers and citizens left to wander Tal without a ruler, without a protector."

"Fine. But since *I* have returned, I expect you to honor your word to me."

The self-appointed king's brow furrowed.

"This is why I wanted to let you spend a few days among our people before this audience. Then you could have judged for yourself whether they want me to step down. They see the results of my rule. They feel safe, happy. I think you'll find that they don't wish to change their circumstances."

"Perhaps," Carol said. "But first I must deliver some foul news. Kragan has returned to the Endarian continent."

"So Derek informed me."

"Kragan has acquired six of the nine fragments from Landrel's Trident."

Hanibal's already pale face blanched at the news. "Isn't that what you went to Sadamad to prevent?"

Arn gritted his teeth at the man's tone. Lektuvu's shimmering eyes shifted from Carol to Arn. A dozen versions of the immediate future painted themselves in Arn's mind. When none of them resulted in violence, he allowed himself to relax.

"We undertook our journey to find Kragan and kill him. That quest has once again changed continents. He has returned with enhanced magical abilities but will need to raise an army. We have a chance to finish him if we act decisively now."

"I take it you want to strip away Tal's defenders to join your hunt."

"We haven't come back empty-handed. Alan and his thousand warriors await us at the edge of the Great Forest. If we augment that force with another twenty thousand soldiers, Prince Galad will speed our pursuit. We can destroy Kragan before he can match our strength in numbers."

"That would leave me to defend the vale with less than half of our fighters when Kragan turns his attention this way."

"Not if he's dead."

Hanibal laughed.

"You just told me that he acquired six of the nine shards and escaped to return here. What makes me think you can challenge his magic?"

A new vision spiraled into Arn's mind.

He pulled the drawstring that released the small pouch from his belt. Opening it, he placed its mummified content into the open palm of his left hand, forcing himself to avoid the visions that sought his full attention. Following Arn's lead, Carol retrieved the matching finger from a pocket. Then they both extended their hands so that Hanibal, Lektuvu, and Jason could see the magical shards.

"As I said, we didn't return empty-handed."

For a moment Hanibal remained speechless. He gaped at the ancient artifacts. Lektuvu stared in wonderment, and Arn sensed the desire that burned within her. Jason's lips curled in distaste at the sight of what he regarded as objects of purest evil.

"And," Arn said, "this is High Lorness Carol's decision, whether you call yourself king or not."

Arn saw the king's gaze shift to the big knife strapped at his side before shifting to meet his eyes.

Carol placed her hand on Arn's arm.

"Think of this as an urgent request," Carol said. "I will spend the rest of today and tomorrow getting reacquainted with my people. If I determine you're correct about their desire for you to remain their king, I will respect our people's wishes. But know this. If you do *not* provide aid to support our mission, Kragan will raise an army. Then, after he crushes Endar and takes the Landrel shard that lies there within a time stone, he will come for you."

Hanibal leaned back in his throne, rubbing his bearded chin with his right hand.

"I will consult with Lektuvu and Jason and make my decision by tomorrow night."

Arn watched his wife give a single nod. Then they turned together with Zaislus and followed Derek out of the dreary fortress.

—⚊—

When Carol stepped out through the castle gates, she welcomed the warm sun on her face and eyes. As frustrating as it had been to delay any challenge she might make to Hanibal's usurpation of her title, she was proud of the self-control Arn had maintained during their meeting.

"What now?" asked Arn.

"I want to visit Colindale, Fernwood, and Longsford Watch to see for myself how our people are doing. I want to spend the night with you in our home within the Fairy Rift."

"You will find it just as you left it," Derek said. "Lonesome and I check in on the house from time to time."

Carol felt her heart race at the thought of home, a feeling she hadn't had for a long time.

When they reached the valley floor, Derek whistled, and Lonesome came loping up to him. Derek hugged the bear's neck, ruffling his coat.

He straightened. "We'll need horses if we're going to visit all three villages and get you home before nightfall. Let me show you to the newest of our stables."

"That's fine," Carol said. "But once you arrange for our mounts, Arn and I won't need you to escort us. I think we can still find our way around."

Derek lifted his hand from Lonesome's head.

"Good. Then I can get back to my rangers."

Midafternoon found Carol and Arn riding toward Colindale, the westernmost of the original three villages within Areana's Vale, with Zaislus trotting alongside. When they rounded a bend in the road and exited the forest, Carol pulled her mount to a halt.

"Wow!"

The small town she remembered had more than doubled in size, as had the cultivated fields that surrounded it.

"It looks like Hanibal has put all the new arrivals to work," Arn said.

She urged her dapple-gray mare forward.

"Let's see what else has changed."

They approached the town's edge, and a small group of onlookers quickly grew into a throng as word of their coming spread, lining both sides of the main street and spreading out in the narrow roads that branched from it. Mothers pulled small children tightly up against their skirts, some putting hands over mouths as they looked at the lorness's blind eyes and the black-clad assassin known as Blade.

They made their way deeper into the village, encountering more and more people she knew as she reached the town center. Carol smiled as she saw the familiar log structure up ahead on the left. A wood sign hung above the wide front door, the image of a rosy-cheeked maiden carrying two foaming mugs swinging slowly back and forth in the warm afternoon breeze. The Flowing Ale Tavern, just as she remembered it.

Carol pulled her horse to a stop outside, swung down from the saddle, and was swept into the arms of Rolf Grombit, the establishment's portly proprietor.

"Lorness Carol," Rolf said, "how I prayed to all the gods for your safe return."

Carol returned the hug and planted a firm kiss on the jovial man's ruddy cheek.

"I missed you too."

But when Rolf released her and stepped back, a look of shock slackened his jaws.

"My girl, what happened to your eyes?"

Ah yes. The inevitable question she had been asked hundreds of times.

She threaded her left hand through Rolf's arm and turned him toward the door.

"Arn and I will be glad to tell you our tale over a couple of mugs of your ale, if you have a free table."

"Never fear. The evening rush won't begin for another few hours. But I would make a table for you even if I had to toss all my patrons out."

Her right hand found Zaislus's head, a habit she almost failed to notice.

"I hope you don't mind my dog accompanying us. He guides me."

Rolf looked down at Zaislus, which felt to Carol as though he were staring directly at her. As familiar as she had become with this odd shift of perspective, it still posed surprises.

"Certainly. I'll fetch him some kitchen scraps and a bowl of water."

Soon Carol found herself seated beside Arn at a table. Rolf sat directly across from her, one of his serving girls having set a flagon before each of them, filled to the brim with the monastery's finest brew. For the next hour they talked, pausing only briefly as they consumed hearty bowls of venison stew, the aroma of which made Carol salivate before she got her first taste. She ignored the stares that her appearance drew.

By the time they took their leave, Carol and Arn had learned from the font of local gossip much of what they needed to know. Rolf had reluctantly confirmed that the vast majority of the vale's citizens were indeed happy to have Hanibal as their king. While there were rumblings of discontent at the way Hanibal had deposed Carol during her long absence, those who complained were in the minority. Derek's arrival with thousands more soldiers and citizens of Tal had cemented Hanibal's popularity.

Despite her best efforts to find the positives in their current situation, a deep melancholy wormed its way into Carol's soul. Arn sensed it and tried to lift her mood by pointing out the dozens of waterfalls that plummeted from the cliffs that lined all sides of the spectacular valley. But as they made their way through Fernwood and then Longsford Watch, she reached out to gently touch the minds of the hundreds of people who stopped what they were doing to watch her.

Although some of these folks harbored fond feelings and a sense of nostalgia for Carol, most regarded her with a mixture of foreboding and dread. The fear in the air was palpable, as if she and Arn were harbingers of ruin.

Carol had to acknowledge that the citizens of the vale were probably right.

—m—

Carol and Arn rode into the wild crevice that had been named the Fairy Rift just as the sinking sun painted the western sky in swaths of magenta and scarlet. Their home was nestled beneath an overhanging section of cliff that looked out over a vista. Across the canyon from the entrance to their log abode, a waterfall plunged two thousand feet from the southern cliffs to feed a rushing stream. And they had their own hot spring. The abundance of white aspen, tinted pink by the sunset, gave the scene a mystical appearance.

The two dismounted and removed their horses' saddles and bridles. They hobbled and released the animals, knowing that they would graze on the deep grass and drink from the stream. Carol opened the door, letting Zaislus enter as she summoned a globe that spread a soft light throughout the single-room structure. As Arn opened the shutters that covered the lone window, Carol summoned an air elemental to dust the interior and sweep the floor.

Arn walked outside to place kindling and sticks from the stack of dried firewood into their rock-lined firepit. While her husband retrieved his fishing line from his pack and made his way down to the brook, Carol brought the pile of sticks to a crackling blaze. Then, turning her back to the fire, she gazed across the canyon to the spot where a bend in the babbling brook had created a deep pool.

As she stroked Zaislus's head, memories flooded through her, unleashing a torrent of emotions. Once again, she felt her father's powerful embrace and watched the warm smile light the high lord's craggy face as he gazed into her once-brown eyes. She had never thought that the commander of the army of Tal, the hero of the Vorg War, could fall in battle. But he and Battle Master Gaar had died together in Endar Pass, swept from the land of the living as they fought Kragan's horde.

She didn't try to fight the tears that cut twin trails down her dusty cheeks. When Zaislus started licking her hand, his rough tongue pulled her back into the present moment in time to see Arn walk into the circle of firelight carrying a gutted eighteen-inch brown trout. His forehead furrowed as he looked at her.

To his credit, Arn didn't ask what was wrong. He merely nodded in gentle understanding, then turned to spit the fish above the coals formed by the dying flames, allowing Carol the space to come to terms with her feelings.

It was the wonderful aroma of the cooked fish that stimulated her hunger and pulled her out of her brief depression. People said that blindness enhanced a person's other senses. She didn't know whether that was true, but her mental connection to Zaislus opened a whole new world of perception.

"Gods, that smells wonderful," she said. "I can't wait to taste it."

"Let me grab some plates and utensils from the cabin," Arn said. "Then we'll find out whether I'm as good a cook as you believe."

Carol seated herself on the aspen log they'd placed near the firepit during the construction of their abode and waited for Arn to return. It took only a few minutes for him to debone the fish, place a lovely fillet on her plate, and sit down beside her. It had been so long since she'd tasted trout that she'd forgotten how delicious it was. She forced herself to eat slowly, savoring each bite and enjoying the look of satisfaction on Arn's and her own face as seen through her dog's eyes.

She gave half her fillet to Zaislus. After he gulped it down, he placed his big head on Arn's knee, extracting a laugh.

"Don't think you can play me for a sucker," Arn said.

But her husband lowered his plate to the ground and let the dog lick it clean.

Carol shifted her mind link to Arn, seeing herself from his perspective. She liked the smile on her face and the way her eyes closed as he leaned in to kiss her lips.

She felt herself lifted in his arms and watched as he carried her back to their shelter. He laid her down on their thick bedding and leaned in to kiss her again as his fingers undid the buttons on her shirt. His rising passion fanned a similar flame within her breast. They took their time undressing each other, and when he gently lowered Carol onto her back, he leaned over her.

Through his eyes she watched him caress every curve of her body. Propped on his elbow beside her, she watched him caress the skin of her arms with the fingertips of his right hand, his touch so light that it sent shivers of anticipation through her body. Then he traced a finger along her armpit and down her side, the palm of his hand barely touching the swell of her breast.

She saw her nipples firm. The agony his caresses generated within her nerves arched her stomach upward. Her lips parted. Her breath came in sharp pants. But still he lingered. Arn watched Carol writhe beneath his gentle strokes, and found that this shared view of her body's reaction only elevated her longing.

His lips brushed her throat. Ever so gradually, his kisses made their way down her body. As they did, low moans escaped her throat. When she could take no more, Carol pulled him atop her and they intertwined their bodies in ecstasy.

She cried out, hearing Arn's loud gasps as they reached a crescendo together. When he finally collapsed atop her, he laid his cheek on her breast. She shifted her mental link to Zaislus to watch as she ran her fingers through Arn's curly brown hair.

The sight of their tangled bodies was the most beautiful thing she'd ever seen.

15

King Hanibal stood before the roaring hearth in his throne room, feeling its flames warm his back. Although the temperature in the cavern remained relatively constant, a deeper chill had crept into his bones.

Having released Lektuvu to dine with her apprentice, he focused his attention on his high priest. Jason stood before him wearing his traditional white robe. Although the man was in his late forties, his thin frame, gray hair, hawkish face, and serious demeanor made him appear much older.

Hanibal had long been one of the high priest's devoted followers. He'd trusted Jason's judgment when the priesthood had deemed Carol to have lapsed into madness through her use of forbidden magic. Back then, the priests' use of therapeutic tinctures would have cured her addled brain. But Blade had come for his fiancée and taken her into the high mountains. Jason's attempt to reason with the assassin had cost him his ring finger.

And it had been Jason who had convinced Hanibal that the people of Areana's Vale needed a king who heeded the priesthood's sage counsel. The high priest had been instrumental in building public support for the new monarch.

"How do you judge the people's reaction to Carol Rafel's return?" Hanibal asked.

"I sent Bishops Williams, Smaith, and Forston to Colindale, Fernwood, and Longsford Watch respectively. I received the last of their reports just before sunset."

"And?"

"As expected, Carol still has many supporters who would like to see her returned to power. But your loyal followers outnumber them. That doesn't even consider the Talian refugees who fill the new towns of River Bend, Granite Falls, and Falcon Peak."

"I trust that the priesthood is actively engaged in reminding people of Carol's dalliance with the darker branches of magic, amplified by the shard of Landrel's Trident she possesses."

"It will be the subject of tomorrow's sermons throughout the vale."

Hanibal nodded in satisfaction. Before he could spend a few moments savoring the feeling, two loud raps sounded from the throne room's double doors. Hanibal didn't try to keep the irritation from his voice.

"Enter."

As the guards outside the doors pulled them open, General Garland strode through the opening, his rugged visage more dour than usual. The commander of the king's army slapped a fist to his chest and executed a slight bow.

"My liege."

"What's wrong?" Hanibal asked.

"My scouts report that more than a thousand warriors emerged from a time-mist just beyond the western entrance to our gorge shortly after sunset. Lord Alan Rafel leads them. His warriors have shaved their heads in the manner of the Forsworn. And Princess Kimber and Prince Galad accompany the lord."

Hanibal felt his fists clench. How dare Alan Rafel make such a provocative challenge? Did the presence of the Endarian prince and princess signify that Carol had the backing of Endar?

"What are they doing right now?"

"Setting up a string of encampments. Their campfires stretch for a league, blocking access to Areana's Gorge. Do you want me to clear them out?"

"No. Carol Rafel is within the vale. Should we attack her brother, she will rain death and destruction on us like few can imagine. Let the so-called Chosen have his insignificant moment. By demonstrating restraint, we show him that he's beneath my consideration."

The general saluted, turned, and exited the throne room.

"What if Carol decides to contest your rule?" Jason asked.

"We're the same age. I've known her since we played together as children. She is far from the hothead her younger brother has always been. Carol will respect the will of the people."

Jason stroked the nub of his missing finger.

"Her husband may not."

"Blade has one weakness. He respects his wife's wishes."

"Unless he perceives a threat to her."

Hanibal placed a hand on his high priest's shoulder.

"Then let us ensure that no such threat occurs."

16

Carol mounted the gray mare as the first hint of dawn lightened the eastern sky. Zaislus watched as Arn swung effortlessly onto his bay horse. It still amazed her how Arn could move so gracefully with Slaken belted on his left side, a throwing dagger strapped to each thigh, and another sheathed inside each boot. So much deadly cutlery should have unbalanced a man. But her husband danced with these knives like lovers.

Her eyes shifted to Slaken's ivory hilt. How different it was from the runed black haft that had once warded his knife. Arn had destroyed that runed handle in a fit of rage at his failure to prevent Carol's blinding. It was the reason he had carved this gleaming white handle for the ebony blade. In his old life he had relied on the elemental wards carved into Slaken's haft to shield him from magic. Since Landrel's newfound revelation of Arn's time-sight talent, that arcane ability warded him instead.

Having seen how things stood within Areana's Vale, Carol intended to ride out through the gorge that protected the gorgeous valley to visit the people of the Kanjou tribe. She longed to visit with Chief Dan; his wife, Kira; and their lovely daughter, Katya. Most of all she wanted to see Dan's stout adviser, Darlag.

Carol remembered those wonderful days when she had taught the children of the cliff dwellers. The memories filled her with a warmth she had long forgotten.

They made their way through the fort that guarded the entrance to the vale from the narrow canyon named Areana's Gorge without incident. Clearly the guards stationed at the gates had been ordered to allow Carol and Arn free passage. For two leagues they made their way along the river that wound between the sheer rock walls. But the scene that confronted Carol when she emerged pulled a gasp from her lips.

"What in the names of the gods . . . ?"

The Forsworn camps stretched out before her in a ragged line that blocked entrance or exit from the gorge. For some reason beyond her ken, Alan had decided to throw down a challenge to Hanibal's authority.

As she and Arn approached the nearest of the encampments, Alan, Kim, and Galad strode out to meet them. Carol pulled her mare to a halt and swung out of her saddle to face her brother.

"Why have you defied my orders to encamp the Forsworn within the Great Forest?"

Alan's face showed no change of expression. Clearly he'd been expecting this rebuke.

"I took that as a suggestion rather than an order."

"Really? What are you hoping to accomplish with this maneuver? Hanibal's command outnumbers us by thirty to one. I hardly think he regards you as a threat."

"I never intended this as a threat."

"What, then?"

"It's merely a reminder of who we are and whom we serve."

"You think Hanibal doesn't remember that?"

"I think there are those under his command who need that reassurance. The ratio of those who would stand against us may be a lot less than thirty to one."

Carol felt her fists clench and then forced her hands to relax.

"I will not cause a civil war among our people, no matter the personal cost. Nothing could aid Kragan more than that."

"True enough," Alan said, "but if we cannot convince Hanibal to restore you to power, then we at least need to recruit volunteers to bolster our numbers. Hanibal shouldn't mind ridding himself of those soldiers who retain their allegiance to you."

Carol paused, turning her attention to Kim.

"What do you think, my sister?"

Kim's eyes sparkled. "At first I doubted the wisdom of Alan's show of force. But I now think it may give us the best leverage over Hanibal's decision."

"Galad?" Carol asked.

"I grow weary of coming back to our lands, hat in hand, begging for the boon of the new lords. I stand behind Alan's actions. However, the final call is, of course, yours."

"I foresee no negative reaction from Hanibal during the next two days." Hearing her husband's voice, she turned Zaislus to look up at Arn, who still sat astride his horse. "After that, my visions become unclear. But I have a strong feeling we should wait and see how the situation unfolds in the next week."

"What about Kragan?" Carol asked.

"His army is moving east, but at a normal pace. I sense that Kragan isn't with his troops. What he's doing, I cannot see."

Carol turned to her brother.

"We cannot change the events you've set in motion," Carol said. "But make no more aggressive moves until Arn and I return."

Then Carol swung up onto her mount and turned her mare southwest, toward the distant rift within which the cliff-dwelling Kanjou people made their home.

—⁓—

Following Zaislus, Carol turned south into a crack in the canyon wall with Arn behind. The way forward tapered through an opening just wide enough for horse and rider to pass. After a few minutes, the narrow crevice opened into a broad, cliff-walled glen. Neat furrows between broad irrigation ditches crisscrossed the farmland. A spicy aroma accompanied the view of fruit and vegetable plants that extended into the distance, row upon row.

High up on the cliff walls, an abundance of caves pocked the area. Rope ladders and bridges connected one to another as if some gargantuan spider had been at work. Other ladders dangled several hundred paces down to the floor of the valley. Dozens of cliff dwellers moved along the ropes.

But the sight of the small group that awaited her filled Carol with joy. Chief Dan and his adviser, Darlag, stood at the fore. The statuesque chief of the Kanjou tribe wore green breeches and a yellow shirt. The grandly plump Darlag wore a bright-red robe and leaned heavily on his gnarled staff.

Dan's wife, Kira, stood a step behind the men. She was towering and lean, with bronze skin and raven locks, her deep-brown eyes flecked with gold, just as Carol remembered her. She wore a cotton skirt and blouse decorated with colorful, intricate patterns and beadwork. Carol hardly recognized the tall girl at Kira's side. Katya had grown several inches since Carol had last seen her and taken on a striking resemblance to her mother.

Carol and Arn dismounted. Dan extended his hand, and Carol took it. Dan's eyes were the same brown flecked with gold as Kira's and

Katya's, but far more penetrating. His face was etched and weathered by wind and sun, making his age difficult to judge.

"My scouts informed me of your imminent return," Dan said, trying to mask the concern that was obvious on the face of everyone in the group at the sight of her eyes. "This is a most joyous reunion."

Carol released his hand and motioned Arn forward. "This is my husband, Arn."

Dan shook Arn's hand and Carol introduced him to the others, exchanging hugs with Darl and Kira. Then Katya threw her arms around Carol's neck and pulled her into a tight embrace. Carol felt the girl's warm tears on her cheek.

When Carol stepped back, she addressed them all.

"I know that you find my appearance shocking. Please don't worry. My magic enables me to see through the eyes of Zaislus."

She leaned down to ruffle the canine's fur.

"His senses are far better than mine ever were."

Dan stared down at Zaislus, his left eyebrow raised as he struggled to come to grips with the concept of such mind sharing.

"Please follow me," he said. "We have much to discuss."

The chief led them past a crowd of onlookers who'd left their work in the fields to marvel at Carol's return. As they reached the base of a cliff draped with rope ladders, Dan stopped and looked down at Zaislus.

"We'll have to lower a basket to bring up the dog."

"That won't be necessary," Carol said. "I can transport Zaislus up to your dwellings, along with Arn and me."

Arn touched her arm.

"Not me. I want to make the climb."

"I volunteer to take your husband's place on the magical ride you promise," Darlag said.

She smirked at the plump adviser who'd become her close friend and confidant during the early days in Areana's Vale. Carol placed a hand on his arm.

"Okay, Darl. Ready to fly?"

"That spell wasn't in the book of magic you allowed me to transcribe," he said, eagerness shining in his eyes. "But yes, I most certainly am."

—◆◆—

Arn watched as Carol, Darlag, and a tail-wagging Zaislus floated off the ground, rapidly rising to the top of the ledge, where a vast and shallow cavern provided shelter for the cliff dwellings within. Katya scrambled up the rope ladder ahead of the adults. The ledge from which the rope ladder dangled was a hundred rungs above her. Arn waited until Dan and Kira followed their daughter up. He waited to begin his climb until the others had almost reached their objective.

As he looked at the marvelous cliff, Arn was sorely tempted to avoid the rope ladder altogether, making the free climb up the sheer rock face instead. Such ascents had fascinated him since childhood. After the murder of his parents, when Arn was only five, he had learned to survive as an orphan within Tal's capital city of Hannington, climbing the walls of buildings to escape the ruffians and gangs who'd roamed less savory neighborhoods.

Arn gripped the first rung and began to climb, the memories washing through his mind like a wave on the Brinje Ocean.

The cliff fell away below him. Sections of wall where the rope ladder dangled free, due to an indentation in the rock, produced a wonderful rush and clarity he hadn't felt for some time. When Arn stepped off the ladder onto one of the ledges upon which the extensive cliff dwellings had been erected, he turned around to gaze out over the sheltered valley, his toes on the very edge of the sheer cliff. He breathed in, filling his lungs with the peaceful air of the refuge.

Carol's gentle touch on his shoulder broke his reverie and turned his gaze toward the beautiful woman who'd stepped up beside him. Her milky eyes added an allure to her face that he hadn't recognized when she'd been so grievously injured. It was one more violation for which he intended to kill Kragan.

Abruptly, the image of the wielder formed in Arn's mind. The intensity of the vision wiped away his current surroundings and sent a spike of adrenaline through his body. He stepped forward, his mind merging with that of the enemy who became more real with each passing moment, Carol's cry of alarm seeming to carry from a great distance.

Arn never felt the wind that whistled past his falling body.

17

Kragan stepped from the rychly time-mists he wielded to gaze up at a sight he hadn't beheld in ages. A rocky pinnacle rose before him. Atop its sheer cliff face, the remains of a crumbling castle loomed above the surrounding terrain.

A steep and narrow trail led up the side of the cliff, and Kragan set his feet upon the treacherous path. What had long ago been a good road had fallen into ruin, large sections of the rock wall having plunged to the valley floor. The path rose steeply and at the crumbled parts narrowed to less than a foot wide. The arduous climb to the top of the rock spire left Kragan winded. Several times he was tempted to use an air elemental to lift him up to the fortress far above. But wielding that much arcane might would be sure to awaken the presence trapped within these ruins. It would awaken the Guardian.

As the sinking sun colored the western horizon mauve, Kragan reached the trail's end. From this angle it seemed that blood oozed from the ancient fortress's exposed timbers. The ruins of the castle's outer wall lay in piles of broken stone. Beyond that, bare wooden timbers and supports jutted upward where roofs had been.

Kragan climbed over and through the detritus into a broad courtyard. The inner castle still stood. He paused, feeling the gooseflesh crinkle his skin. Far Castle.

In long-lost ages, when Kragan had first set foot upon the Endarian continent, this had been the kingdom of Tal's proud western outpost. The lord of Far Castle, Baron Rajek, had gone quite mad, his mind twisted and warped by Draken, a wielder of powerful black magics. Only Landrel's direct interference had thrown the castle into ruin.

But at the height of Draken's desperation, he had summoned a creature from the netherworld, taking the being's form for his own, an action that left him without the intellect or desire to reverse his condition. In an action as merciless as it had been just, Landrel had left Draken to prowl the mazes and tunnels beneath Far Castle for all eternity.

Even now, as Kragan stood peering through the opening where massive doors had fallen from rotted hinges, he could feel the creature's malevolent presence lurking somewhere within.

Kragan walked through the opening and into the blackness. He summoned a globe of silver light before him and willed it forward. Scattered piles of bones and rusted bits of armor lay among withered and broken furniture. He stepped across a skeleton that still gripped the haft of an ancient sword. The particles of mildew and dust that rose with each step glittered in the light and clogged his nostrils.

He placed a hand on a fallen timber that leaned against an interior wall and ducked underneath it. His footsteps carried him through halls and rooms until he found what he sought, a stone stairway leading down into a bleakness that even his magical light struggled to push back. Steep and narrow granite steps led steadily downward in twists and turns. The air took on an oppressive weight that left Kragan with a sense of being watched.

Kragan reached out with his mind, searching for the source of his uneasiness. The awareness he sensed seemed to emanate from somewhere in the depths, radiating outward through the very walls. A foul odor grew stronger as he descended, an odor of decaying and rotten flesh. But underlying that stench lay an acidic smell that burned his nostrils.

Turning a tight corner on the stairs, Kragan banged his head on a rusted hook that jutted from the wall at an odd angle. With a curse that echoed through the confined spaces, he reached up to touch his forehead, his fingers coming away damp with blood.

Kragan ignored the wetness that trickled down the left side of his face and stepped off the stairs into a passageway that branched left and right. A low sound rumbled through the hallway, a fleshy, rasping sound of something dragging itself through distant tunnels.

He turned right, relying on his senses of smell and hearing to guide him through a series of turns and passages toward the thing that hunted the intruder within its lair. He found another set of stairs that led down and began a wary descent, his left hand clutching the withered fingers that dangled from his necklace.

The stairs ended in a large room that had been carved from a natural cavern. Kragan sent the globe floating out to the center of the chamber, increasing its brightness as he did so. Ten paces from where he stood, the floor of the room dropped away into a pit that blocked all forward access. The slurping sounds echoed up from below, growing louder with each moment. The cloying smell grew worse, drawing Kragan forward until he stood on the very edge of the vertical drop.

A dozen paces below, a rough-hewn floor extended to a wall where a narrow passage opened into darkness. From that bleak place, a monstrosity emerged, its body a boneless thing that squished out from the hallway, spreading out across the cavern floor in an undulating blob. Atop the squirming mound of flesh, a bulbous appendage emerged, something that vaguely resembled a head.

Psychic waves of desire and depravity washed over Kragan, and he barely resisted the urge to step back from the ledge. This was no denizen of the elemental planes. Nor had it risen from the land of the dead. This was a being that had been summoned from the realms of the gods, something akin to the deity trapped beneath the temple of Mo'Lier.

The wielder found himself overwhelmed by a sense of awe at the audacity and power of the spell that could have plucked this creature from its nether home. The blob moved its vast bulk toward the rough wall that led to the spot where Kragan looked down upon it. As it began to creep up the rock face toward him, the globe of light dimmed to pale red.

Kragan took a deep breath, forcing a calm into his voice that he didn't feel. Reaching out with his mind, he touched the man who still existed within the god.

"Draken. I have come far to speak with you."

The mound paused, most of its bulk still resting on the cavern floor. Ever so slowly, a mouth formed in the slimy appendage atop that body. A voice wheezed, as if it issued from a constricted throat.

"Draken? It's been a long time since I have heard that name evoked."

"I've come to set you free."

A raspy sound that Kragan interpreted as a laugh echoed through the chamber.

"Pitiful fool. Why would I wish to return to human form when the hungers and pleasures of this existence dwarf such a feeble life?"

"Because I can help you resurrect the vast magic you once wielded."

Kragan felt the psychic touch of the Draken thing brush his consciousness, allowing it to delve just deep enough to absorb his memories, to know him.

"I no longer wield magic. This form feeds off magic as readily as it consumes flesh. You see the effect my mere presence has on the fire elemental who provides you with your feeble light. Can you not feel that being's fear?"

"It may fear the foul god who's enslaved you, but I do not."

"Then you're a bigger fool than I perceived."

The blob surged forward, its bulk flattening out, flowing up the rock as easily as it squeezed through tight hallways and moved across the floor. Kragan backed up to the portal from which he had entered the room, summoning Dalg to pull liquid stone from the floor and ceiling to create a granite wall between him and the creature.

Something was wrong. Although Kragan's will chained Dalg here, the wielder felt the searing pain that cascaded through the elemental as it touched the evil god. It was as if the immortal thing that had consumed Draken now feasted upon Dalg. As Dalg's essence drained away, Kragan felt the power he put into his spell flow directly into Draken's repulsive form.

Kragan dismissed Dalg to the earthen plane and called forth an air elemental, hurling forth a dozen invisible scythes that sliced through the gelatinous body, cutting it into squirming chunks. One ethereal blade chopped off the thing's head, which plopped to the floor in a shapeless mass.

The blob flowed forward, the severed chunks merging. The translucent blades wavered and lost substance as the foul god fed upon the elemental Kragan had summoned from the plane of air.

Kragan backed up the stairs from which he had come, his mind churning in search of a solution as a new head oozed from the creature's bulk. Draken spoke again, his voice mocking.

"Kragan. Wielder of magic. You hold six of the nine fragments of Landrel's Trident. Yet you cower in impotence before me. I feast upon your elementals. I will devour your flesh and entrails before sucking the marrow from your bones."

Kragan stopped, snapped his necklace with a jerk of his left hand, and held his arms wide, amplifying his voice so that it boomed through the corridor and echoed in the chamber.

"Then take me if you can."

The blob surged forward to engulf him. Everywhere its flesh touched his skin, pain exploded.

The two fingers of life magic grew ice cold in Kragan's fist as he channeled his will through them, drawing energy from the creature to heal his wounds as fast as the god could inflict them. Pustules formed across the being's mass, grew large and burst open, spewing hot liquid into the air. Draken's mouth opened in a wail of pain and suffering that matched Kragan's own.

For what seemed an eternity, the two remained locked in a battle of endurance where agony was the weapon of choice. But the harder the god tried to devour the wielder, the more it consumed itself.

When the Draken beast released Kragan, it roiled away, thrashing against the walls. Such was its agony that it lost control of its movements, its head continuing to screech.

Kragan merged his mind with the creature's, noting with satisfaction how agony had washed away the desires and urges to which Draken had become addicted. If he was going to be able to do this, the time was now.

"Draken. Allow me to help you free yourself from this suffering."

A burst of clarity that felt human surged from Draken's mind into Kragan's.

"How will you help me? I'm far beyond redemption."

"If you let me, I can channel some of my arcane might into the part of you that's still human. It will allow you to send the being back to his bleak realm in the same way you summoned him."

Facial features formed on flesh. Squirming lips opened, and a slurping voice spoke barely intelligible words.

"There is so little left of me, I can hardly manage to make myself heard. Tell me what I must do."

"With my mind linked to yours, you can use the two shards of mind magic amplification. But you must act now, before the god recovers and enslaves you."

Kragan felt Draken seize the lifeline. Raw energy pulsed from two of the shards within Kragan's hand as Draken gradually reversed the spell with which he had summoned this thing into his world. Immediately above the foul god's body, a fist-size black portal appeared in the stone ceiling. It pulsed and swirled as a gentle breeze stirred the stale air, growing stronger with each passing moment.

The whirling cauldron expanded again. Wind howled down the stairs from behind Kragan, whipping his hair into his eyes and stinging his cheeks. The blob's wet skin rippled across the revolting bulge of its head, then distended as the whirlwind sucked it into the inky hole, as if it were being siphoned into a drain.

The monstrous blob shrank in upon itself. It shimmered, became transparent, and then, with a slurp that vibrated the walls, disappeared into the void. In its place stood a slender man in black robes, his shoulder-length tresses and closely trimmed beard as white as fresh snow. Draken looked down at his liberator, relief replacing the anguish that melted from his face. He sank to one knee, his gray eyes locked with Kragan's.

"Lord Kragan, I find myself deeply in your debt. What do you desire of me?"

Kragan placed a large hand on Draken's shoulder.

"To conquer the world, together."

PART III

Daughter of prophecy, assassin of time, dame of necrosis . . . my murderer seeks thee. The death lord stands at his right hand. But the faith of the chosen will control our destiny.

—From the *Scroll of Landrel*

18

Carol was standing at the cliff's edge, her hand on Arn's shoulder, when she felt him suddenly stiffen. Then he stepped over the precipice and fell. For the briefest of moments, she failed to react while Zaislus moved to her side, giving her a clear view of Arn's fall. Her mind lashed out, ripping Lwellen from the plane of air and thickening the air below her husband, gently arresting his fall.

He came to rest facedown, fifty feet above the ground, a sight that pulled a ragged gasp of relief from her lips. Only then did she hear the startled cries from those around her. He just lay there, suspended in air, unmoving. With her heart trying to beat its way through her chest, Carol raised him back to the ledge, turned his body over, and lay him on the smooth stone.

Carol knelt beside her husband as Dan, Kira, and Darl stood in stunned silence a dozen paces away. Arn's brown eyes were open, his gaze shifting back and forth as she had observed during those times when he was locked in a deep trance. What shocked her was that he had succumbed to such an intense vision while the artifact that amplified his time-sight remained in the pouch at his belt. Even more disconcerting, she had never seen him fall while under the influence of a waking dream. If she hadn't caught him, he would have died.

Fury engulfed her form. This was Landrel's doing, and now the ancient master seemed to be actively trying to kill her husband.

Carol ignored the urgent inquiries from those gathered around. She reached out to place both hands on Arn's cheeks. Her touch failed to rouse him.

She inhaled deeply, found her center, and gently touched his mind with hers. Arn's body jerked and he sat up, startling her. He blinked and looked around, a look of surprise on his face.

"Why am I sitting down?"

Carol was speechless. Rather than respond, she decided to show him, psychically replaying the image of him plummeting from the ledge and her last-second rescue.

"Oh," he said.

"Is that all you can say?" Carol asked, trying to dampen the anger in her voice.

Arn rose to his feet.

"One moment I was standing there," he said, pointing to the spot, "and the next I was a rider in Kragan's mind. Somewhere between those two instants, I lost myself."

"You think?"

"Now that it has happened, I know what to watch for. I won't let it happen again."

"Tell me what you saw."

Arn glanced at the still-startled faces of the Kanjou chief, his wife, and his adviser. He shook his head.

"I don't think we should trouble your friends further. We can discuss this tonight, in private."

As Carol started to respond, Arn turned and walked toward Chief Dan, spreading his hands.

"I apologize for fainting," he said. "It's quite embarrassing."

Dan nodded in understanding.

"Heights have a strange effect on certain people."

Darl slapped Arn on the back, a relieved grin on his face.

"Don't worry. We've learned that our high home can take some getting used to."

Dan turned and led them back toward the place where long buildings were stacked one atop the other in stairstep fashion against the back wall of the wide but shallow cavern. Wood ladders allowed the people to access the different levels. As she walked beside Arn, Carol finally managed to get her beating heart back under control.

They spent the next two hours in a meeting with Chief Dan and Darl, speaking of all that had happened since Carol had last seen the pair. The news that Kragan had commanded the protectors to launch the attack on Areana's Vale, and that Arn had killed him only for the body hopper to rise again in his true form on Sadamad, came as a shock to the men. Worse was the news that Kragan had returned to the Endarian continent to continue his depredations.

When Dan finally rose from the intricately woven carpet upon which they sat, the others did likewise.

"I will think on all you've said. In the meantime, Darl has something he wants to show you."

Then the chief turned and walked out of the room. Carol shifted Zaislus's gaze to the face of her red-robed friend. Gone were the worries Carol's news had put there. His barely contained excitement surprised her.

"Okay, Darl. What is it you want me to see?"

"This."

Darl held out his hands, palms up, his high forehead furrowing in concentration.

When twin balls of flame came into existence, one a foot above each hand, Carol's mouth dropped open in surprise.

"How?"

The adviser dismissed the flames, cupping both hands together. They filled with water that ran between his fingers to splash down on the floor. Darl gestured and a stiff breeze whirled through the room, flapping Zaislus's ears.

The display of the arcane stopped as quickly as it had begun, the broad smile on Darl's face a testament to how much he'd longed to show her the skills he'd acquired.

"I've studied the copy I transcribed from your book of magic. It took me six months of meditation practice before I felt confident enough to perform the Ritual of Terrors."

"You could have killed yourself doing that without a mentor to watch over you!" Carol said. "What were you thinking?"

The joyous look on Darl's face faded.

"I was thinking that you might never return to us. I was thinking that if I were to learn whether I possessed the talent for magic, it was up to me. I was thinking that if our people were ever to be safe, they would need someone of magical ability to protect them. I have worked long and diligently to improve my skills in the craft. And I have found four others who show some of the same ability."

The stout man put two fingers to his lips and issued a sharp whistle that hurt Carol's ears and caused Zaislus to growl. With her ears still ringing, she saw four slender teens enter the room. She recognized each from the days when she had taught reading to the Kanjou children. They stopped before her, lined up as if for inspection. Three girls and a boy.

Legin, an eighteen-year-old woman with shoulder-length flaxen locks, stood on the far left. Havana, also eighteen, stood beside her friend. Then there were Havana's siblings, Khai, a girl of sixteen, and her twin brother, Thienlam. Both sisters and their brother had straight raven hair, although Thienlam's was cropped to the base of his neck.

The young women wore the brightly colored traditional skirts of the Kanjou women. Thienlam was clad in an orange shirt and green pants, much like Chief Dan's. Each of the teens displayed the wiry strength that work in the fields and the climbing of rope ladders yielded.

Darl cleared his throat.

"Carol, I'm proud to introduce my four young acolytes. I believe you remember them."

"I do indeed," Carol said.

"Legin and Havana began training with me shortly after I completed the ritual. The twins drove me to distraction until I tested them and determined that they too possessed their older sister's aptitude.

"I'm proud to say that both Legin and Havana have completed the Ritual of Terrors and have each demonstrated skill casting several spells. Khai and Thienlam are approaching a level of proficiency with meditation where, shortly, they too shall be ready to undergo the trial that will unlock their ability to perform mystical feats."

Carol found the idea of a relative neophyte wielder taking on four apprentices disconcerting. Then again, she had only studied under Hawthorne for a short time before he'd died in the blizzard that had almost killed their entire caravan. So what entitled her to be critical of Darl's actions?

She smiled at the four eager students, recalling how long Lord Rafel had forbidden her to undergo the training. In a way she envied these young people.

"Legin and Havana, as the oldest of Darl's apprentices, you'll need to take special care in monitoring the practice sessions of Khai and Thienlam. Darl cannot focus on everyone at the same time. Will you make that commitment?"

"Yes!" they answered simultaneously.

"Khai and Thienlam, do you promise to follow Darl's instructions to the letter and obey the direction that Legin and Havana will provide?"

"Yes!" the twins answered, their eyes beaming with delight.

"Good. If you follow through on your commitments, then someday I may call upon your talents."

Carol stepped forward, eschewing their extended hands to hug all the apprentices. When she released them, Thienlam's cheeks flamed scarlet, a sight that brought a snicker from his twin.

"Children," said Darl, "you may now return to your studies."

Carol watched the four teens file out through the door, disciplined yet calm and joyous, wishing that she could linger to participate in their training. Would she ever again know such peace?

Shrugging aside the heaviness that tried to drape her shoulders, she hugged Darl and kissed him firmly on the cheek.

"You continue to amaze me, old friend," she said. "I hope that you and your apprentices never need to use your magic in battle."

His brows lowered in concern. "I would wish you the same, but—"

"That's not to be."

"Farewell and safe journeys to both of you."

Then Darl turned and left the couple alone in the council chamber.

Arn slid his hand into hers and squeezed, sensing her somber mood as the reunion came to an end. When they walked outside, Carol saw that the sun was only a hand-span above the cliffs that lined the western edge of the valley.

"Tell me of the vision that almost killed you," she said.

"Let's get our horses and head back to the vale. If we hurry, we can get there by nightfall. We can discuss ill tidings on the way."

The look on Arn's face sent a chill through Carol's bones. His next words did nothing to alleviate the feeling.

"I think it's time to force Hanibal's hand."

19

Just after sunset, Kim saw Carol and Arn ride into Alan's camp, their horses flecked with the foam of a hard ride. Alan moved to meet them, and Kim hurried to join him.

"What's wrong?" Alan asked. "Are you being pursued?"

"Arn had another vision," Carol said.

"We're running out of time here," Arn said. "Tonight we need you, Kim, and Galad to accompany us back to the vale. You can leave Tudor in charge here."

"Fine," Alan said. "Kat and Quincy will accompany me."

Kim fought to keep the scowl from her face at the mention of Kat. She had expected them to come. The bald woman and the lanky swordsman considered themselves the Chosen's personal bodyguards.

"We'll leave the horses here," Carol said. "We've run them pretty hard."

Arn and Carol slid out of their saddles and handed the reins of their tired mounts over to a member of the Forsworn whom Kim didn't recognize.

"Quincy," Alan said. "Go get Galad and Tudor and bring them back here."

He turned and trotted off into the gathering twilight.

Kim approached her sister and saw Zaislus turn his head toward her. The big dog was panting but didn't appear to be as exhausted as the horses.

"What did Arn foresee that's brought you back with such urgency?" Kim asked.

"Kragan will enter Far Castle," Carol said, "if he hasn't already."

The mention of the evil ruin pulled forth the memory of a story Galad had told Kim to scare her when she was a little girl. He'd painted the terrible scene in her young mind in exquisite detail.

The mighty fortress was perched atop a rocky pinnacle in the wild borderlands west of the kingdom of Tal. Far Castle was haunted by an immortal being plucked from the abyss, summoned into this realm by a mad wielder of forbidden magic. Over the centuries that followed the entity's arrival, it had consumed anyone foolish enough to enter the ruins. A vorg raiding party composed of hundreds of warriors and several magic wielders had invaded the castle in search of the vast treasure rumored to rest beneath it. None had returned.

Galad had told her how the shades of all whom the vile god had consumed still roamed the ruins and the tunnels beneath it. He filled her head with horrifying images of boneless people who squirmed along the floor like soft, spineless sea creatures, their lips opening into mouths devoid of jaws or teeth. At night their tormented wails could be heard throughout the valley that surrounded Far Castle.

When Kim had asked one of the archivists about the legend, he had confirmed much of what Galad had said. She had been unable to get the repulsive images out of her head, enduring nightmares for weeks thereafter.

"Why would Kragan go there?"

"To release Draken from the curse he placed upon himself. Alan and I have been inside those ruins. The creature that Draken became almost slew us both."

Kim saw Carol shudder.

"Together, Kragan and Draken will wage war on Endar," Arn said. "We must stop them before they raise an army to seize the artifact that rests inside the time stone within the Endarian royal palace."

A memory crystallized in Kim's mind, that of a walled city that straddled the Banjee River at the northeastern edge of the Mogev Desert.

"Lagoth," she whispered.

Arn nodded.

"Kragan will return to the city he founded."

Kim shuddered at the memory of the city that everyone in Endar had thought destroyed four hundred years ago. An absolutely monstrous place founded upon slavery. Kragan, wearing one of the many bodies he'd taken over the centuries since he'd first arrived on the Continent of Endar, had founded the extensive, walled city. Populated by hundreds of thousands of humans and vorgs, it had been the launching place for his wars of conquest.

Four hundred years ago, an army of Endarians and humans had surrounded Lagoth. A group of the most powerful Endarian time-shapers had cast a spell to destroy Kragan and his city. But the wielder had managed to deflect the casting into his enemies. The spell had aged a vast swath of land on the western side of the Kanjou River and created the Mogev Desert.

A couple of years ago, Kim, John, Ty, and Arn had stumbled upon the city everyone believed was destroyed and had fallen under Kragan's spell. They had barely escaped with their lives.

She forced her thoughts back to the present.

"He already stripped Lagoth of most of its soldiers to raise the army we defeated in Endar Pass," Kim said.

"True," Arn said. "But tens of thousands of human and vorg citizens remain there. Kragan will no longer care whether the city remains viable. To get what he wants, he'll strip Lagoth of everyone able to wield a weapon or cast a spell. We need to reach him before he can complete that task."

"What if Hanibal refuses to give us the soldiers we need?" Alan asked.

The seeds of a new idea took root within Kim's mind, born of a secret she had kept from all her companions.

If Hanibal's decision was the key that would enable them to stop Kragan from raising his army, she would have to make sure he chose wisely.

Quincy returned with Galad and Tudor, and Alan took Tudor aside, giving him instructions to have the Forsworn ready to integrate reinforcements and march on short notice.

Then Kim followed the rest of the small group into the time-mists that Galad summoned. They made their way back through the gorge, stopping just short of the fort that blocked the entrance to the vale. The time-mists dissipated, giving them a clear view of the torches that burned along the top of the wall that rose before them.

Carol summoned a light that allowed the guards to see them clearly. Moments later, the gates opened, and the guards stepped aside to allow them entrance. A captain whom Kim didn't know stepped forward, slapped fist to chest in salute, and introduced himself to Carol and Alan.

Kim turned her attention to the dozens of soldiers who guarded the wall and manned the gates. When she began to funnel the health from them, she did so with subtlety. To these men and women, it would feel like a passing faintness, momentary headache, or disgruntled stomach. Nothing to take particular note of.

But as she continued wielding her magic, drawing from a fountain of life, Kim felt her aura strengthen in preparation for the delicate soul-binding she would soon attempt. The warmth that built within her was accompanied by elation. She felt so light that her feet barely touched the ground as the captain led them through the streets of the fort and out into the vale.

—⟶⟵—

King Hanibal paced slowly back and forth within his throne room. Tonight, he wore a blue tunic and red trousers tucked into shiny black boots. Having been informed of the party that had arrived at the castle, he had sent runners to summon Lektuvu and High Priest Jason to his side. Until his two trusted counselors arrived, he would leave Lorness Carol, Lord Alan, and the Endarian royals waiting in the adjoining room.

Lektuvu was the first to enter his chamber, her iridescent robes rustling softly as she approached the throne where he now sat. Without bothering to speak, she took her position at his side. She had been an active participant in the discussion where Hanibal had come to a decision on Carol's request and needed no further clarification.

By the time Jason made his entrance, annoyance had crept onto Hanibal's face. He didn't bother keeping the irritation from his voice when he spoke to the captain of the guard.

"Let us not keep our guests waiting any longer."

The captain opened the door and then stepped aside to allow the Rafel party into the throne room. Carol, her dog, and Arn were the first to enter. Then came Alan, flanked by two of his Forsworn. High Lord Rafel's son had added even more muscle since Hanibal had last seen him, something he wouldn't have thought possible.

Prince Galad and Princess Kimber entered last. Standing six and a half feet tall, the prince radiated authority. Even the stump of his missing left hand failed to detract from it.

But it was the princess who captured Hanibal's full attention. It was as if he had never seen her before. Beauty radiated from Kimber and, when her dusky eyes met his, he couldn't pull away from her gaze. Hanibal tried to swallow and failed.

He found himself stepping forward before realizing that he had risen to his feet. The princess extended her hand and Hanibal bent to kiss it. When his lips touched her skin, an electric charge stood the fine hairs on his arms and neck.

Noting the wide-eyed stares of the others, Hanibal raised himself to his full height and awkwardly turned to Galad.

"Prince Galad, Princess Kimber," he said, struggling to gather his thoughts. "I welcome you to the kingdom of Tal. If there's anything I can do to make your visit more pleasant, don't hesitate to ask."

"As a matter of fact," Kimber said, drawing his eyes back to hers, "there's a boon that only you can grant. It is why I'm here."

Her melodic voice held Hanibal in thrall. He barely heard Jason's voice from somewhere behind.

"A word, my liege—"

Anger at the interruption turned his glare on the old priest.

"Silence."

Then he beheld Kimber once more.

"Ask it of me, dear lady. If it is within my power to fulfill, I will gladly do so."

Kimber's face grew serious, worry furrowing her brow.

"Highness. I am here on behalf of the kingdom of Endar. Not that many seasons ago, you fought alongside us against Kragan and his army. Now he has returned to threaten Endar once again. We have one chance to stop him, but we must hurry. I ask that you grant Lorness Carol's request for reinforcements to aid us in this quest."

Hanibal's mind fogged. He struggled to remember today's discussion with Jason and Lektuvu about this very request. The decision he had believed in so firmly until just moments ago suddenly seemed ill considered.

"How many soldiers do you need?"

Kimber's hopeful look wiped away his confusion. She placed a hand on his arm, invoking an electric thrill.

"I've learned that you've gathered more than thirty thousand troops here. Endar would never expect you to leave this valley and its people undefended. But if you can find it in your heart to place half of your force at our behest, my gratitude would know no bounds."

The sheer size of the request immediately sobered Hanibal. He heard Lektuvu hiss. But then Kimber's grip tightened, imparting the depths of the princess's desperation.

"Highness," she said, "please don't regard this as sacrificing half your kingdom's defenders. If Kragan succeeds in conquering Endar, he will seek to consolidate power throughout all these lands. Our preemptive strike is the best chance to prevent that."

He paused, looking around at the rest of Kimber's party. Except for Galad, they seemed as stunned by her entreaty as Hanibal. He realized that none of Kimber's companions had uttered a word since entering the throne room. As much as he was tempted to appease this divine spirit, he needed time to collect his thoughts and consider all the ramifications.

"You and your companions must be hungry. Dine with me and we will discuss this."

Kimber relaxed her grip on his arm but didn't release it.

"Thank you, Highness. We accept your gracious hospitality."

When she removed her hand from his arm, Hanibal felt as if a piece of his soul had been cut away. No woman's touch had ever moved him so.

20

Areana's Vale
YOR 416, Late Spring

Alan greeted the new dawn flanked by Kat and Quincy. The three days that had elapsed since their dinner with Hanibal had been filled with activity. During that time he had recovered from the shock of seeing Kim weave her seductive spell on Hanibal.

Having enjoyed an intimate connection with Kim, he knew what it was like to be the object of her desire. He told himself that jealousy had nothing to do with his disdain for Hanibal. The sheer ease with which she had captivated the self-proclaimed king of Tal was what rubbed him raw.

But even Kim hadn't been able to extract everything she had asked of Hanibal. He hadn't promised to provide fifteen thousand soldiers. What Hanibal had offered was to let Carol and Alan recruit as many volunteers as they could convince to follow them. Even Alan had to agree that it seemed on its face to be a fair offer.

It would have been if the high priest and his minions hadn't, according to Derek Scot, been spreading the notion that the gods had blinded Carol in punishment for her pursuit of foul magic. Hanibal had made sure that rumors of the curse of the Chosen had circulated throughout the army, spreading the fear of serving under Alan. Other soldiers were reluctant to leave their families to take part in a long and dangerous expedition that would take them far from their loved ones. And Hanibal's wielders had elected to remain with their king in the vale.

Despite those problems, the three days that Alan and Carol had spent recruiting veterans from Rafel's legion had swollen their ranks by more than eight thousand soldiers. Alan worked with the officers to organize these volunteers into a single regiment composed of four battalions with five companies each. Alan placed Commander Vontay, a leader who had performed heroically during the battle at Endar Pass, in command of this regiment. Vontay would report directly to Alan, as would Derek Scot, who commanded the rangers, and Tudor, who commanded Alan's Forsworn.

According to Kim yesterday, Hanibal had begged her to remain behind with him. She had rebuffed the king's advances. Although he'd failed to give her the support she'd requested, Hanibal had provisioned their force, even providing the oxen and wagons needed to haul the supplies. He seemed eager to have the Rafel loyalists out of his valley.

Now Alan marched out through Areana's Gorge at the head of the column of veterans who had fought under his father's command and remained loyal to the Rafel family. These soldiers weren't his Forsworn, but they had a score to settle with Kragan. He and his vorg army had killed their high lord and their battle master.

Alan rounded the last bend and emerged from the gorge into a broad valley. In the distance he saw what he'd expected. Arn, Carol, Kim, and Galad waited. Behind them, Tudor and the thousand Forsworn stood in formation, their bald heads glistening in the morning sun. The warriors had their weapons sheathed or slung across their backs.

As they approached those who awaited their arrival, Alan turned to Commander Vontay.

"Commander."

"Yes, lord?"

"Position your regiment behind that formation. Derek's rangers will lead my battalion of Forsworn with your regiment and the wagons behind them. Prince Galad will wield the time-mists through which we'll march."

"May I ask our destination?"

"Back to Endar. But first we'll visit Val'Dep. I need to speak with the khan."

—◊—

Chief Matron Loraine had one mission left in her life, to protect the children who had survived the desolation wrought by the dark-magic wielder. She had lost consciousness after witnessing the mass sacrifice of her people on the valley floor beyond Val'Dep's walls. She had come to, wedged within the crenel, in the bright light of day. The wielder and his legion had departed some time during the night.

Loraine had struggled back up onto the wall, every joint and muscle in her body a mass of pain and bruises. The burns on the left side of her neck and face were the worst of her injuries. When she put her fingers to her blinded left eye, she had recoiled in horror. The eyeball had burst. What was left had dried in the socket.

She had limped back into the city and found the medical stores she required to treat her worst injuries. She washed her wounds in cold water. Loraine applied a disinfecting salve to her eye socket before applying a bandage. A chocolate-brown liniment that smelled of camphor dulled the pain of her burned flesh.

She pulled herself together and spent the rest of the day roaming through the streets and buildings of Val'Dep, calling in as loud a voice as she could manage for survivors. She had not found the thirteen children hidden behind rubble in a basement until late the following day.

She had moved these traumatized babes into the house that had been her home since she had been named chief matron.

Food and water weren't a problem. But the raiders and the resurrected dead had looted the city armory and treasury. They had stolen all the horses, some oxen, and many of the ox-drawn carts to haul away the spoils of their attack.

The oldest of the children was a twelve-year-old girl named Esper, who'd proved to be a responsible, sure-footed helper. Whenever Loraine had to go out, Esper filled in as caretaker of the children.

In the days since then, her eye socket had begun to heal. But the blistered skin of her face and neck and melted ear continued to inflict agony. Loraine interspersed caring for the children with her continued search for any more survivors. She had finally come to accept that she and the thirteen small ones were the last of her people.

Only when she left the children in Esper's care to roam the empty city did Loraine allow herself to cry. Today, for the first time since the night of horrors, she shambled out onto Val'Dep's great outer wall.

Standing atop it, she looked out at the twin ramps that had been lowered across the chasm and the fertile valley beyond. The tall grasses bent and waved in the stiff morning breeze. She felt . . . alone.

Loraine straightened her back, turned, and walked the length of the wall, ignoring the stench that permeated the air. Every couple of steps she would pause to look down at the mangled and decaying corpses of people she had known. She couldn't give them a proper fiery funeral. But she would not just leave them lying here atop these battlements.

Loraine bent her back to the task that she dreaded. One by one, piece by piece, she lifted the bodies to the nearest crenel and pushed them through, sending them tumbling into the depths beyond.

The afternoon sun was sinking low when she finished the grim job. When she had pushed the last of the brave defenders from the wall, Loraine put her back against the outer battlements and sank down upon the walkway.

Shaking with exhaustion, Loraine sat there, back against the wall. Then she put her face in her hands and wept, slowly rocking herself back and forth.

—⁓—

The afternoon waned as Arn stepped out of the time-mists beside Carol and Zaislus, alongside the front of Alan's legion. As the fog dissolved around them, he caught his first sight of Val'Dep's outer wall a league in front of them. Although he couldn't make out details from such a distance, the heavy hand of dread settled on his shoulder, pulling him to a halt.

"What is it?" Carol asked.

Arn studied the wall with growing concern. Shouldn't the khan's scouts be riding out to meet them?

He called upon his time-sight, looking into the recent past instead of trying to decipher the future. The gift showed him something only when he focused on a particular target or when a specific event triggered his intuition. The easiest visions to reach were those closest to the present and nearest his physical location. When he branched out further in time or distance, the effort strained his talent.

An image formed in his mind of a middle-aged woman weeping atop the outer wall, one side of her face puckered with burns that had left her minus an eye and ear. Filth covered her long dress, her hands, her arms. Her hair was so matted he couldn't make out its natural color.

She was alone atop the wall. What had happened here?

Arn extended his sight toward the city. The fields were empty. The streets were empty. Other than the flags flapping in the wind above the city towers, nothing moved.

He stepped back to earlier in the day, watched the woman walk out of Val'Dep and make her way across the parade ground and up the ramp that carried her to the top of the wall. Decomposing corpses littered the battlements. Arn watched her lift the bodies and dump them into the ravine.

After several moments, he pulled himself back into the present.

"Something terrible has happened here," Arn said.

"What?"

Arn unleashed a new dreamscape.

The women warriors of Val'Dep lined the top of the torchlit battlements. All along the wall, catapults launched their deadly loads of heavy stones into the horde. Lightning and fireballs answered the volley, setting the catapults ablaze. Then Kragan raised his hands, levitating hundreds of vorgs up onto the broad wall.

The defenders leapt upon the attackers, but without magical support, they had no chance whatsoever. He watched the ensuing slaughter until no Val'Dep warrior remained standing.

Arn pulled himself back to the present.

"Kragan killed them all."

"Oh no."

Carol took Arn's hand in hers and squeezed. But even the feel of her gentle grip couldn't dampen the rage that clenched his gut.

—ᘓ—

Alan ordered his legion to halt a thousand paces from Val'Dep's outer wall. He lifted his far-glass to his eye, studying the ramparts. Arn was right, nobody was defending the city's battlements. Having spent considerable time and effort defending that wall alongside the men and women of Val'Dep, he couldn't shake the tightness the sight put in his gut.

The ramps were down, but nobody had ridden out to challenge the legion of nine thousand that Alan had marched onto the khan's doorstep.

"Tudor," Alan said.

"Yes, Chosen?"

"Keep the Forsworn here, at the ready. I'll pass the same order to Commander Vontay and his regiment. I'm going into Val'Dep with my sister and Arn."

"Alone?" Tudor asked, concern in his voice.

"Kat and Quincy will accompany me. I'm not going to march a thousand Forsworn up those ramps and into Val'Dep. That sight would traumatize whatever survivors might yet remain in the city. I daresay my sister can provide us cover, should we need it. If you see magic roiling the skies, come running."

Tudor slapped his right fist to his chest, rattling the chain mail that draped his torso.

"As you command."

Alan, with Kat and Quincy trailing, walked over to his sister.

"Ready?" Alan asked.

"Yes," Carol said.

"Then let's not be shy."

Alan led the way to the leftmost of the twin ramps that provided a path to the top of the great wall of Val'Dep. When the group reached the top, they found the battlements splattered with dried blood and gore. But the defenses were unmanned. The sight left Alan queasy. He walked to the rear of the wall and gazed back toward the city.

Val'Dep stretched out before him, climbing the canyon walls on the right and left in a series of steps carved into steep hillsides that ended at the cliff walls. The city looked like a multitiered cake cut in two, a narrow gap separating the sections. The buildings had been constructed of white limestone, offering peaked tile roofs.

A lane twenty paces wide between high walls was blocked by a series of iron gates. The defense was augmented by fortified city walls on either side, from which arrows could be fired from the hundreds of crenels lining their tops. More of the cantilevered ramps connected the opposing city walls, allowing troops to traverse Val'Dep above those jammed into the killing zone below.

High on the steep slopes of the right-hand portion of the city, a white palace perched, its turrets and rooftops covered with brightly colored tiles. A prominent flag showing crossed ivory axes on a bloodred background fluttered above the tallest tower.

Like Areana's Vale and the home of the cliff-dwelling Kanjou tribe, the sheer cliffs had been carved eons ago by the glaciers from which the mountain range had gotten its name. Half of this pastoral canyon bottom was farmland, while the other side was used as grazing land for several thousand horses. Here the roadway split, with one portion leading along the city wall on the left and another branching along the city wall on the right.

But what froze Alan's bones was the utter emptiness of the scene. He saw no people, no horses, no activity whatsoever. He'd spilled his own blood and that of many enemies fighting atop this wall alongside the women and men of Val'Dep. Now the people he had grown to love were gone.

He didn't know for sure who had attacked Val'Dep, but one name sprang to mind, of course. Kragan. But why hadn't the evil bastard burned the city? As Alan surveyed the scene, he understood. Its pristine appearance only served to make its emptiness all the more haunting.

Beside him he heard Carol's exclamation.

"Gods preserve us."

"Let's go," Alan said, only now realizing that his right fist held the haft of the ax he'd unslung. "I need to get into that city."

Alan led the small group along the lane between the split halves of the city, passing through the open iron gates. They made their way along the road until they entered the box canyon on the north side of the city. The broad and fertile canyon had been divided into fenced farmland and extensive pastures.

Although cattle and oxen still grazed in the pastures, only a few of the khan's many horses remained. No women worked the fields, some of which looked ready to harvest.

Here the road branched left and right. Alan took the rightmost path, skirting the city wall until he reached a ramp that led up through a gateway beneath a raised portcullis. He roamed the cobblestone streets, past the rows of connected houses and shops separated by narrow alleys. Colorful cloth curtains flapped from open windows in the evening breeze.

The oppressive silence of the city weighed on him. Even if Kragan had killed all the warriors, what had he done with the noncombatants? What had the wielder wanted with all the old people and children?

When the group reached a bend in the street, Alan turned onto the broad avenue that meandered upward toward the gleaming walls of the palace. There he halted and turned toward his brother-in-law.

"Arn. Can you tell me what happened here?"

"I'll have to rewind the days in my head. It's not something I've practiced much."

"Give me what you can."

Arn nodded and seated himself, leaning back against the wall of a building.

"This may take a while."

As the assassin closed his eyes and grew still, a cold gust whipped the banners atop the tallest tower, chilling Alan to his core.

—⚇—

Arn immersed himself in a dream of the past, directing his mind at the city within which his body now sat. He watched the woman whom he had seen weeping atop the outer wall leave a large home not far from the palace, then backed up to see what she had done before that.

His vision shifted to the house interior. She moved among the children sleeping inside the home, instructing the oldest girl to care for the others while she worked outside. He moved steadily back in time, saw the woman spend days searching the city for survivors until she located the hidden group of thirteen kids.

Arn turned back the clock again and saw thousands of vorgs and men gathered in the valley beyond the battlements as they herded thousands of Val'Dep's citizens down the ramps. He watched in horror as Kragan sacrificed them to raise an equal number of vorg warriors from the dead. Then they looted the city and departed.

The fury that built within his chest pulled Arn from the dream and back into the present. This had been a replay of what Kragan had done to the denizens of the fishing village. He had sacrificed his own people to raise hundreds of sea-dragons.

Arn opened his eyes, blinking to allow them to adjust to the globe of light Carol had summoned to drive back the night. He rose to his feet to meet the curious stares of the others.

"Did it work?" asked Alan. "Do you know what transpired here?"

"It was Klampyne all over again, but on a much larger scale."

"Oh no," Carol said. "What did he raise from the dead?"

"The beginnings of the army he seeks to gather. Four or five thousand vorgs."

Alan kicked the door of the small shop, breaking its hinges and sending it hurtling inside. Zaislus wheeled toward the source of the sound, a snarl curling the big dog's lips to reveal his long canines.

"In addition to the woman I told you about," Arn said, "thirteen children survived. She's caring for them in a house not far from here. I can lead us there."

"They must be traumatized," Carol said. "We should be careful not to scare them even more than they already are."

"The people here know me," Alan said. "Maybe not the children, but the woman will recognize me. I should go in first."

"Maybe we should wait until morning," Carol said. "Someone knocking on the door at night in an empty city will startle them."

A new vision formed in Arn's mind, the woman grabbing a butcher knife and whirling toward the door as children howled and cowered behind her.

"That would be bad."

"Quincy," Alan said, "I need you to run back to the legion and let Tudor, Vontay, and Derek know we'll be staying in the city for tonight. Tell them to make camp where they are but be ready to march by midmorning."

"On my way."

Quincy turned, his long stride carrying him out of sight around the bend.

Then the night's silence was broken by distant screams.

21

Carol heard the chorus of terrified children's voices, the sound amplified by Zaislus's sensitive ears. She whirled toward the noise. Zaislus's gaze locked on the entrance to a side street a hundred paces before the palace doors.

As her companions broke into a run, Carol levitated, hurling herself and Zaislus through the sky with all the speed the air elemental she'd summoned could manage. Even her mental soothing failed to stifle the big dog's whimpers. She slowed and dropped to the ground in front of the building from which the cacophony echoed, bathing the street in brilliance.

The front door stood open, sagging on its hinges, revealing a vorg who had twisted his head to look at her. The woman Arn had described lay on the floor, clutching a butcher knife and struggling to roll to her knees. The children's cries continued unabated.

The big vorg turned to face Carol, sword in hand, a snarl on his jutting muzzle. She gestured, lifting the warrior a foot off the ground, pinning his arms to his sides with invisible strands, and pulling him out through the door to float before her. Carol increased the force that wrapped the vorg's sword arm, squeezing so hard that she pulled a howl of pain from the evil thing's throat. The sword clattered to the cobblestones.

Just then, Alan and the others rounded the corner.

"I have the vorg," she said. "Help those inside."

Alan slowed and stepped inside with Kat right behind him.

As Carol shifted her attention back to her prisoner, she heard Alan's startled exclamation.

"Tell me why you're here instead of with your horde," Carol said.

The vorg spat, but a gust of air spattered the wad back into his face.

Then Arn stepped to her side, Slaken in his right hand.

"Leave the interrogation to me," Arn said. The icy tone of his voice was that of Blade. "You don't need to see this."

With a flick of her will, Carol hammered the vorg down, leaving him breathless, faceup on the cobblestones. From the corner of Zaislus's eye she saw Arn straddle the vorg, Slaken's tip cutting a thin trail of blood just beneath the thing's left eye.

Then she released the vorg and walked into the house, magically closing the door behind her and shutting out the disturbing sounds that tried to follow her inside.

—⚍—

As Kat moved to calm the children, Alan knelt beside Loraine in the candlelit room, examining the chief matron of Val'Dep with careful hands. She bled heavily from a long cut down her left forearm, but he found no other recent injuries. He could do nothing for the scars that marred the left side of her head.

She opened her good eye, her lips working themselves into a weak smile.

"You have no idea how I prayed for your return. Alas, Chosen, you've arrived too late."

"Don't talk," he said, gentleness in his tone. "Rest now."

Loraine closed her eye and sank back.

Alan, working quickly but with shaking hands, tore a long strip from her dress. Seeing the blood spurting from her wrist in rhythm with her heart, he tied the cloth around her arm just above her elbow and twisted it into a tourniquet. But as he finished the task, Loraine shuddered and issued one last breath.

Alan went cold. As he looked down at that scarred and battered face, memories of this woman came forth, the ill-fitting chain mail tunic draping her stout chest as she fought alongside him atop Val'Dep's great wall.

Face it, Chosen. How many of your friends have you failed to save? How many more will die following you into battle? This is your destiny.

Alan heard Carol enter as a rasping voice outside began to shriek. Then the door closed, somehow shutting out the agonized howls.

"Loraine?" Carol asked.

His answer came out as a croak.

"Dead, like Val'Dep."

He took Loraine in his arms and rose to his feet. Alan carried the injured woman into the next room and gently laid her on her bed, carefully covering her with a thick blanket, as if the dead could feel cold. Alan had been in the chief matron's house only one time before. On that evening she had schooled him on the importance of women in Val'Dep society, a lesson he'd internalized.

He stood looking down at her marred face and bent to kiss her forehead.

Alan walked back into the living area, noting that Carol and Kat had managed to calm the frightened children. Several still whimpered, but the combination of Carol's soothing mind magic and the way the two women gathered them into their arms was working. Alan watched how tenderly Kat cradled three of the smallest waifs. The sight tightened the vise that gripped his throat.

Noting that the children would be unlikely to find his grim appearance soothing, Alan walked to the door and pulled it open. When he stepped outside, it was as if he passed through a curtain. Suddenly he could hear the desperation in the vorg's rasping voice.

"Blade. I have told you all I know. Kill me and be done."

In the pale light of the rising moon, the vorg warrior lay on his back. The assassin in black held the tip of a dagger to the leftmost of the empty eye sockets with his left hand. Arn's right fist gripped Slaken, blood dripping from the knife's black blade. Strips of flesh hung from the vorg's sliced cheeks and forehead.

Alan stared down at his brother-in-law's handiwork, feeling no pity for the vorg. Suddenly Arn shifted his weight, driving the dagger hilt-deep in the bloody socket where an eye had once rested. The vorg's body spasmed and lay still.

Arn wiped the blades of the two knives on the vorg's shirt, rose to his feet, and sheathed them.

"You probably don't want Carol to see that," Alan said.

"She knows what I am," Arn said. "But you're probably right."

Alan reached down, grabbed the vorg's corpse by its belt, and carried the body around the side of the house. He dumped it facedown in the gutter. For several moments Alan just stood there staring down at the body.

Loraine's words flooded his eyes with tears. She had been right. *Alas, Chosen, you've arrived too late.*

22

Lagoth
YOR 416, Late Spring

Kragan and Draken stepped out of the rychly time-mist a half league
north of the majestic walled city of Lagoth. From this ridge their twilight view of the battlements was clear. Hundreds of torches lit the
ramparts, revealing armored guards moving atop the fifty-foot-high
wall that ringed the jumble of buildings below the temple atop the hill.
Regularly spaced towers jutted skyward along its perimeter.

The Banjee River split the city from north to south, spanned by
seven bridges. The river passed through a tunnel in the wall and a vast
portcullis that could be raised during periods of flood or lowered in
seasons of drought.

"Well, here we are. Now what?" asked Draken.

"Now we announce my return."

The two wielders approached the city, avoiding the wide and heavily rutted road that led to the city gates. Instead they swung wide,
moving toward the western portion of the wall, cloaking themselves in
invisibility. That spell was imperfect. While it worked well at a distance,
they would be visible to anyone who came within a couple of paces.

Kragan knew his city, and he brought them to a place where several abandoned warehouses lay on the opposite side of the wall.

"Up and over?" Draken asked.

"Yes."

Kragan floated over the wall, his veil masking him from the guards atop the battlements. Draken followed him through the air, then down into a murky alley. Having bypassed the guards, Kragan and Draken dropped their spell of invisibility.

Kragan led them through alleys and backstreets before turning south onto the main avenue. This time of night, most of the inhabitants had made their way back to their homes. But the carousers and ruffians were out and about, as were the soldiers who helped keep order.

Unlike any other large city, Lagoth had an almost equal distribution of vorg and human citizens. A city within the caverns and tunnels beneath Lagoth housed thousands of enslaved people who did most of the work. Kragan's throne room occupied a cavern of its own, but he had no intention of visiting the chamber.

They bypassed the plaza with the pyramid at its center, crossed three more streets, and turned east down another broad avenue. The street ended a hundred paces in front of them, at the gates that provided access to the palace grounds.

Kragan led the way directly toward them, pausing only when the captain of the palace guard uttered his command.

"Step into the light and state your business."

Kragan walked forward, Draken at his side.

The vorg captain directed his words to Draken, showing that he assumed the taller man in wielder's clothing carried the authority.

"I'm here to see Bohdan," Kragan said.

The captain shifted his gaze down to Kragan, a scowl forming on his muzzle.

"Quiet, imp. I'm speaking to your master."

Kragan narrowed his gaze and the vorg grabbed his throat, trying to tear free the invisible rope that tightened around it, cutting off the blood supply to his brain. When he dropped to his knees, a dozen guardsmen leveled their crossbows at Kragan and Draken.

Kragan loosened the magical noose. The captain coughed twice, then gasped in a lungful of air and struggled back to his feet.

"Kill them."

The crossbows twanged, sending the bolts streaking toward their targets. They embedded themselves in the air three feet in front of Kragan and the white-haired wielder who stood beside him. Kragan released his will and the bolts clattered to the ground in front of him.

"I prefer not to kill my own warriors, even fools such as yourselves," Kragan said. "But my patience wears thin. Go tell Bohdan that Kragan has returned and wishes to speak with him."

The vorg captain's eyes widened at the mention of the name that everyone in Lagoth knew well.

"You? Kragan?"

Kragan slowly lifted his right hand, a red ball of flame growing within his palm, radiating heat that singed the vorg's hairy jaws and eyebrows.

Suddenly the captain dropped to one knee and bowed low, face solemn.

"Forgive me, my lord. My deepest apologies. I expected to see you wearing the same body as when last I saw you. I'll personally relay your words to our city master."

Kragan let the fire die.

"Apology accepted. Do *not* keep me waiting."

—∭—

Kragan stepped into the chambers of the vorg wielder whom he had long ago made caretaker of Lagoth. The room was the size of an average cottage but empty of furniture. The walls were bare stone and mortar with neither tapestries nor adornments, matching the ceiling and floor.

Bohdan sat cross-legged on a ten-foot circular black rug patterned with red snakes that seemed to crawl away from his body in all directions. He wore the familiar scarlet robe he favored and stared outward, his black-flecked yellow eyes shifting from Draken to Kragan.

"Which of these bodies do you currently inhabit, my lord Kragan . . . if such you truly are?"

Kragan touched Bohdan's mind, placing a sequence of visions there.

Bohdan standing beside Kragan atop Lagoth's great wall as he deflected the time magic cast by hundreds of Endarian time-shapers into the army of Endarians and humans who'd laid siege to Kragan's city.

Kragan wearing the seven-foot-tall body and feline face of Kaleal, the primordial Lord of the Third Deep, standing before Bohdan in this very chamber.

Kragan rising from his coffin in Sadamad, having returned to his original body after falling to Blade's killing blow in Endar Pass.

Kragan stepped into the circle formed by Bohdan's rug.

"If you doubt the visions I've shown you . . ."

Kragan pulled the necklace from beneath his tunic, cupping the six shards in his upturned palm.

Bohdan's extended jaws dropped open, and he climbed to his feet. He reached out as if to touch the artifacts, snapping out of his trance only when Kragan closed his left fist around the shards, bathing himself in a brilliant curtain of magic. The energy raised the gooseflesh on Bohdan's skin as tiny blue sparks crawled across him.

The vorg's eyes widened, and he dropped to one knee, head bowed. "Forgive me, my lord. Welcome home."

23

Galad's time-mists carried a group that included the children of Val'Dep through the gorge, where an unseasonably warm morning welcomed them back to Areana's Vale. Each of the adults carried a child in each arm, leaving the oldest girl to walk along beside them. Soldiers offered to help with the children, but the Rafels and their companions refused to relinquish the traumatized babes to a new set of strangers.

Kim marveled at Carol's ability to soothe the minds of the young ones, putting them into a dreamless sleep where no demons could trouble them. Carol and Zaislus led the way toward the one family she said she could entrust the orphans to.

Onlookers gathered as they passed through Colindale, Fernwood, and Longsford Watch. But the small group left them in their wake, not slowing until they reached the farm where Henry, Mary Beth, and their five girls lived in their multiroom log cabin. Mary Beth was the first to see the travelers approach and came running to meet them, apron strings flapping.

"By all the gods," the motherly woman said, "what's happened?"

"Can we get these children inside?" Carol asked. "After they're settled in, we can talk without disturbing them."

"Certainly."

Henry and their five daughters hurried to help carry the children into the house. Within moments Mary Beth and her daughters had laid out blankets for the sleeping babes to rest upon. Then the daughters gathered around the oldest survivor, hugging her and wiping away the torrent of tears that she finally released.

Kim left Carol and Mary Beth tending to the children and stepped outside to find Alan, Galad, and Arn locked in conversation as Kat looked on.

"We need to brief King Hanibal on Val'Dep," Galad said. "Perhaps what happened will encourage him to provide more support for our mission."

"It's a waste of time to try to talk sense to this so-called king," Alan said.

"If we don't ask, the answer is certainly no," Kim said.

"I'm not crawling to Hanibal."

"I'm not asking you to. Galad and I will talk to him."

"Fine."

Alan turned and walked away, taking Kat with him.

"I'll let you two handle those negotiations," Arn said. "I have something I need to do before we begin our journey."

Kim watched Alan and Arn walk away and shook her head. How could those two be so hardheaded and prideful? She'd made some real inroads with the king in the one evening she'd spent in his company. Now that the opportunity presented itself, Kim was determined not to waste the chance.

She stepped into the gray rychly mist that roiled into existence, leaving the thickness of normal time behind. She and Galad avoided the towns, skirting the woods on their way to the road that led up to the ledge upon which Hanibal's castle rested. Only a few minutes passed in the real world.

Galad laid his hand on her arm, and she turned to look at him.

"I will let you handle this, Sister."

Kim studied him. There was no hint of mirth on his face or in his midnight eyes. He merely stared back at her as if what he'd said was the obvious answer to a particular problem. No wonder he had been such a successful commander of the Endarian mist warriors. He saw things as they were, not as he might wish they would be.

Kim reached up to place her hand on his cheek. She gave a slight nod. Then the mists gathered to sweep her brother away.

—⚬⚬⚬—

When Kim reached the castle gate, the captain of the guard sent a runner to inform the king that she desired an audience. Moments later, Hanibal surprised the Endarian princess by walking out of the fortress to greet her.

Hanibal beamed. He extended his arm, inviting her to take his elbow. Kim nodded and slid her left hand into the crook of his arm. His touch sent a thrill through her, an expected side effect of the soul magic she'd expended upon first meeting the king. That spell had been a gentle casting but had nonetheless forged a lasting connection between them.

"I thought we could share the warmth of this sunny day and the beauty of this valley as we walk and talk," he said.

"Lovely."

They strolled down the road that wound its way to the valley floor. When they reached the verdant land at the base of the cliffs, Hanibal left the road and led her east into the tall pines. The tangy scent of sap and pine needles filled her with life, almost as if she had tapped their energy. Slanting shafts of sunlight speared down between the branches to puddle on the forest floor.

For a while they walked among the trees without saying anything. When they came to a stream, Hanibal turned to follow its winding path. A flowering meadow opened before them, and the king ushered her to a seat atop a flat boulder that had long ago plummeted from the cliffs that towered above them. The twitter of birds in the trees accompanied the babble of the brook.

Seating himself beside her at an angle that allowed him to gaze into her face, Hanibal finally spoke.

"I often come here when I need a quiet place to sit and think."

"It's beautiful."

He took her hand in his. "Thank you."

"For what, Highness?"

His cheeks flushed ever so slightly. "For not hating me."

Kim looked into his eyes and understood. He had usurped Carol's position as leader of the Talian people. Alan hated him for it. Kim was Carol and Alan's half sister. He could hardly have expected her not to feel the same way. He started to speak, but she held up her hand.

"I was angry when I first learned that you'd named yourself king. Certainly. But I have seen for myself the improvements you've made here, how you've strengthened the vale's defenses and gathered the refugees from Tal. The people of Areana's Vale respect you. I like that."

"But Alan and Carol—"

"Carol, Arn, and Alan have their destinies. I cannot see that any of their futures include ruling Areana's Vale or the kingdom of Tal. Neither do I see myself leading the Endarian court."

A sudden look of concern spread across Hanibal's face.

"Do not so quickly eschew all courtly life. There may be one that you could come to love."

Kim nodded. "Perhaps."

Then she grew serious.

"I have troubling news to relay."

Hanibal leaned back a bit, as if she had slapped him to kill the mood that had been building between them.

"Can we not delay such revelations for another time? Why should we spoil this moment?"

Kim looked down, debating his request. But when she raised her gaze to meet his, her resolve firmed. She slid her hand from his gentle grip.

"Kragan has massacred the people of Val'Dep."

"What?"

"Kragan overran the city and sacrificed its citizens to raise a legion from the land of the dead. We've just returned from the site."

Hanibal's mouth dropped open. For several heartbeats he seemed too stunned to speak.

"Were there no survivors?"

"Only the thirteen children we carried back with us."

"Dear gods."

Kim leaned in close, taking both of Hanibal's hands in hers and looking directly into his eyes.

"You can help save my people. You can help save me."

Hanibal shook his head but didn't release her hands. If anything, he squeezed them tighter.

"I've given Alan and Carol the eight thousand soldiers who volunteered to serve under Alan's command. Would you have me order thousands more to serve against their will?"

"Their duty is to enforce the will of their king, not do whatever they wish."

Anger crept into Hanibal's voice, and now he did release her hands.

"Do not school me on a soldier's duty. I have lived my entire life as one."

Kim stood up.

"Yes, but you've been sovereign for less than a year. You've done well for your people, but I must ask that you open your eyes to the wider world."

She pointed toward the gorge that led out of the vale.

"Evil is out there. It ate Val'Dep. If I do not enjoy your full support, Kragan will most certainly destroy Endar. I will perish with my family and allies. Then he will come for you and yours. Think on it, dear king."

Then Kim turned and left Hanibal sitting there. Her magic had not been enough to cause the king to fully commit, had not bound her so stoutly to him that she couldn't leave his side.

A single tear trickled down her left cheek, but she made no attempt to wipe it away.

—⁓—

Arn skirted the town of Longsford Watch and made his way to the cabin that High Lord Rafel had built for Carol. It had stood empty since Arn had carried her from the priestly edifice within which she'd been confined.

He stepped onto the porch and stopped to right the overturned chair. When he opened the door, its hinges squealed in protest. He stepped inside, blind to the dust that his boots raised and the spiderwebs that draped the rafters. A stack of dried-out sticks and kindling were stacked next to the dead hearth, but in his mind he saw the blaze that he had lain in front of, holding Carol in his arms.

He moved to the bed where they'd first made love. This was the place where he'd asked her to be his wife and where she'd said yes. It was the house where he'd given her the ancient book of magic that almost robbed her of sanity.

Arn ran his hands over the bed, then lay down to stare up at the ceiling. He got up and walked out onto the porch. If he could go back in time, would he change the past? Perhaps, with his growing ability, he could alter events, never give her that magical tome, prevent all the subsequent death and destruction that followed.

But if he hadn't given her the book of magic he'd left here on her porch, she might not be his wife today. Now the world might fall. Kragan might become a god. He and Carol might both die. Regardless, he wouldn't change one single thing in the past that had brought them together.

Arn sat down upon the chair and looked out through the woods and up at the cliffs that towered above the verdant valley that he'd fallen in love with. He wouldn't change the past. But he might be able to choose the future.

His fingers fumbled at his belt, removing the small pouch that held the shard. He could almost feel the terrible power of the thing radiating through the soft leather. His index fingers and thumbs plucked at the drawstring, slowly loosening it until the mouth of the pouch yawned open in his lap. For several moments he took deep breaths and performed the mental exercises that calmed him.

Then, when his mind had achieved a stillness that Carol called finding one's center, he lifted the pouch and dumped its skeletal contents into his open palm.

—⚬—

A kaleidoscope blossomed before Arn's eyes, the futures whirling out before him in a dizzying, multicolored cascade. Arn spoke the word of focus.

"Kragan."

He felt himself sucked into one of the myriad visions as the others melted away. He stood on a broad avenue along which a mob of vorg soldiers had chased him and Ty three years ago. A seemingly endless column of vorg and human soldiers marched by, streaming north toward the city gates.

He turned around, his eyes searching for the target that had brought him here. High up on the side of an apartment building, Kragan stood on a balcony with a pair of companions, staring over the railing at the troops marching out of the city.

The white-haired man standing on Kragan's left had a neatly trimmed beard of the same color and wore a black robe. Arn recognized him from a previous vision.

Draken.

A red-robed vorg stood on Kragan's right, an evil gleam in his yellow eyes.

Leave it to Kragan to surround himself with the foulest magic wielders he could find. And now he's gathered an army to augment his legion of resurrected dead.

Still locked on Kragan, Arn stepped forward in time.

The scene faded away as a new one took its place. Kragan's army stood in formation outside Lagoth, tens of thousands strong. Kragan and the two other wielders stood at the forefront, three paces in front of Arn. Kragan reached inside his shirt, pulling forth the necklace from which dangled the shards of magic amplification. He selected two, closing his left fist around them. Then he turned to Draken.

"I need you to direct into me the sorcery you used to call forth the corrupt god."

Draken raised an eyebrow. "For what purpose?"

"Even with these two shards of time magic, I cannot summon enough time-mist to engulf an army of this size. But you can widen that channel, one of the reasons I made the journey to collect you from Far Castle."

"It might be dangerous for you."

"A risk I'm willing to take."

Draken inclined his head. "As you wish."

The white-haired wielder lifted his hands, palms out toward Kragan. The air shimmered between his splayed fingertips. Kragan's face tightened and his breath panted out, as if he were in the midst of a desperate footrace. For several moments Kragan's image blurred.

Draken lowered his hands and the distortion faded away.

"It's done," Draken said.

"I feel it. How long will the effect last?"

"I don't know."

Kragan grinned. "Let's find out."

Then the rychly time-mist formed, flowing like a murky fog over the wielders and the army while a lighter pomaly mist trailed behind it.

Arn watched the fog bank race away, just south of west. What in the realm of the vile gods was Kragan doing? He wasn't headed for Endar Pass but toward the northern tip of the Glacier Mountains.

A lump formed in Arn's throat.

Kragan wanted to cut off any forces from the south that might try to come to Endar's aid. Arn knew what Kragan intended to do.

Divide and conquer.

—∽—

Arn stepped out of the dreamscape and back into his seated body on Carol's porch. He lurched to his feet. Arn needed to collect his wife and companions. Whether or not Kim had been able to extract a promise of more help from Hanibal, they could dally here no longer.

Even if his vision of Kragan was still a day or two weeks from happening, Arn, Carol, and their companions had just run out of time.

169

24

Alan looked out over the mountains that formed the southern boundary of the kingdom of Endar. He had just marched nine thousand soldiers out of Galad's time-mists and across the Endarian border. Alan knew that the Endarian scouts had watched. Right now they would be sending mist runners to report the armed incursion.

Galad and Kim had been unable to gain their king's permission to enter Endar on their first attempt. Now they and the accompanying legion needed to demonstrate their loyalty to Endar by defending its southern border against Kragan. In the meantime Alan and company would have to hope that Endar chose not to attack them from behind.

This was the craziest strategy Alan had ever envisioned. He had positioned his legion to act as a covering force for Endar, making Kragan commit his forces in order to break through. But unless Kelond opened the way into Endar Pass, Alan would have no place to retreat should things go badly.

Arn liked the plan, but that did little to reassure Alan that he wasn't about to get everyone who fought under his command killed. Hanibal wouldn't have approved of this tactic, but Hanibal wasn't here. So to the deep with him.

"Lovely place for an ass kicking," Quincy said from just behind Alan.

"Long as it's not ours," Tudor added.

"You two are disturbing the Chosen," Kat said. "He needs to focus on planning."

"The plan seems to be clear," Quincy said. "We have the high ground, but our backs are against the proverbial wall. On the positive side, our troops should be highly motivated. Knowing what happened at Val'Dep, surrender isn't an option."

This last comment drew a low chuckle from Alan. The truth was, the Forsworn needed no additional motivation. The same was true for the bulk of the veterans from High Lord Rafel's legion who'd volunteered to serve under Alan's command. Everyone who manned these battle lines had been in multiple life-or-death fights.

"Derek, any word from your long-range patrols?" he asked.

"No sign of the enemy yet."

"Commander Vontay," Alan said, "are all your troops in position?"

"They stand ready, lord."

"When Kragan comes, he will bring his army through the timemists. But those warriors will be far less experienced than the Forsworn at fighting within the mists. We will bloody their noses while you hold your troops in defensive positions. Should we survive, we will pass back through your lines here. You have my permission to kill anybody who pursues us."

Alan clapped his hand on Commander Vontay's shoulder.

"In this fight, shock will be our only ally. Let's make it count."

—⁓—

King Kelond looked around at the seated circle of high councillors, trying to judge their emotions. Beside him he could feel Councillor

Sersos's anger radiating from his thin body in waves. But Devan's expression was unreadable.

"I believe you've all heard the rumors of an incursion across our southern border. I have called you together to tell you what I've learned so that we can discuss possible courses of action.

"Our scouts report an armed force almost ten thousand strong has crossed into Endar, setting up defensive positions in the mountains there. Lord Alan Rafel leads the legion. Lorness Carol Rafel and Blade are with them, as are former prince Galad and princess Kimber."

Sersos leaned forward, his mouth drawn into a thin line across his hawklike visage.

"There's no need to discuss this provocation. Galad and Kimber have returned with a much larger force, intent on restoring their mother to power. We must meet this threat with force, lest they perceive weakness."

"Nonsense," Devan said. "The Rafel legion is setting up defensive positions, and from the reports I've heard, those defenses are oriented toward the south. They have their backs to us."

"True," Kelond said. "An odd way to make a threat, don't you think, Sersos?"

"The point is," Sersos said, "they've illegally invaded our territory. If the Rafels think they have a legitimate reason for this action, why have they not sent an emissary to request your authorization?"

"Perhaps," Devan said, "because of the way we treated the emissaries Alan and Carol sent on their last visit. If you recall, we banished Galad and Kimber from the kingdom."

"Yet another of your edicts that the siblings have violated, my king," Sersos said.

A murmur arose within the council chamber, a buzz that Kelond allowed to continue while he pondered both sides of the argument. With each passing moment, it became clearer that, once again, the High Council found itself divided.

The king admitted to himself that the affront to his authority infuriated him. But he'd always prided himself on making decisions based on reason rather than emotion. The mark of a good king rather than a tyrant.

Rafel's legion had turned its back upon the obvious threat of a violent Endarian response to its incursion. That made no sense . . . unless . . .

The king steepled his fingers, touching them to his lips. Then he clapped his hands to signal silence. All eyes turned to Kelond.

"I'm inclined to defer this decision until the situation clarifies itself. In the meantime we'll send two emissaries under flag of truce to meet with Lord Alan and Lorness Carol in order to assess their intentions."

"I object to this," Sersos said. "I see no reason—"

"Silence!"

Sersos quit speaking.

"My two emissaries shall be High Councillor Sersos and High Councillor Devan. You'll depart within the hour. A time-shaper and six of my royal guards will escort you."

King Kelond eyed Sersos and Devan, seeing each nod in turn.

"Twenty thousand soldiers will be readied for combat should the outcome of these talks fail to satisfy my concerns. Questions?"

Silence curtained the room.

"The council is dismissed," Kelond said.

He waited until the chamber cleared, leaving him alone. As he sat, the memory of Galad and Kimber's warning about Kragan needled him. It was not feasible that in mere weeks the ancient one could have gathered a large enough force to again threaten Endar and marched it all the way here.

Not possible.

And yet the Rafel legion faced south.

—⚍—

Even with Draken's magic increasing Kragan's ability to channel the time-mists, he was growing tired. That was okay. He could rest when his army made camp on the southern border of Endar. A couple of days there would allow the army and its wielders to rest also and to organize for the assault on Endar Pass.

The risen Dread Lord was an ever-growing source of Kragan's fatigue. The being's will strained against the life force of the thousand Val'Dep warriors whom Kragan had sacrificed to summon Ty from the land of the dead. At the moment the warrior with the great ax strode at the head of the thousands of vorg and human warriors who stretched for leagues in his wake.

The power of the demigod's aura inspired all who served him to be better than they otherwise would be. Kragan had placed Ty in command of every warrior he'd recruited. Only Draken, Bohdan, and Kragan himself were impervious to his supernatural ability to inspire.

"You seem pensive, lord," Draken said. "Or is it worry I perceive?"

Kragan directed his gaze at the wielder in black who strode at his right side.

"Your perception is no concern of mine."

"But you do have concerns. Pray, tell me of them."

Kragan mulled this request. Draken had once been the second most powerful wielder alive, lesser only than Landrel. Even at the moment when Landrel had defeated him, Draken had summoned a malevolent god to merge with him, denying Landrel ultimate victory. Kragan couldn't ignore the threat the mage in black might pose should the man choose to go rogue.

Walking on his left, Bohdan listened attentively. Through the centuries of his life, Kragan had almost grown used to subordinates watching for an opportunity to supplant their master. Kragan sneered. If these two worked up the nerve to challenge his authority, he would splatter their remains beneath his feet.

But Draken's prodding wasn't a real challenge. Kragan could see no harm in enlightening the two wielders.

"I've told you of Carol Rafel, the blind witch whom Landrel prophesied would destroy me. A few months ago, she and the assassin Blade came close to fulfilling the foretelling. During that battle the witch cast a spell that somehow blended mind and time magic in a way I've never witnessed. I have to assume that, since then, she's gotten better at wielding her power."

"She frightens you?" Draken asked.

Kragan laughed and pulled the necklace from beneath his tunic.

"No. But even with these, I won't dismiss the threat the sorceress poses. Do so at your own peril."

—⁂—

"Kragan comes," Arn said, watching the vision of Kragan leading his horde through the time-mists play out in his mind.

"How close?" Alan asked.

Arn pulled his mind fully back into the present moment, looking out across the valley that marked the southern border of the kingdom of Endar.

"Just beyond those distant hills."

Alan turned and issued his order to Tudor, who immediately brought the thousand Forsworn to attention, weapons held at the ready. The other eight thousand Talian soldiers remained in their defensive positions along the ridgeline at Alan's back.

"Wait for it," Arn said to Carol and the Endarian siblings. "Any moment now."

The gray mists rolled over the hilltops, three leagues from where they stood, hurtling forward at great speed.

"Now," Arn said.

Galad summoned the mists, rolling them out to intercept the enemy on its left flank instead of head-on.

"Forward," Alan yelled and led the Forsworn into the familiar fog.

Arn and his companions entered alongside the bald warriors.

When Galad's mists merged with Kragan's, Alan's next command echoed through them.

"Charge."

The leading ranks of vorgs suddenly found a thousand battle-hardened warriors crashing into the left side of their march formation. Lightning crawled overhead, splitting into an inverted tree. Its branches speared down into the vorg ranks, littering the battlefield with smoking corpses.

Thunder shook the earth, drowning out the battle cries of the Forsworn and the wails of the dying. The vorgs milled in confusion as they tried to react to the assault.

Arn placed a hand on Galad's arm, drawing his attention.

"Kragan is about to dispel his mists," Arn yelled.

Galad nodded and stood ready to react. He dismissed his own time-mists. Daylight blossomed over the battlefield only to be blotted out by black clouds that rolled into existence at the behest of the wielders who summoned them.

The Forsworn were now so intermingled with the enemy that Arn lost sight of Alan and Kim. The vast bulk of Kragan's army was blocked from entering the fray by its own troops. The surprise attack and the close combat rendered his archers impotent.

He felt Carol's mind link with his, her mental voice clear.

"Show me what's about to happen."

Arn understood. He released the now in favor of the next. As those visions formed in his mind, he heard Carol's sigh of satisfaction.

"Aaahhh . . ."

—⚶—

Kim stayed within a half dozen paces of Alan, at the tip of the spear that the Forsworn had made of themselves. All around, the blows of their hammers, swords, and axes sent the vorg formations roiling like wounded animals.

Her life magic flowed out from her in ethereal snakes that plunged into the Forsworn wounded and the enemies who fought against them, exchanging injuries for health, life for death. The pain and pleasure that coursed through her body left her gasping and dizzy, yet she continued to extend herself as more and more of the Forsworn suffered wounds.

Thus far Alan remained unscathed. The vorg and human enemies whom he confronted shrank before the crescent-bladed ax that split shield, armor, and flesh with each ferocious blow.

Something flashed across the corner of her vision and she ducked to the side, but not quickly enough to dodge the thrown dagger that embedded itself to the hilt in her stomach. A geyser of pain fountained through Kim, dropping her to a knee. She snatched the blade free, creating a matching wound in the knife thrower's gut as her stomach knitted itself back together.

She rose to her feet as her attacker slumped to the ground, trying to keep his guts from crawling out onto the soaked earth. Kim looked for Alan. She spotted Quincy, locked in combat with a man almost as tall as he was, the blades of their swords locked together, chest to chest.

Suddenly the momentum of the battle changed. Many of the Forsworn had fallen, leaving knots of them isolated from their compatriots. Most were beyond the range of Kim's magic. She saw Tudor lead a group of Forsworn clansmen toward one of the nearest isolated clusters, his war hammer rising and falling in dull, wet thuds.

The Chosen burst through a cluster of five vorgs, sending a pair of heads spinning into the air. Alan kicked another of the vorgs in the chest, his boot launching the she-vorg into three of her compatriots, sending them sprawling.

Alan's stentorian yell rang out above the din of battle.

"Forsworn. To me!"

A great burst of pride filled her chest at the sight of the Chosen, his shaved head and body bathed in blood. She took two steps toward him.

Then the earth beneath Alan's feet liquefied.

—⁂—

Kragan didn't realize that his army was under attack until he noticed the lead elements had separated from the columns behind them. Looking back, he realized that a section of his time-mists had merged with mists he hadn't summoned. All around that point of penetration, his columns of soldiers milled about in wild confusion.

The Endarian mist warriors had somehow mounted a preemptive attack on his forces. This bore all the hallmarks of the hit-and-run tactics of the commander who'd harassed the army Kragan had last marched toward Endar. He'd tortured the name from Endarian captives. Prince Galad.

Now this same warrior harried him while he was tired. Wonderful. So much for rest and recuperation within the foothills while he readied his troops for an assault upon Endar.

Kragan allowed his time-mists to dissipate, illuminating the scene with the bright light of day. The Endarian time-shaper followed his lead, fully revealing the situation. Kragan lensed the air into a far-glass that pulled the distant scene toward him. Madness.

The attackers numbered perhaps a thousand, no more. Yet they had thrown themselves into the flank of an army almost a hundred times their size. To be sure, the ferocity and surprise of that assault was wreaking havoc upon the midsection of Kragan's columns. But even if he hadn't been present, this bold thrust would have been suicide.

Then a new sight brought a hiss to his lips. These were not ebony-skinned Endarian mist warriors. These were the warriors who had conquered the combined armies of three of the five city-states of Sadamad. The sun glinted off their pale, shaved heads as brilliantly as it reflected from their weapons. And the one they called Chosen was leading the charge.

"Draken, Bohdan," Kragan said, magnifying the ax wielder's image so that the others could see his target. "Kill that man. I will handle the blind witch."

Kragan summoned Jaa'dra and hurled a fireball at the woman who'd just levitated herself, Blade, and a dog above the battlefield. The heat of the flames caused the air around the bounding inferno to pop and crackle as it streaked outward. But thirty paces from its target, it collided with a huge globule of water that materialized in the air. The fire fizzled out as if Kragan had just tossed a candle into a pond.

Then he was wreathed in lightning, barely erecting his shielding in time to deflect the bolts into his own troops. From the corner of his eye, he saw the Chosen sink waist deep into the ground beneath his feet. A dozen silvery darts streaked from Draken's outstretched hands toward the partially immobilized warrior, but once again Carol reacted, redirecting the bolts into the vorgs who stood before the Chosen. Her accuracy was uncanny. Twelve heads exploded upon impact.

Bohdan reached toward the Chosen, the fingers of his right hand curling inward, sending the liquefied earth and stone crawling up the warrior's body toward his head. Suddenly he uttered a cry and dropped to his knees as something siphoned the muck from the Chosen's body and set him back on solid ground.

Kragan pulled his necklace from beneath his tunic, clutching all six shards in his left fist. Their power surged through his body like one of the witch's lightning bolts. Indirect attacks weren't working. It was time to get personal.

—∞—

With Arn filtering his near-future visions, showing her the best course of action, Carol touched the mind of the caster attacking Alan. She recognized the taint of Draken's mind from when he'd pursued her and her brother through Far Castle in the body of a vile god. Carol ripped control of the earth elemental from Draken and forced it to undo the earth magic with which it had ensnared Alan.

The battlefield faded away, replaced by a vision of Kragan reaching into his shirt to pull forth a necklace from which shards dangled. The dreamscape shifted. Carol saw herself clutch her head in both hands and scream as she, Arn, and Zaislus plummeted to earth.

The present reclaimed Carol, and she snatched the small purse from her belt and dumped its contents into her left palm.

Please, gods, let this go better than last time.

She reached into the elemental plane of fire and summoned the strongest elemental she could sense to earth a dozen paces from Kragan. Instead of releasing it in a panic as she had done before, she gave the being a target before setting it free.

For a moment she felt Kragan wrap her in bands of power that she barely resisted. Then he broke contact.

Beside her, Arn spoke. "Tell Alan it's time to go. Then cut the Forsworn a path for retreat."

Carol shifted Arn's gaze to where Alan fought. The surviving Forsworn warriors had answered his call and fought their way back to his side. But the enemy warriors had recovered from the shock of the initial attack and had Alan and his followers surrounded.

She lowered her small group to the ground behind Alan. She sent a fireball bouncing westward through the vorgs, cutting a smoking path of destruction that forged a gap through the enemy lines. Carol's mind touched her brother's.

"I've opened a way for us. Get the Forsworn out, now."

Alan didn't hesitate.

"Follow me," he yelled and rushed through the gap, cutting down warriors who attempted to block his retreat.

Tudor and two hundred Forsworn fanned out in a rear guard. Then Galad's slowing pomaly mist flowed over their pursuers while the Forsworn fled through a gray rychly fog.

25

One moment Kragan gripped Carol with all the amplified magic he could summon, and then the impossible happened. An elemental being stepped through a portal from the plane of fire to a spot a few paces from where he stood.

What in the deepest pits? . . . Impossible.

Elementals could only produce effects in the physical world. They couldn't be transported out of their realms. But somehow Carol had gated a being from the ethereal planes into the physical world. This was bad.

Kragan dropped his attack upon Carol and erected a shield bubble around himself and Draken just as the lion-shaped creature of living flame turned its face toward him and exhaled. A river of fire flowed from the thing's open maw. The heat grew so intense that the wind howled around the wielders, racing upward in a vortex of flame that spiraled into the sky. It chewed at the invisible wall that held it back and continued pouring over the duo from a seemingly endless reservoir.

Kragan felt exhaustion from having wielded the mists to transport his entire army. Fatigue crawled through his limbs, leaving his arms feeling like dying snakes. He heard his own breathing as ragged gasps. His shield wavered, and a burst of heat torched his eyebrows.

Draken augmented Kragan's will with his own. He thrust his shield out at the elemental, who stopped breathing fire to rake the invisible barrier with its flaming claws.

Kragan shifted to attack, drowning the fire creature with a sudden torrent of rain. But the water evaporated without touching its incandescent skin. Kragan understood why. While it was possible to drown the fiery magic an elemental could wield from its home plane, the creature itself was the forge that kindled the flame. And this one was angry.

Draken launched a barrage of spear-tipped ice shards at the thing, pulling forth a crackling screech that hurt Kragan's ears. But he saw its chest work like a bellows and once again called forth the ethereal shield that had saved them from the inferno.

Kragan touched the elemental's mind with his own, seeking to master it as he did whenever he took control of an elemental to cast a spell. But this thing's mind was a blank slate to him. Whatever Carol had done to pull the being from its astral home had created a barrier he couldn't penetrate.

The force of another fiery blast pushed Kragan's bubble backward. Something crunched beneath Kragan's boot, and he looked down to see the charred skull and bones that had once been Bohdan. The vortex of fire hadn't killed him. Kragan suspected that Carol Rafel had shredded the vorg's mind as she had done to other wielders who had fought alongside him in the past.

The roiling flames died out, and the lion's incandescent skin took on the fading orange of dying coals. Then, as Kragan prepared to drop his shield to launch a fresh attack, the elemental shimmered and disappeared.

"Abyss spawn," Draken gasped as he sank to the ground. "It seems that your witch pulled a new trick from her spell book."

Kragan felt him withdraw the will that had shored up his own and took a seat beside the wielder in black. He tried to still the tremors in his hands but gave up. He felt wrung out, as weak as a newborn babe.

An unpleasant conviction framed itself in his mind.

Somewhere, somehow, Carol Rafel had acquired one of Landrel's shards.

26

Endar Pass
YOR 416, First Day of Summer

Alan led his Forsworn out of the time-mists a hundred paces from the forward lines of the bulk of his legion. Derek Scot and a half dozen of his scouts guided them to the place where they would make the passage of lines. He greeted Commander Vontay, and the two watched as Tudor led the Forsworn past the forward defensive positions. As his warriors walked by, Alan counted the survivors.

Despite Kim's incredible efforts, every member of the Forsworn had suffered injury. Of the more than one thousand who had gone on the raid, only 487 remained alive according to a hasty count. Alan had lost more than half his fighters.

The price these brave warriors had paid added to the weight on his shoulders that made it difficult to breathe. That all those who pledged their lives to serve the Chosen knew exactly what they were signing up for didn't lessen his responsibility. Alan's only consolation was that Kat, Quincy, and Tudor still lived.

He lifted his far-glass to his eye, focusing on the masses of Kragan's army struggling to restore order. They weren't preparing to attack, at least not this evening. They spread out horizontally for leagues, setting up camps as more of the rear columns arrived.

Commander Vontay placed a hand on his shoulder.

"I'm sorry to trouble you, Lord Alan, but two Endarian emissaries have arrived. They've made urgent requests to speak with you and Lorness Carol."

"What about Prince Galad and Princess Kimber?"

"They weren't invited."

Considering how the siblings had been treated on their last visit to their homeland, he wasn't surprised. Alan looked down at himself. He was covered with blood in varying states of dryness, some of it his own. He hadn't even had time to sponge the gore from his ax.

Every part of his body ached, and he was hungry. But his thirst dominated. Early in the fight, something had punctured his waterskin and he hadn't wanted to ask one of his followers to share what they carried.

"I need water. Then you can take me to the emissaries."

Vontay handed Alan his full waterskin, watched him take a long pull, and then refused its return.

"Keep it. I'll get another."

When Alan reached the spot where a tent had been erected beneath the pines, he pulled back the flap, surprised to see that Carol and Arn were seated on the ground beside the two Endarians. Carol looked pristine in her color-shifting Endarian uniform, and Arn's black pants and shirt were unstained.

Alan noted that he carried a variety of odors into the tent with him, blood, sweat, and offal among them. He was too heartsick and weary to care.

Carol spoke first.

"Lord Alan, let me introduce you to High Councillors Sersos and Devan."

Alan seated himself beside Carol. He remembered the white-haired Endarian woman, but if he had seen Sersos when he had been in the Endarian palace, he didn't recall.

Alan merely nodded. They were members of the High Council that had overthrown Queen Elan and expelled Kimber and Galad from their kingdom. So yes, that was all the respect he would show them.

Sersos broke the awkward silence. "King Kelond bids me to tender his regards to you, Lord Alan, and you, Lorness Carol. However, I will be blunt. Our purpose in coming here is to ascertain the motives which drove you to violate our borders, bringing thousands of armed warriors and two banished former members of Endarian royalty."

"Did you get here in time to observe today's battle in yon foothills?" Alan asked, pointing back through the tent flap.

"We watched most of the engagement," Devan said.

"Then you know," Carol said, "that had we not established our defenses here, Kragan and his army would be here right now."

"Why march all this way to come to Endar's defense?" Sersos asked. "Why, if you're truly committed, did you not bring more of your army?"

"Because these volunteers were all that King Hanibal would give us," Alan said.

"King Hanibal?" Devan asked.

"Long story."

"Why did you attack with such a small force today?" Sersos asked, derision in his voice. "It was foolhardy, accomplishing little."

This pompous ass was starting to roil Alan's blood. He battled back the urge to lean forward and grab the Endarian man by the throat and squeeze respect into him. Carol caught his eye and gave a single shake of her head.

"The surprise attack forced Kragan to dispel the time-mists through which they raced toward Endar Pass. It has given us time to prepare to further delay and disrupt his plans. If King Kelond and the High

Council take advantage of our actions, then together we may yet emerge victorious."

Sersos laughed.

"Your attack was like a beesting on the nose of a cave bear. Tomorrow that army will roll over you in a tide that will wash away your few thousand troops."

"Perhaps," Alan said. "But we're not the invaders of Endar. Kragan and his horde hold that title. We've made our choice clear. We're here to fight and, if necessary, die to prevent Kragan from achieving his aim of conquering Endar and stealing the artifact that sits in Kelond's throne room. King Kelond must now decide what to do."

Alan stood, glanced down at the two surprised emissaries, and walked out of the tent.

—⚊⚊—

Carol watched Alan depart without comment. Nor did she apologize for his behavior.

"High Councillors Sersos and Devan," she said, "unless you need further clarification of our intentions, then I believe we're done here."

"Indeed," Sersos said.

"One final question," Devan said.

"Yes?"

"Should our king open the way into Endar Pass for your legion, how quickly can you get there?"

Carol considered this for several moments.

"I suppose," Carol said, "that depends on how quickly his decision is relayed to us and how heavily our forces are engaged when that happens. As High Councillor Sersos so directly stated, time isn't on our side."

Then she and Arn both stood, an action that the emissaries mirrored. Carol walked the Endarians outside into the gathering gloom of evening, said her farewell, and watched their time-shaper summon the mists that swept them away.

"Well, that went well," Arn said.

"Didn't it, though?"

They walked forward to a vantage point where they could see the line of distant campfires that spread out across the far side of the valley that lay between them and their enemies. A tightness formed in her chest as she thought about what would happen come sunrise.

"I almost failed us out there today," Carol said.

She felt Arn's left hand gently clasp her right hand.

"But you didn't."

"When Kragan attacked my mind, his will was . . . strong. Even more so than when we fought him below the royal palace in Paradiis."

"We beat him there," Arn said. "He needed Landrel's help to escape. We'll beat him again."

"I should have been working to master the shard I possess."

"It's a dangerous thing to practice with."

"Yes," she said. "And now our time has slipped away."

She suddenly felt Arn's gentle grip on her hand tighten uncomfortably. Carol looked at her husband's ghostly outline in the semidarkness.

What new dream has swallowed you now, love?

—∿—

Landrel appeared on Arn's right, while Carol stood frozen in place on Arn's left. Arn looked at the long-dead wielder in surprise.

"Did you just stop time?" Arn asked.

"You did that. Just as you summoned me here."

Arn shook his head. He hadn't done either of those things. Had he? He realized that he now held the skeletal shard in his right hand. Arn had no memory of removing the artifact from its pouch. He replayed his thoughts just prior to Landrel's arrival.

Carol had been talking about how time had slipped away. Her words had triggered a mental response that Arn hadn't uttered.

Not if I can help it.

Then time had frozen and Landrel had stood beside him.

Arn stared out across what would probably be tomorrow's battle-field. The campfires no longer danced and leapt. Absolute silence ruled the night.

"Dawn should not find any of you here," Landrel said.

"Why not?"

"See for yourself. I see the same futures that you will, if you only open your inner eye and look."

Dawn broke before Arn's eyes. Alan's legion and the remnants of his Forsworn stood ready. Their enemies came running across the valley, stretching for leagues to Arn's left and right. Carol struck out at them, but Kragan and Draken had changed tactics, focusing all their energies into shielding their warriors from her arcane attacks.

It was clear to Arn from the onset that the torrent of vorgs and humans numbering more than ten times Alan's soldiers would over-whelm these defenders. Then his eyes were drawn to a shirtless warrior. He rode atop a palomino stallion at the front of the charging horde, carrying a great ax in his right hand.

Recognition pulled an audible gasp from Arn's lips.

"Ty!"

The man leading this army's attack was Arn's old friend, the man with whom he had shared blood in a ritual that had enabled them both to grasp Slaken's haft and escape from Lagoth. Arn felt his stomach roil.

The Chosen must have seen Ty at the same time, because he stepped away from the defensive lines and strode forward to meet the charge. He hefted the crescent-bladed ax that had once belonged to Ty in his right hand. The muscles of Alan's neck and forearms corded in outrage. Then, with a yell that became a defiant howl, the Chosen ran to meet the man that the horse warriors of Val'Dep had named Dar Khan, the Dread Lord.

Arn continued to watch the scene play out before him. In a clash of titans, Alan faced off against Ty, whirling in a dance of axes, only to slip and fall. Ty's ax swept down, putting an end to the Chosen. Carol shrieked her fury and despair. Her momentary loss of concentration weakened her shielding. Kragan's mystic darts tore her and Zaislus to pieces.

Shift.

Another vision supplanted the first, and then another, over and over. In none of the variations did a single person who fought at Alan's side survive.

Arn extracted himself from the dream storm. He turned his head to look once more upon Landrel. The man inclined his head ever so slightly. Then Landrel's image wavered and faded away.

The evening breeze ruffled Arn's locks. He felt the pulse in Carol's hand and heard her exhale as he watched the distant campfires leap and dance.

Arn turned back toward Alan's headquarters. He pulled Carol with him, ignoring the deep snarl that rumbled from Zaislus's chest.

"What is it?" Carol asked, hurrying to keep up.

"Wrong time, wrong place," Arn said. "We need to get to Endar Pass, tonight. I have to tell Alan some horrible news."

27

Endar Pass
YOR 416, First Day of Summer

King Kelond stood atop the Endarian palace's outer battlements as deepest night replaced twilight. The stars glittered overhead in such abundance that a portion of the sky looked as if someone had spilled salt across the heavens. So much beauty despoiled by such foul tidings.

Having been briefed by Sersos and Devan, he'd needed to get outside and breathe the cool night air. Now a group of armed guards hurried along the castle wall toward him, accompanied by two torchbearers. In their midst strode Lord Alan Rafel, his ax slung across his broad shoulders. Dried blood caked his chain mail and streaked his bald head.

The young lord looked every bit the mighty warrior Kelond remembered. He had watched the man fight to defend this very wall last year. The group halted three paces from Kelond.

"My king," the captain of the guard said, "the legion from Areana's Vale has exited a time-mist outside the entrance to Endar Pass. Lord Alan has agreed to be brought before you alone, under armed guard. He urgently requests an audience with Your Highness."

The king had spent the last hour wrestling with the decision that this man would now force him to make. Kelond met Alan's gaze. The lord bowed his head and dropped to one knee.

"Highness," Alan said.

"Rise, Lord Alan. My emissaries have told me of your battle and of your request, but I didn't expect you so soon."

Alan stood. His face grim.

"The situation has changed. My brother-in-law, the man you know as Blade, has had a vision that foretold disaster unless we made this march tonight."

"You believe he is prescient?"

"I do. He possesses one of the artifacts from Landrel's shattered trident. He has used it before, and his foretellings have yet to be wrong."

Kelond's heart jumped.

"King Kelond," Alan said, "I offer to ally myself and my people with you in defense of your kingdom."

"You would submit to my command?"

"I so pledge."

This changed the balance of the scale upon which Kelond had been weighing his decision. Despite Sersos's reservations, Kelond trusted the so-called Chosen's word.

"Very well. I accept your offer. Bring your legion through the portal into Endar Pass."

"There's one more thing I would ask of Your Majesty."

Kelond raised an eyebrow. "Yes?"

"As you're aware, the former princess, Kimber, is my half sister. She and former prince Galad are part of my retinue. On my word, they will do nothing to undermine your rule, should you allow their admittance as part of my command."

"You ask much, Lord Alan."

"And I offer much. Their abilities will be crucial to the outcome of the fight that Kragan is bringing to this place. You know what they can do."

Kelond knew very well what the time-shaper and the wielder of necrotic life magic were capable of. Against Kragan, those talents would be valuable indeed.

"Their compliance with my will shall rest on your head."

"So be it."

The king turned to his captain.

"Escort Lord Alan back to his people, then instruct your commander to admit the lord's legion, and the former prince and princess. We have a long night's work ahead of us."

—⁂—

Seeing two torchbearers lead the way, Kim watched Alan return with the guardsmen who had escorted him into Endar Pass and breathed a sigh of relief. She hurried to join Carol, Arn, Vontay, and Tudor, who walked forward to meet him. Carol lit their path with her magical light.

Alan stopped before them and pointed back toward the mist-shrouded tunnel that led through the glacier-capped mountain into Endar Pass.

"King Kelond has accepted my proposal for an alliance," Alan said. "He's granted the legion admittance to Endar Pass. Vontay and Tudor, get your people moving. I want the whole legion inside the pass and occupying the defensive positions King Kelond's army commander designates by dawn."

Alan shifted his gaze to Kim.

"Kelond has also lifted his order that banished you and Galad."

Kim felt her heart stutter. This was the first truly hopeful news she'd heard since they'd set foot on the Endarian continent. But perhaps she was overreacting.

"What conditions did he place on that?" Kim asked.

"I agreed to two conditions. First, my legion and I will submit to Kelond's commands. Second, I've given my word that you and Galad will do nothing to undermine the king's rule while you remain within the pass."

Kim almost said something she knew she would regret but swallowed hard and forced her anger down. There were far bigger things at stake than her personal agendas.

"Galad will not be coming with us," Carol said. "Arn has asked him to return to Areana's Vale with one final appeal for Hanibal to come to our aid."

"And," Kim said, "I've given him a personal note to the king."

"What did it say?" Alan asked.

"That's between Hanibal and me."

Kim saw the brief scowl that crossed Alan's features and understood. Despite his attachment to Kat, she still had a hold on him. But right now, Hanibal had to be the focus of her attraction. She had scrawled the message in her own blood, infusing the redness with life magic as she visualized the words.

Her essence would linger there as long as she still lived.

28

Endar Pass
YOR 416, Second Day of Summer

Kragan awoke before dawn from the deepest sleep he'd allowed himself in months. He dropped the wards he'd placed around his tent, stepped outside, and stretched his arms overhead. His back popped and it felt good.

He saw Ty sitting atop his stallion thirty paces away, dimly visible in the predawn twilight. The barbarian stared across the valley that separated Kragan's horde from the Chosen's defensive positions on the distant hills. It was still too dark to discern the enemy lines from where Kragan stood. Stern voices rang out from multiple directions as Kragan's subordinate commanders rousted vorgs and men into battle formations that stretched for a league to his left and right.

Draken stepped up beside Kragan.

"Something isn't right," he said.

Kragan looked around, but failed to see anything that caused him concern.

"What?"

"I don't know. It's just a feeling I've had that's been growing for the last hour."

"Well," Kragan said, "if the blind witch and her brother are up to any tricks, we'll find out as sunrise approaches."

Then again, why wait for that?

Kragan summoned a pair of elementals, one of air, another of fire. The ball of flame he created emitted almost no heat, but it shone like a small sun, turning night into day for everything within a hundred paces. It leapt from his hand to streak across the valley and cast its brightness on the hills where his enemies awaited Kragan's attack.

Then the air elemental lensed the air, seeming to pull the scene toward Kragan. He couldn't find where the Chosen and his soldiers had gone. He moved the globe of light left and right but found nothing.

"Do you think they swung wide around us in the night, in order to attack from behind at daybreak?" Draken asked, turning to look in the opposite direction.

A much more worrisome idea jelled in Kragan's thoughts. He silently cursed himself for his foolishness.

"No. They've tricked me, but in a much more subtle way."

"Explain."

"The Rafels surprised me yesterday when they attacked our flank as we traveled through my time-mists. The blind witch used one of Landrel's shards against me. Then they retreated to where their legion had arrayed its troops in defensive formations.

"I was tired, my forces were in disarray, and the day was nearing its end. It did not occur to me that the Chosen was only pretending to make his stand here. They slipped away after nightfall. By now they're back within Endar Pass."

"Does it matter," Draken asked, "whether we kill them here or at the Endarian citadel?"

Kragan mulled the question. The sorceress and her companions had proved time and again that they shouldn't be underestimated. But that had been before Kragan had acquired six of the nine shards.

"I suppose not. I should thank Carol Rafel for showing me that she has one of the artifacts. I will shortly take it from her corpse."

29

King Hanibal finished his inspection of the thirty thousand troops who stood in formation in the valley, just east of the fortress that blocked the upper end of the narrow gorge. He pulled his mount to a halt before General Garland.

"Excellent. Dismiss the troops and send them back to their regular duties."

Then Hanibal trotted his chestnut charger back to the fort, dismounted, and handed the reins to a groom.

In the past, military duties such as this had fulfilled him. These troops were ready to defend the valley should Kragan decide to attack. So why did he feel such emptiness? He didn't really want to answer that question, but he couldn't stop his mind from pulling forth an image that had haunted his dreams.

Kimber.

He recalled how she had looked as they walked through the woods and meadows on that brilliant, sunlit day. The grace with which she moved was magic in and of itself.

Hanibal couldn't quite understand the main source of his attraction to the princess. Perhaps it was the quiet confidence she exuded. Or maybe it was the way she reached out to trail a hand across the vegetation they passed, a loving touch that spoke of worship. Had he imagined what he saw? At her touch the shrubs and flowers had seemed to firm and brighten, as if they'd just been given a cool drink of water.

But her mere presence was what had robbed him of breath. Kimber had practically pleaded with him to go with her to save Endar. No matter how much he told himself that he had done his duty to his people, Hanibal couldn't shake the feeling that he'd made the biggest mistake of his life.

Her last words to him replayed in his brain.

Evil is out there. It ate Val'Dep. If I do not enjoy your full support, Kragan will most certainly destroy Endar. I will perish with my family and allies. Then he will come for you and yours. Think on it, dear king.

Hanibal felt the gaze of the guards atop the walls and of others who moved about the fortress, realizing that he'd been standing in the street for uncounted moments. Not an image likely to inspire confidence in his subordinates.

The king straightened, then strode out through the back gate, making his way back toward his castle beneath the cliffs. His advisers, including Lektuvu and Jason, had pushed him to have guards accompany him wherever he went. But Hanibal was the son of Battle Master Gaar. He had been and always would be a warrior who lived up to his father's expectations.

The hike from the valley floor up to the entrance invigorated him. The gate guards slapped right fists to chests as he passed. Hanibal had forbidden those on guard duty to bow before him. Such actions took their eyes from their duty.

When he reached his throne room, lit by torches and the log fire that burned in the great hearth, he seated himself and leaned back, his red locks draping his shoulders. Alone in the chamber, Hanibal settled into the gloom. The dankness fit his mood as the sunlit valley did not.

He surrendered to his nature. No thoughts touched his mind. For endless moments Hanibal sat there, feeling the cavern's damp air on his skin, listening to the hiss and sputter of the burning pine log, smelling the smoke, tasting it on his tongue, and watching the shadows leap and dance.

A loud *rap-rap* sounded on the door, pulling him from his reverie, sparking anger at the unwanted interruption.

"What is it?"

It hadn't been an invitation to enter, but his captain of the guard apparently had taken it that way. When he stepped into the king's chamber, Hanibal understood why.

Prince Galad stood at the captain's side. The tall Endarian's uniform shifted colors to imitate its background, creating the illusion that Galad's head floated above a ghostly body. Galad moved forward until he stood a single stride from the throne, then inclined his head in a brief bow.

"Majesty," he said, holding out a rolled sheet of parchment. "My sister tasked me to carry this message to you."

King Hanibal's breath caught in his throat so that his words came out in a harsh rasp.

"What does it say?"

"It's for your eyes only."

Hanibal leaned forward and gently took the message from Galad's hand. But before he could open it, Galad spoke.

"Kimber said you were to be alone when you read it. Your captain and I will wait outside for your summons."

Then, without asking permission, the Endarian prince turned, and the guard captain followed him out, closing the door behind them.

When Hanibal looked down at the small scroll, he was surprised to see that his hands were shaking. Ever so slowly, he unfurled the parchment. The flowing script had been written in blood that appeared to still be wet, although it hadn't smeared. He gently touched the writing with his index finger. As he made contact, smoke curled from the page, coalescing before his throne.

Kimber stood there in all her beauty, looking as solid and lifelike as she had appeared in person. Hanibal's heart thundered in his chest. He couldn't take his eyes off her, wouldn't have done so if he had been able to. Her lips curved into a sad smile. Then she approached him, her gaze still locked to his as she took his right hand between both of hers.

Great gods. She was real.

"My dear king," Kimber said. "This may be my last chance to tell you what I longed to say in Areana's Vale. I ran out of time."

She lifted his hand to her lips, the soft touch of them to his fingertips sending shivers through Hanibal's body and robbing him of the ability to speak. Again her deep-brown eyes met his.

"When I first met you upon our return to the vale, I used my life magic to forge a bond of attraction between us, hoping that I could sway you to lead your army to help us in our fight against Kragan. The price of such a casting is that the bond works both ways. Now I find myself as caught in your web as you are in mine."

A single tear trickled from Kimber's right eye to cut a glittering trail down her cheek.

"It was not a bond made lightly, considering all that I have endured, the loss of love I have suffered, and the freedom, the sweet life I have come to cherish." She paused. "But I do what I must. Kragan has come to Endar. I fear that, in the coming days, we won't be able to prevent Endar's fall. Even within Galad's mists, you will be unable to arrive before Kragan destroys us. But if you make haste, you may be able to attack Kragan while he's weakened. It's the only way you can save your people from his ultimate wrath."

Once more that brief smile graced her lips.

"Judge me as you will, I had to confess what I have done. Even though my love is the result of the spell I used to bind us together, it is nevertheless a powerful thing. Do not blame yourself for my fate. I have no regrets."

Then Kimber melted into smoke, curling back into the bloody words he held in his trembling left hand.

PART IV

When the Endarian palace is Kragan's, the dead shall rise from the catacombs. And sorrow shall reign throughout the kingdom.

—From the *Scroll of Landrel*

30

Endar Pass
YOR 416, Early Summer

Carol stood atop the outer wall that protected the Endarian palace and the city that occupied the island near the lake's south shore. Zaislus stayed by her left side while Arn stood to her right. It broke her heart to look out across the lake to see the withered forest that had once been so verdant.

Kim and the other Endarian wielders of life magic had drained the plants and soil to heal wounded soldiers. In the end desperation had forced Kim to use her talent for the forbidden necrotic sorcery that had now become her specialty.

Carol recalled her naive belief that Endar was far superior to other monarchies. The beginning of her disillusionment had been the attempted assassination of Queen Elan by a member of the sect that embraced life magic. The High Council's overthrow of the queen while Carol and her companions had been away had further shifted her opinion. The land had its own imperfections and tumult, matters not easily resolved even by the Endarians and their ancient culture.

She shifted Zaislus's gaze to the thousands upon thousands of Endarian soldiers who manned the city wall and waited in reserve in the courtyards and avenues. With the help of Carol's mind magic, Arn had shown King Kelond a vision of how Kragan would attack the pass.

Kragan wouldn't tunnel through the mountain with earth magic as he'd done last time. Using the six shards he possessed, he would use dozens of air elementals to flood his horde over the glaciers and then down into Endar Pass in waves. Although Carol could block one or two branches of such an attack, she couldn't stop them all.

Some of the attacks would flank the defenders. So King Kelond had abandoned his previous battle plan and ordered Alan's legion and the entire Endarian army to withdraw into the walled city. This would be their only stand, and one way or the other it was going to be final.

She placed her right hand on Arn's arm, then slid it down to intertwine her fingers with his. Carol knew her husband, understood how he wanted to fight alongside Alan or infiltrate the enemy army to try to get to Kragan. But his persistent waking dreams had driven him to stay beside her. Only that way could he gift her with knowledge of what was about to happen.

"They come," Arn said.

"Where?"

"There," he said, pointing to the southwest and shifting his hand to indicate several other places along the glacier-capped mountains.

"How long until they come?"

"Soon."

Three breaths later, she saw what appeared to be tendrils of mist flowing down into the basin like waterfalls. But when she focused the air to magnify the scene, Carol saw the same sight that Arn had previously shown her and the king. Tens of thousands of vorg and human warriors drifted down from atop the glaciers, settling to the valley floor thousands of feet below the bitterly cold heights. As their enemies touched the ground, they sprinted forward to clear space for those who followed.

Arn had been right. The streams of Kragan's warriors that descended from the heights were so widely separated that she couldn't have stopped more than one grouping. But here in these much more limited confines, Carol could block that magic and send any whom Kragan lifted into the icy waters of the lake, where the weight of their armor would drag them to the bottom.

Besides, she was going to make sure that Kragan and his fellow wielder were otherwise engaged.

—◊◊◊—

Kragan stood atop the glacier, separate from the flood of his soldiers, having sent Draken to a place leagues to the north to transport those distant troops down to the valley floor. The far greater amount of magic that Kragan channeled was a steady drain on his reserves, despite the two shards that amplified his mind magic. Only those artifacts allowed him to control the number of air elementals now locked to his will.

What had surprised him was that the Endarian army had not been deployed to try to engage Kragan's horde when it first entered this wide basin. Instead it had made this part of his attack much easier than it should have been. This had the stain of Carol Rafel's hands all over it. But try as he might, Kragan could not work out what the devious witch was up to.

He peered over the edge to watch as his army blossomed to its full size thousands of feet below, his breath issuing forth in billowing puffs in the chill summer air. As the forces marched to reassemble in combat formations, he saw the bare-chested rider canter back and forth. The Dread Lord might not like doing what Kragan directed, but he was good at it.

When the last of his warriors set their feet on the ground, Kragan released his hold on all but one of the air elementals and stepped over the precipice. With a grin he allowed himself to plummet toward the forested slope far below. Wind whistled in his ears and billowed his leather tunic.

The floor of the basin hurtled toward him, the pines growing with each passing moment. Kragan slowed himself so gracefully that he swooped in to land lightly on the balls of his feet. He stepped into the narrow channel of rychly mist he summoned to carry him around the thousands of assembling warriors.

Only when he was certain he was out in front of them did he dispel the fogs. He stepped out of the region where time passed faster, feeling as if he were walking through a wall of mud. The day blossomed bright all around him. From his vantage point in a meadow atop a gentle rise, he could see the ivory fortress on the island in the center of the lake.

The gleaming white walls rose hundreds of feet into the sky, brilliantly colored pennants flapping from the tops of four towers. A single bridge of the same white stone crossed a wide expanse of water, connecting the south shore to the island fortifications. Warriors lined the span, standing erect along both sides of the bridge. The castle battlements were fully manned, the archers and warriors watching Kragan's approaching army.

The walls came right to the water's edge, leaving no shoreline upon which an enemy could disembark from boats. The last time Kragan had assaulted the fortifications, his efforts had ended in disaster. While he had been engaged in magical combat with the Rafel witch, Blade had delivered the blow that had killed Kragan's borrowed body, sending his essence back to the crypt in Sadamad.

But if Kragan died in this, his real body, his quasi-immortal existence would be over. That was the risk that came with the choice he had made to wield Landrel's shards, something that no borrowed form could withstand.

Ty rode over to where Kragan stood, nudging his steed to a halt with the pressure of his legs.

"How long until the army is ready to march?"

The Dread Lord glanced at the sun's position in the sky.

"They'll be formed up by early afternoon. We should be positioned for the assault by sundown."

Kragan put the shards that dangled from his necklace back beneath his tunic, feeling their unnatural chill from recent casting.

"Good. Move out as soon as they're ready."

Ty whirled his horse and loped away. Kragan shifted his gaze back to the ivory fortress in the lake. As anxious as he was to get inside, he would force himself to wait for sunrise to launch his attack.

31

Alan stood at the center of his Forsworn, positioned directly over the tunnel that led from the white bridge through the time stone wall and into the courtyard. A heavy portcullis had been lowered and barred in place where the bridge connected. Another had been dropped over the tunnel exit into the fortress. The interior of the passage was flooded with slowing pomaly mist. Kragan's forces wouldn't be gaining entrance that way, having to go over the walls.

Alan glanced up at the tower within which Arn, Carol, and Zaislus waited. The arched openings through its walls were barely visible in the dim predawn light. It was the same place from which she'd shielded the city from magical attacks months ago. Now Kragan was back, far more dangerous than before.

In a perfect world, Carol and Arn would have finished Kragan when they had him at their mercy beneath the palace of Paradiis. But Landrel had somehow reached through time to put a stop to that.

Alan looked to his left and right. The wall atop which he and his Forsworn occupied the central position was at least twenty paces thick.

Endarian bowmen were positioned at crenels with more archers lined up in rows behind the warriors who manned the forward battlements. The rest of Alan's eight thousand soldiers occupied the wall on either side of the Forsworn.

Beyond them, many thousand more Endarian warriors spread out along the wall, backed by reserves that filled the courtyards and avenues stretching into the city.

The first rosy glow of the new dawn gradually spread across the mountains ringing the east side of the basin. And the thunder of enemy swords, axes, and war hammers banging on shields accompanied dawn's arrival.

Alan tightened his grip on the ivory handle of his ax and shifted his shield higher with his left arm. Quincy, Kat, and the rest of the Forsworn shifted their shields into position to weather the storm of projectiles that their enemies were about to unleash on them.

One moment the cacophony hammered his ears. The next an eerie stillness took hold. It lasted for a handful of heartbeats. Then the wind howled out of the west, pulling forth roiling thunderheads that moved across the lake, shrouding the white citadel in shadow.

Lightning spiderwebbed across the low ceiling, branching as it struck down toward the fortress. But two hundred feet above the heads of the defenders, the bolts scattered along an invisible barrier, arcing into the lake and flashing so bright that Alan's eyes were dazzled. With a sound like shattered drum skins, thunder echoed through the battlements.

The magical bombardment increased as fireballs streaked down onto Carol's tower, only to be reflected toward their origin. There was a blur in the air beyond the bridge as a new cloud rose up to arc toward Alan and his warriors. Arrows rained down upon the shield wall that the Forsworn and the Endarians erected, clattering off to skitter across the ground, an attack that Carol must have been too magically harried to deflect.

A torrent of rain and hail cascaded down upon the enemy forces, and the arrow storm subsided. Then the shields behind Alan parted as Endarian bowstrings thrummed, sending thousands of shafts streaming into the enemy lines.

A white-haired, white-bearded wielder in a black robe stepped to the edge of the lake and touched its surface with his staff. The air grew so cold that Alan had to flex his fingers to keep the blood flowing as the lake between his forces and the southern shore froze over.

—⚡—

Carol marveled at the raw power with which Kragan battered the wall of force she'd erected. Ohk, an elemental lord from the plane of air, howled pain and fury into the wind, but maintained the shield despite Kragan's battering.

Carol siphoned off a bit of her focus to unleash rain and hail upon the archers attacking the defenders atop the wall. She knew what Kragan was trying to do. If he could force her to pour all her power into blocking his attacks, Draken could wield his magic unchecked against the defenders.

Then it happened. She saw Draken step to the edge of the lake and place the tip of his staff into the water. The staff jerked in his hands as brilliant worms of flame crawled along its surface. The water between the shore and the fortress froze solid.

Draken lifted his glowing staff, pointed it directly at her tower, and sent forth a river of flame. As the hissing wall of fire reached for her, a part of Carol's consciousness shifted to the plane of water, pulling a geyser of ice from the frozen lake. The two elemental forces met, turning into a jet of steam that climbed straight up into the clouds.

But the combined attacks from Kragan and Draken strained her ability to react. As they shifted tactics, Carol felt herself struggling.

It was time to do what she wanted to save for later.

—⁓—

Kim watched in fascination as the lake froze over. Despite volley after volley of arrows that dropped vorgs by the hundreds, they continued to stand waiting on the lake's south shore.

With a sound like a thousand teakettles boiling, a geyser of ice intercepted a river of fire that rushed toward Carol's tower. Then she saw Draken raise the hand that didn't hold his staff, sweeping it outward, palm down.

Bubbles formed on the surface of the ice. Then they began to pop. From each of these icy pustules, fist-size blue-and-white spiders emerged to scuttle toward the great wall by the thousands.

Kim leaned forward through a crenel to peer down. When the first wave of the creatures reached the wall, they froze to the time stone. The ones who followed climbed over the bodies of their frozen fellows until they stuck to the vertical surface a little higher. A burst of understanding pulled a gasp from Kim's lips. These things were building a lattice up the wall.

No wonder the distant vorgs weren't carrying ladders.

She stepped back to allow the archer she stood beside more room to aim and fire. She positioned herself behind a knot of Forsworn that had Alan, Kat, and Quincy at its center. To her right she saw Tudor grip his war hammer and yell.

A shirtless warrior stepped out onto the lake, an ax in his right hand. It seemed as though he stared right through her. Dear gods, how she had wept as the funeral pyre had burned his body to ash.

Just as Arn had said, Ty was reborn.

—⁓—

Arn had seen the results of the ice-spider spell before it had been cast, seen the vorgs swarm up the walls to fall upon the defenders atop it.

But in any of the visions where Carol diverted energy from defending herself against Kragan's attacks, she died. So he gripped the shard that amplified his time-sight and concentrated on showing her only the most pressing of futures. Too much and the visions would overwhelm her.

A new dreamscape blossomed so brilliantly in Arn's mind's eye that it drew his focus away from Carol. Vorgs climbed the wall in dozens of places. Kim stood behind Alan, slaying vorgs to heal wounded allies. But a hundred paces east of where the Forsworn held their ground, Ty reached the top of the wall at a seam between the Endarians and Alan's legion. Ty's ax split an Endarian warrior's shield and armor. The blow hurled the warrior backward with such force that it knocked down a half dozen of his fellow defenders.

Ty shifted and spun, his ax felling three defenders with one stroke. No blade touched his skin. Vorgs surged into the opening Ty created, throwing themselves into the gap between the legion and the Endarians in waves. The Endarians fell back before the furious assault. Their lines buckled and failed. Vorgs poured down into the courtyard before the reserves could block their advance.

In moments the situation went from bad to disastrous as Ty led a charge that trapped Alan's legion atop the wall, where it was attacked front and rear. And the vorg breakthrough also isolated the tower within which Carol fought.

Arn hadn't meant to share his vision with Carol, but she witnessed what was about to happen and reacted in desperation. She directed Arn's gaze toward the spot where Alan fought in the present, linked her mind to her brother's, and showed him what she'd just seen.

Arn tackled Carol to the ground as a dozen silvery bolts streaked into the spot where she'd just stood. Agony exploded in his left shoulder and his blood sprayed Carol's face as he landed atop her. He tried to catch himself, but his left arm buckled.

Arn's head slammed into the wall and the world spun away into oblivion.

—⟋ɲᴧ⟍—

Alan bashed the biggest of the vorgs who faced him with his shield, knocking the warrior backward over the wall. His whirling ax took the head of the second vorg, while Kat hamstrung the third and then cut its throat as it fell.

The sound of steel on steel, the battle cries of the living, and the wails of the dying formed a cacophony that almost drowned out the thunder. Almost.

Then his sister was in his head, delivering one of Arn's visions of what was about to happen. He stumbled, and Quincy stepped past him to impale the next vorg who climbed over the battlements.

Alan straightened and bellowed the command that would shock his followers to their core.

"Abandon the wall. Fall back to the courtyard."

For a moment everything seemed to freeze. Then Tudor and Commander Vontay echoed his call. All around him, the Forsworn and the rest of his legion began withdrawing from their former positions. The rearmost soldiers descended to the courtyard quickly while Alan and those at the front fought a delaying action to give the others time to retreat to fallback positions among the Endarian rear guard.

His shield deflected a crossbow bolt that nicked his left temple as it hurtled past. Like all head wounds, it bled more than it hurt, dimming the sight of his left eye behind a red curtain. Alan expected to feel Kim's healing magic, but a rearward glance showed she was no longer nearby.

Alan bellowed his rage at his enemies, dropped his shield, and attacked. He split one vorg from head to belly, caught the sword arm of another in a bone-crushing grip and sent him screaming from the wall. He wielded the great crescent-bladed ax with both hands, gripping its blood-soaked ivory haft.

Then, as Alan threw himself into a cluster of vorgs, their battle cries transformed into dread-filled moans.

—◊—

Kim felt the undulation in life force like a wave breaking on shore. There was no doubt in her mind what had produced the disruption. As much as the thought of leaving Alan and his men to fight without her healing presence disturbed Kim, she had no choice but to obey the call that summoned her.

She pushed her way through the soldiers and down the steps to the courtyard below. Among the Endarian soldiers who waited in reserve to get into the fight, she saw several of her fellow life magic wielders. Many more were already on the outer wall, wielding the necrotic version of life magic that had long been forbidden within Endar.

But Elan was no longer queen, and desperation had driven King Kelond to command that it be used against this enemy. They had little choice. Too little vegetation remained alive here for life wielders to draw upon, so they would steal it from their enemies.

Kim ran back through the palace gardens, past the fountains, and up to the massive front doors. The captain of the guard held up a hand to halt her. But as he did so, Kim gently funneled a bit of health from the three dozen guards who stood in formation behind him. The rush of holding that extra life essence within her pushed back the pall of gloom the thick clouds had produced.

She wove the magic into her voice as she spoke.

"Captain Jovec. Has King Kelond not instructed you to allow me access to the palace?"

The captain's eyes widened, as if he were seeing her for the first time.

"Indeed, he has."

"Please have your guards stand aside. I have an urgent message for the king's ears alone. He will be angry if I'm delayed. Would you escort me to the throne room?"

For a moment the captain stood there in indecision. Then he turned away.

"Follow me."

When they reached the throne room, Jovec again ordered the guards on duty to stand aside as he ushered Kimber through the twelve-foot-tall double doors. The king sat on the jade throne atop the terraced dais that elevated it two paces above the floor.

Kim's eyes took in the room with which she had grown so familiar over the years of her mother's rule. Flying buttresses in groups of four supported arches that braced a ceiling laced with the constellations of the night skies. A turquoise carpet with an elaborately embroidered sun at its center covered the floor. With the exception of a lone pedestal against the western wall, the chamber was unfurnished.

Jovec bowed and Kim inclined her head to the king.

"Excuse me, Highness," Jovec said. "The former princess has come from the battle atop the wall bearing an urgent message. She says that you alone shall hear it."

King Kelond's slate eyes regarded Kim. Then, with a wave of his hand, he dismissed the captain. When the doors closed behind Jovec, Kelond spoke.

"What news of the battle brings you to me?"

"It's not of the battle that I shall speak. I came because I was summoned."

Kelond frowned. "Summoned?"

Kim raised her arm and pointed to the time stone atop the pedestal.

"By that. Do you not see the discoloration that grows more distinct with each passing moment?"

The king's eyes narrowed as he peered at the white block of time stone. Its ivory-colored surface was now marred by a murk that seemed to ebb and flow within it. King Kelond's mouth opened, but no words came forth.

He stood and, motioning for Kim to accompany him, made his way to the pedestal.

"By the gods . . . ," he said.

"It's dissolving," Kim said. "The shard within has beckoned me here, when I really need to be fighting at the city wall."

Kelond quoted Landrel's Scroll, his voice so soft she had to listen closely to hear the words.

"The last of the three fingers of life magic shall rest within a time stone inside the Endarian palace until the day Endar falls. Only then shall it summon another life master to wield it."

Kim laced a bit more of her magic into her voice.

"And here I am, to answer that call."

King Kelond's hand trembled as he picked up the time stone. He stared at it, shifted the block within his hands. Then he slowly turned and handed it to Kim.

When the block touched her hands, the smoke that seemed to flow within it billowed out to swathe her arms in cool mist. Then it was gone, leaving a mummified finger resting in her palm.

Somewhere in the back of her mind, Kim heard Landrel's delighted laughter.

32

Endar Pass
YOR 416, Early Summer

Carol felt Arn's blood splatter her face while she saw what happened through his eyes. Then she landed on her back and lost her connection to her husband. Scrambling wildly, her hands found Zaislus's furry head, and she shifted her mind link to him. The sight of Arn's body sprawled facedown took her breath away. But he would have to wait.

She fumbled with the cord that fastened the pouch to her belt, slid it free, and dumped the shard into her palm. Carol shifted her concentration to the plane of air, found Ohk, the powerful air elemental she sought, and completed the summoning.

The being coalesced inside the tower as a shimmering whirlwind of force.

"Stay here. Defend this room and strike back at anyone who attacks it."

Her will, amplified by the shard, tightened a vise on the elemental's mind.

Then Carol moved to Arn's side and gently rolled him onto his back. He bled from a deep wound in his left shoulder and from a gash at his hairline. But he was breathing. She grabbed one of the daggers and cut both sleeves from his Endarian shirt, balling one into the cut in his shoulder and binding it in place with the other. The necessity of maintaining her grip on the dead finger made the task difficult.

Then she spotted the shard that had fallen from Arn's hand. Working swiftly, she returned it to the pouch at his belt, pulling the cord that closed it inside.

She heard the sizzle-pop of a fireball striking the tower, but the wind roared outward and its flames failed to reach her. She sucked in a breath and stood. This location was about to become untenable. She had to get out of here before the vorgs surrounded them. And with Kragan out there with a clear line of sight to the upper portion of the tower, she couldn't attempt to fly them to the ground.

Instead she touched the mind of Nematomas, casting the spell that helped her lift Arn onto her shoulder. It was awkward, but she managed to descend the spiral staircase with Zaislus leading the way. She felt her hair stand on end as lightning hit the floor they'd just left behind. Again the ethereal defender Ohk deflected Kragan's attack. The boom of thunder rattled her teeth and sped her feet downward.

Halfway down she almost tripped, and she leaned against the wall to catch her breath. Long before she wanted to, she resumed her labored descent. This time she didn't stop until she staggered out into the crowded courtyard. The noise of the battle was deafening. She staggered past Endarian warriors rushing to fill the latest breach in their defenses.

Carol watched as time-mists congealed, shielding the warriors from magical attacks from beyond the mist boundary. But she didn't seek time-shapers. She needed to get Arn to Kim or another of the Endarian life-shifters.

She reached out with her mind, using the special link to her half sister that didn't require Carol to see or touch her. Just then a warrior backed into her, knocking Carol to the ground.

"The wall has fallen," someone yelled. "Fall back to the palace!"

Zaislus snarled and leapt over Carol, the big dog's teeth tearing out the throat of a vorg who bore down on her in the confusion. He moved in front of her as Carol erected an invisible shield around the dog, Arn, and herself, something that was far more difficult than it should have been. Her summoning of the magical defender she'd left guarding the tower had drained her reserves.

She considered calling down lightning, but thousands of vorgs, Endarians, and warriors from Alan's legion had become intermingled in the time-mists within which Carol now found herself. She couldn't stay here.

Carol once again called upon her magic to lift Arn onto her shoulder and support most of his weight. Then she began wielding her shield to shove aside the combatants, giving Zaislus a clear path to lead her around the side of the palace.

She needed to find someplace clear of the battle where she could lay her husband down. Once he was safe, she would contact Kim and get herself back into the fight.

—⁂—

"Alan!" Kat yelled into his ear. "The wall has fallen. We have to go, now."

Her words barely managed to penetrate the fury that consumed him. Vorgs moved around him, trying to stay outside the reach of his ax. Alan waded through corpses toward the body of his friend. Quincy Long had fallen defending Alan's back. He swept Quincy up in his left arm as if the tall swordsman weighed nothing. He wouldn't leave him here to be defiled by these foul beings.

Kat, Tudor, and several dozen of the Forsworn had stayed with Alan, even after he'd gone into a battle rage. Now they were helping their Chosen chop his way back to friendly lines.

Knots of vorgs were intermingled with warriors from Alan's legion, but with every passing moment, the enemies his people faced grew in numbers. As Alan led the final withdrawal into the city, the thousands of vorgs atop the wall howled their victory to the skies.

Alan fought his way toward the palace, and the enemy parted before him, either widely skirting the group of bald warriors or making their way to the land of the dead.

"Trouble," Kat said, pointing back at the distant wall.

The white-haired wielder in black stepped to the rear edge of the wall and raised both hands. Before he could cast his spell, the mists of time enfolded the Forsworn.

—⁓—

Kragan deflected the magical darts that were similar to the volley he had launched at Carol a short while ago. It irked him that she'd survived the attack. He had seen her lose focus. His missiles of crystallized air should have cut her down. But Blade had reacted more quickly than humanly possible, as if he had known what Kragan was about to do, and had tackled Carol, carrying them both out of Kragan's line of sight.

He dared not levitate himself so that he could see directly through the high tower windows. Kragan had learned the dangers of doing so against a talented wielder on Sadamad. Instead he locked an elemental from the plane of water to his will. Although he couldn't pull such a being from its plane of existence and into this one, as Carol had done with the fire elemental, he could force it to exercise its powers. This one pulled fist-size chunks of ice from the frozen lake, catapulting them at the arches by the hundreds.

They burst in midair, hammering themselves into an icy mist against an invisible shield. The wind roared in Kragan's ears, increasing in intensity, pelting him with sticks and debris from dead vegetation. Kragan reached out to link Ohk to his will . . . and failed.

The wind roared. A rock hit Kragan in the thigh, dropping him to one knee. In desperation he clutched the shards and transferred the injury from himself to the nearest of his personal guards, who'd taken cover behind a tree.

Kragan barely avoided a tree branch that whistled past with enough energy to impale him.

"Enough," he growled, thrusting his hand to the earth, which flowed up all around him, hardening into stone.

For several moments the wind continued to batter his earthen shield before dying out. Something bothered Kragan about what had just happened. He had tried to link to the air elemental Ohk and failed to make the connection. Even if another wielder happened to already control the elemental, it should have come down to a battle of wills to determine which master Ohk would serve. It was as if the elemental was no longer a resident of the plane of air.

Carol Rafel had used her shard to summon Ohk, just as she had done with the fire lord during their last encounter, binding it here until the energy expended in that casting used itself up. Now that he thought about it, every spell that had been cast in Kragan's direction since Blade had tackled Carol had been one an air elemental could wield.

Of course. She wants me to think she's still in the tower.

Ohk was wielding magic against Kragan only in response to his attacks. The devious witch had slunk away while Kragan tired himself fighting a being he couldn't kill.

Kragan dispelled the earth shield. It melted away, leaving the ground around him as it had been. He walked out of the stand of dead trees and across the ice to where his army flowed up and over the city wall. His soldiers stepped aside to allow him to pass those who waited for their turn to climb the wall. Then he let his anger lift him from the ground and set him atop the battlements.

The time to end this had come.

33

Exhaustion muddied Galad's thoughts, but this was a task that only he could finish. Hanibal had emptied Areana's Vale of soldiers except for a skeleton crew augmented by citizen soldiers to man the fortress. He had also left only one of his six magic wielders behind. The army of Tal had marched through Galad's time-mists, twenty-five thousand strong. Now the leading elements had reached the mist-filled tunnel that was the southern entrance into Endar Pass.

Even though Hanibal had bunched them as closely as possible along this narrow road that wound up the cliffs, it had stretched Galad's time-shaping ability to the breaking point. He glanced down at his withered stump of a left wrist. He had been here before, and that had *not* gone well.

Galad allowed the mists to dissipate. The view that confronted him filled the former prince with dire portents. The tunnel stood unguarded, the time-slowing pomaly mist that filled it looming pale in the afternoon sunlight. Distant thunder pulled Galad's gaze up to the glacier that draped the tops of the cliffs. Slate thunderheads loomed over the peaks and extended northeast toward Endar Pass.

King Hanibal stepped up beside Galad. It was one of the things about the man that Galad respected. Hanibal had led his troops into battle in the last war that Kragan had launched upon Endar. Now that he'd named himself king of Tal, he was leading from the front instead of issuing orders from a position of safety.

"No guards," Hanibal said.

"That means trouble on the other side."

"Do you think Kragan will be guarding the far end?"

"He didn't bother last time. I don't think he'll do so now."

"So how do we do this?" Hanibal asked.

"It will take too long to march your army through the pomaly mist. It would take too long even if there were no time-slowing mist within. The passage has to be made quickly."

Hanibal turned his eyes on Galad, concern etching his features.

"You look tired. Perhaps if you rest a bit we could—"

"Every moment I rest, more of my people and your people die. Kimber might be one of them."

King Hanibal gave a curt nod. "Then let us not keep Kragan waiting."

"I'll have to move your soldiers through in groups of a few thousand at a time," Galad said.

"How will you do it?"

"I will envelop the first group in a matching fog and they will march into Endar Pass. Then I will go back and bring the next bunch through. I will repeat this cycle until I have transported all soldiers into the pass."

Galad saw the concerned look return to the king's face. Then Hanibal nodded and turned to give orders to his commander. The tunnel again drew Galad's gaze. He took a deep breath and channeled time.

As the slowing haze cleared, a slate rychly mist replaced it and a balancing bank of pomaly fog formed in the canyon below where Galad stood. If he had been fresh, this wouldn't have been a big challenge. But now the effort left him panting.

He watched the first batch of Talian warriors march into the tunnel, then went back for the next group. Each time he repeated this, he had to go farther and farther down the road. Despite the coolness of the mountain air, sweat rolled down his face and stung his eyes. Galad gritted his teeth and continued. When he followed the last of the soldiers into the tunnel, he allowed the mists behind him to disperse. Staggering, he forced himself to take one step after another.

His knees wobbled, and he couldn't still the tremors that crept up his arms and into his shoulders. Every muscle in his body began to shake, but he kept going.

Just a few more paces. The end is near. Just a few . . .

His legs gave way and he felt his knees slam onto the rocky tunnel road. Pain exploded through his body and Galad felt himself lose control of the mists. He looked down as his arms crumbled to the same ancient dust that had aged his left hand out of existence. Then the accelerating mists took his legs and he toppled forward. He took one last breath as his face hit stone.

Then Galad, son of Elan, was no more.

34

King Hanibal watched the last of his twenty-five thousand march out of the tunnel as the time-mist dissipated behind them. Galad stumbled to his knees, purest agony showing in his face. The last of the mists swirled around his body, blackening as they churned.

Galad's mouth opened as if he wanted to scream, but no sound issued forth. Then the mists flowed from his arms onto his legs.

Hanibal stumbled back two steps as the tall Endarian's arms turned to dust. His legs melted beneath him, and his torso toppled forward. The mist crawled over what was left of the man. It curled away, smoke on the wind. Where Galad had just knelt, nothing but a rust-pitted sword blade remained.

"By the gods," Hanibal muttered. "That's no way for a warrior to die. Especially one of royal blood."

The king's guards recovered from their shock and raced to surround him, facing out, swords drawn as if to fend off monsters.

Hanibal shoved his way past them to kneel beside the remains of the ancient weapon. Ever so slowly, he reached down to touch it. The brittle metal crumbled beneath his fingers. Hanibal jerked his hand away as if bitten. His heart pounded in his chest, and he felt bile rise in his throat.

He swallowed once . . . twice . . . then rose to his feet.

Hanibal raised an arm, signaling for his general to come forward. The rumble of thunder pulled his eyes toward the distant lake, but from this position, a low ridge masked his view of the fortress.

"General Garland, scouts out. Get my army moving. Be ready for combat when we top that ridge. Lektuvu stays with me. I place the other four wielders under your command."

The general pounded fist to breastplate, then spun away to execute his king's orders. Hanibal's slender female mage walked to his side, pointing at the thunderheads that gathered in the east.

"Those clouds aren't natural."

"I didn't imagine they were. Can you do something about them?"

"Perhaps, when I get close enough to see our enemies."

"At that point they'll be able to see us. You've experienced Kragan's magic before. Carol says he's much stronger now."

Lektuvu lifted her head slightly, sending electric pulses dancing through the short spikes of her blonde hair. The sneer that formed on her lips told Hanibal that the wielder looked forward to testing the truth of that statement.

—◊◊◊—

Arn opened his eyes to find Kim standing over him in the unnatural twilight. He blinked to clear his vision. He felt tired, but there was no more pain. Arn touched his forehead. The blood there was sticky, but no other sign of the wound remained. He rolled his previously injured shoulder and sat up.

Zaislus licked his face with a rough tongue. The big dog was glad to see him well, or maybe it just liked the taste of his blood.

Can Carol taste it too?

Arn shoved the thought from his mind as his wife knelt to hug and kiss him.

"Can you stand?" Kim asked.

A sudden fear shook Arn. Where was his time shard? He touched his pouch and sighed with relief and placed his hand on Carol's cheek.

"Thank you."

Then he climbed to his feet and looked around. They stood beside a fountain at the far end of the palace gardens, well away from where the battle raged amidst the roiling time-mists. Lightning crawled across the sky, repeatedly striking down toward the mists, unable to reach the warriors who fought within the fogs.

But the mists were moving in the direction of the palace. That could mean only one thing. Alan's legion and the Endarian army were being pushed back.

"From outside the mists, I can't help Alan," Carol said.

"And neither can I," Kim said.

Arn removed the shard from his pouch and closed his left hand around it while his right hand drew Slaken. Then he closed his eyes and called upon his time-sight.

—⁂—

"My lord Kragan," the she-vorg messenger said as she raced up to where he stood beside Draken. "Another army has just crested the rise a league southwest of here."

Kragan channeled a bit of his sorcery, pushing aside the warriors who were trying to force their way toward the battles raging in the streets and courtyards below. He walked through the path he created to the south edge of the city wall. He stepped up onto a pile of bodies and leaned out to look through a crenel.

Lensing the air, he scanned the disciplined formations of soldiers that marched down the nearside of the distant ridgeline. He made a quick estimate of their numbers, judging them to number fewer than thirty thousand.

He spotted at least two wielders of magic among them. He was familiar with one of these, having been troubled by the silver-robed woman during the battle months ago.

"Should I alert Commander Ty?" the messenger asked.

"No. I want him to focus on crushing the remaining Endarian defenders. Tell Commander Bator to take thirty thousand of my warriors who are still waiting to get into the city and block the Talian force from reaching the citadel. He doesn't have to defeat them, just slow them down. I'll deal with the Talians once my victory here is complete."

He turned to look at Draken, who'd joined him at the outer battlements.

"Go with him. Keep the newly arrived wielders busy."

Kragan gestured and lifted Draken and the startled messenger into the air, then set them down in a clear spot on the south shore.

From the direction of the palace, a furious yell echoed above the chaos of battle. Kragan hurried to the inner edge of the wall to see what was happening. One of the time-mists within which a battle raged suddenly dissipated to reveal Ty, striding forward dragging a dead Endarian by the neck with his left hand. Ty hurled the corpse to the ground, and Kragan's vorgs poured around him to attack the shocked mist warriors.

Then Ty, bloody ax in hand, strode into another wall of mist. And hundreds of battle-maddened vorgs followed his lead.

Very soon now, the Dread Lord and his followers would overrun the Endarian palace. Then Kragan would hunt down Carol Rafel and end the threat she posed. He thought of Landrel and smirked.

"Tell me, time seer, what do you think of your prophecy now?"

Having laid Quincy's body on the palace steps, Alan stepped back into the mists within which his Forsworn fought a hopeless battle. Only threescore remained fighting alongside several hundred Endarian mist warriors. And this group of Endarians had just lost their last healer. It took Alan only moments to reach the place at the center where Tudor dealt death with each swing of his hammer.

But as he stepped into the gap where one of Tudor's clansmen had just fallen, he heard Kat cry out on his left. He saw her collapse onto her back. Her hands clutched at the blade of the sword with which a big vorg had just gutted her. Then, for the briefest of moments, her eyes locked with Alan's, just before they froze, wide open. The vorg pulled his sword free, bared his canines, and howled.

Alan lost his mind.

He leapt forward, the great ax whistling through the air to cleave the vorg's shield and bury itself in his sternum. Alan kicked the warrior back into those who pressed forward to get at him. One moment he was standing there. The next he whirled, his ax blurring into a sweep that cut three enemies in half.

Before the nearest of the vorgs could realize that they were next, Alan was on top of them, a savage yell tearing itself from his lungs. Blood fountained to rain down on him and everyone around him. Kragan's warriors tried to retreat before him, but the press of their fellows blocked their flight. Alan seized one by the neck, snapping it in one motion as his ax took the head of another. A blade penetrated his side, but he barely felt it.

Suddenly the vorgs parted before him, revealing a man Alan had never thought he would meet again in this life. Every other warrior stepped aside.

Ty stepped forward, his hands gripping an ax, his chest and body bathed in blood as well. Alan saw recognition and something that might have been sorrow in those blue eyes.

Tudor stepped to his side but backed off when Alan angrily signaled to him to get away.

Alan matched Ty's stance. They moved as one, their ax handles meeting with bone-jarring force. They grappled, each with one hand on the other's weapon. As Alan pressed his ax slowly toward Ty's neck, the taller warrior tripped him. Locked together, they tumbled into the side of a fountain. Ty landed atop Alan, driving his back into the stone rim of the bowl.

Pain exploded in his left side, and he sucked in a ragged breath. When he exhaled, a bloody froth bubbled to his lips. Ty leaned all his weight into his ax, driving its blade ever so slowly toward Alan's throat.

Alan shuddered, then glanced back at Kat's prostrate form. He gritted his teeth, ignored the pain, and heaved. The metal gauntlets on both his wrists burst open as he lifted Ty into the air and slammed him down to the ground. Alan rolled atop his onetime friend and mentor.

Now it was his turn to press all the weight and muscle of his massive chest behind his ax. Ty grinned up at him, even as Alan drove the weapon down, bit by bit.

He froze. A vivid memory blossomed in his mind.

—⁂—

Ty lay in Alan's arms, bleeding out through a jagged hole through his stomach and out his back. The barbarian grinned feebly before erupting in a fit of wet coughing that splattered Alan with more blood. Ty's head turned, and his arm stretched out in the direction of his ax, unable to reach it. Alan jumped to retrieve the weapon and placed it in Ty's hand.

The Kanjari clutched it to his chest with both hands, a broad smile once more on his lips. "Glorious."

The word rasped from Ty's mouth as his steel-blue eyes shone with a savage light. He reached a hand out to clutch Alan's wrist, the power of the grip threatening to break bone.

"I'll await you on the other side. When I have made the crossing, let no other touch my ax. I want you alone to use it. You can return it when we meet again. Do I have your word?"

"You have it."

Alan gripped Ty's face in his hands so that he looked directly into the barbarian's eyes. "I am so sorry that I was late arriving. If I had only been here a little sooner . . ."

Ty's lips moved, but with the words on his lips only half formed, the light in those savage eyes went out.

And as the Kanjari who had saved both his and Carol's lives died in his arms, Alan's yell of despair echoed from the cliffs.

—w—

The vision ended, leaving Alan staring down into those same eyes, clutching the same ax that Ty had given him. When he spoke, his voice rasped out.

"I honor my word."

Alan released his grip on his ax.

Ty's eyes widened as he accepted the weapon. He stared at the rearing stallion etched into the bloody crescent blade, then returned his gaze to Alan.

"Chosen of the Dread Lord. I see that I chose well."

—w—

With the return of his ax, the vow that Ty had extracted from Alan on that rocky pinnacle was fulfilled. He felt the thousand souls that chained him to Kragan's will struggle to contain the power that the honored vow funneled through the Dread Lord.

He looked up at Alan, watched him cough bloody phlegm, and let his Chosen slump to the ground beside him. Then the Dread Lord snapped the soul bands that held him in this world, taking the others whom Kragan had resurrected back to the land of the dead with him.

35

Endar Pass
YOR 416, Early Summer

Kragan staggered, feeling as if he had just been kicked in the head by a stallion. The jarring sensation left him shaken and dizzy. He dropped to his knees, retching violently. The contractions of his stomach continued, even when his wet heaves changed to dry. He was dimly aware that the magically summoned storm clouds had cleared but couldn't work up the energy to care.

When he finally managed to stand up, he gazed across the top of the wall through blurry eyes. The four thousand Resurrected from Val'Dep who had formed his personal regiment were gone. Sometime during the episode with his stomach, he'd released his grasp on the bone necklace. Now it dangled freely outside his leather tunic. Kragan tucked it back in so that the six fingers all touched his skin.

Kragan stood by himself atop a two-hundred-pace span of the south wall. Everywhere he looked lay piles of armor, weapons, bones, and ash. How had this happened? Had the Dread Lord been deceiving him, gathering his strength and storing it up until he had enough to break free of Kragan's will? Even if so, how had he freed the others?

Then he was no longer alone. The vorgs and other warriors who had been stacked up on the lake side of the wall began pouring over.

A snarl formed on his lips as he directed them down into the courtyards and avenues where the fighting still raged within the time-mists. Strangely, Kragan found that, as he recovered from the trauma the Dread Lord had inflicted, he felt stronger than before. Apparently the unconscious effort of keeping the horse warrior and the other four thousand bound to his will had drained him more than he'd thought.

He summoned an air elemental, wrapped himself in an invisible shield, and lowered himself into the courtyard. Since he didn't know where Carol Rafel had hidden herself, it was time to involve himself directly in the fight. Kragan magically shoved his way through the knots of his warriors who were trying to push their way into the nearest of the time-mists.

Then Kragan stepped through the layers of swirling miasma.

—⁊⁊⁊—

Kim watched as Arn stood before her, his eyes having taken on the glassy appearance they sometimes got when the time-sight weighed heavily upon him. When the sky cleared, it happened so fast that Kim had to squint while her eyes adjusted to the brightness of the late-afternoon sunshine. She reached out to place a hand on his arm, as if to steady herself.

"What just happened?" Kim asked, a note of panic in her voice.

"I don't know."

A deepening sense of dread clutched at her heart.

Arn's urgent words startled her.

"We can't stay here. Follow me. Both of you."

Arn turned away from the palace and set off at a rapid walk, heading deeper into the city, with Zaislus, Carol, and Kim at his heels.

"Where are we going?" Carol asked.

"To the place where the Endarians will make their last stand."

"But . . . the palace," Kim said.

Richard Phillips

"The palace is overrun. The royal guard has already taken King Kelond and the rest of the High Council out the back way. They're falling back into the catacombs. It's important that we get there before Kragan does."

The catacombs. The burial place that held the bones of the capital's residents and any Endarians who'd died defending their land. Galad had given Kim a tour when she was a little girl. Its winding tunnels had frightened her.

Arn began to jog, keeping himself at a pace Carol could maintain and Kim easily matched. As Carol worked to keep up with both of them, Kim could hear her half sister breathing hard. They turned onto a narrow street that dead-ended into the squat time stone entrance fifty paces ahead. Soldiers crowded into an arched opening in the wall. To either side, a twelve-foot statue stood guard, feet spread shoulder-width apart. Each grasped the hilt of a longsword that rested tip down on the paving stones.

Between each guard's booted feet rested a carved stone skull.

Arn slowed to a walk, allowing Kim to take the lead. She recognized the female commander who stepped out to meet her.

"Commander Namon," Kim said.

"Former princess. Your skills and those of your companions are sorely needed here if we're to have any hope of holding this place. King Kelond and the High Council will be glad to see you."

Kim heard no hope in that voice, nor did she see any indication of it in the woman's stern features.

Namon turned to the soldiers who guarded the entrance, speaking loud enough that her voice echoed down the steps to the ranks of soldiers that extended around the bend in the torchlit tunnel.

"Stand aside. Let the former princess and her companions pass."

"Thank you," Kim said.

Then she led the others into the endless, bone-lined crypt.

—※—

236

King Hanibal stood at the front of his assault formations, looking through the far-glass at the thousands of vorgs and men maneuvering to keep him from getting to the city. He shifted his view to the city walls that had already fallen to the enemy that swarmed up and over. If he let the legions that moved against him get set, then Endar would fall.

With a twist of the far-glass, he focused on the vorgs and brigands who shambled along at a double-quick pace. The formation was ragged, ill formed. They tripped over each other's feet. They were hardly the veteran, disciplined soldiers under Hanibal's command.

He turned to Lektuvu. "Let's get this started."

She raised her hands, summoning a ball of flame the size of an oxcart and sending it streaking out toward the other army. It exploded into a shimmering wall, then dropped to the ground, setting the dead forest ablaze. Three of the other four wielders under his command followed Lektuvu's example, sending forth a rain of fire that forced Kragan's wielders to extend the protective shield across all the marching horde.

The first fireball to penetrate the barrier was Lektuvu's second casting. It bounded through the enemy ranks, leaving a smoking trail of death and destruction, setting more of the forest ablaze.

"Keep them on defense until we close ranks. After that I leave it to your imagination."

Lektuvu sent another ball of flame hurtling in an arc into the enemy.

King Hanibal drew his sword and raised it high above his head, a move that the flag-bearers across his formations echoed. He brought his sword down with a rapid motion and pointed it directly at the enemy. The flags were lowered and Hanibal charged forward, his army matching him stride for stride.

Only one of his wielders didn't focus on the attack, instead providing his king with a protective bubble that moved. Hanibal leapt over a fallen log and raced toward the turmoil that his early attack had inflicted on the enemy.

A swarm of shimmering bolts struck at him, only to be deflected. A hundred paces ahead, the enemy unleashed a swarm of arrows. Hanibal made himself the most inviting target, drawing hundreds of bolts that would have been put to better use against the men behind him.

Then the vorgs surged toward him in a charge of their own. Hanibal shifted his steel shield higher and yelled his own battle cry. The wielder who had been tasked with defending him dropped the shielding as Hanibal and the rest of his warriors charged to meet their foes.

Once again storm clouds boiled into the sky, unleashing a torrent of rain that doused the fires and turned the ground to slippery mud. Wind howled out of the southwest, driving the rain into the faces of the vorgs and brigands. Lightning crackled into Hanibal's lines, killing soldiers by the dozens.

Then the two opposing forces merged with a crash that echoed from the hills.

As Hanibal parried a blow and cut the vorg down, a single thought filled his mind.

Stay alive, Kimber. I'm coming.

—⚞—

Kragan burned the last defenders at the palace entrance to ash, then followed his warriors as they flooded inside. He saw a pair of vorgs rip down an ornate tapestry and surrendered to cold fury. Silvery bolts flashed from his fingertips, cutting the offenders to the floor.

His amplified voice thundered through the building.

"Touch nothing. Damage nothing, on pain of death. Spread the word. This palace is mine."

As he opened the doors and stepped into the throne room, his heart hammered in anticipation. It froze when he saw the pedestal that Landrel's Scroll had described. It held nothing. The Endarian king had taken the time stone and fled.

He turned and gave a command at the same volume as the first.

"The Endarian royals have fled into the city. Find them. Send word of where they're hiding. I'll set up my command here."

His warriors streamed out of the building to pass Kragan's directive on to those outside. Kragan walked to the jade throne and levitated himself to sit upon it. He leaned back, clasping his hands in satisfaction.

This was exactly as he had imagined it.

—m—

Kim followed the soldier who guided them down the winding torchlit passage to the imperial crypt, where all royal and High Council dead were interred, trying to ignore the skulls and bones stacked from floor to ceiling along the walls. Zaislus, Carol, and Arn walked closely behind her.

Another time stone archway opened into the chamber that contained an ornately decorated tomb carved from rose granite. She and her companions stepped inside to find the king and the dozen members of the High Council with their royal guards.

When King Kelond stepped forward, Kim bowed her head, and the others followed her example.

"I never thought I'd see the day when Endar falls," Kelond said, his voice filled with resignation.

"That's yet to be determined, my king."

"Majesty, have you heard from my brother?" Carol asked, trying to mask the concern in her voice.

"I haven't received word of him or his legion," Kelond said. His eyes widened, and a sad little laugh escaped the king's lips. "It matters not. We shall meet death in this chamber. Kragan has routed our army. Thousands of his warriors are already within the city. They have taken the royal palace. It is only a matter of time until they find this place. When they do, they will force their way in and kill us. Or they can wait outside for us to die of thirst."

To Kim's right, Carol gestured toward a carved fountain that adorned the tomb. As they watched, it filled with water.

"I don't think that will be our fate," Carol said. "Hang on to hope."

"Hope? What makes you think I have any reason to hope?" Kelond replied.

A new worry formed in Kim's mind.

"Where's my mother? Did you leave her in the palace while you and the rest of the High Council fled here?"

Devan spoke up.

"No. I had Elan's guards escort her deep into the city before the palace fell to our enemy."

Relief flooded through Kim. She reached into her pocket and extracted the mummified finger from Landrel's Trident, then opened her palm to display it. Carol and Arn opened their pouches to mirror Kim's stance.

"Kragan seeks these final three shards. He will not wait us out," Kim said. She pointed back toward the hall through which they'd made their way. "We three will stand together to make sure he fails."

The king just shook his head.

"Do as you please. The High Council and I will make Endar's final stand right here."

"So be it." Kim was unable to keep the disgust from her voice. This man was no king, was a mere shadow of her mother.

Then she and her companions walked out of the imperial crypt and back down the hall of bones to the entrance.

—w—

"My lord Kragan." The vorg captain's excited voice boomed as he entered the throne room. "We've found them. The royals have taken refuge in a crypt not far from the palace."

Kragan slid from the throne, feeling his boots thud onto the sun carpet.

"Has anyone verified that the king and his council are inside it?"

"The force that guards the entrance wears the colors of the royal guard. We have surrounded the area and have an assault force ready. They await your arrival."

"Take me there."

When Kragan reached the narrow street packed with hundreds of his warriors, he made his way to the front. His left hand plucked the necklace from beneath his tunic. When he stepped past his commander, Kragan came to an abrupt halt. Carol Rafel stood in the entrance to the catacombs, in front of the royal guards. Blade, the former Endarian princess, and a wolflike beast positioned themselves at her side.

The blind witch sent a barrage of sparkling shards of ice streaking out to strike the shield that Kragan erected. She widened her spray, striking down dozens of his vorg warriors before Kragan could extend his protective barrier across the street. He funneled the chest wound of the vorg at his feet into Carol, seeing her eyes widen in shock.

His elation lasted a fleeting moment, when he felt his own chest open as Carol's wound healed. Kragan stole the life of the nearest vorg as his gaze shifted to the princess. Ah, another master of necrotic magic. He squeezed the shards in his left fist and shifted the head wound from another injured vorg into the Endarian wielder.

But as quickly as the wound formed on her head, Kragan felt it mirrored upon him. He funneled more health from the Endarian in a contest of who could suck the life from the other more quickly. Then the Rafel witch struck again, this time with a river of fire meant to burn through his shielding.

As wounds blossomed on all three of his enemies, the princess placed them upon him. Kragan tightened his shielding around himself and moved against the building to his left. The shift had no effect on the life magic, but it opened a path for his warriors.

"Kill them all," he yelled.

The vorgs poured through the gap. Kragan felt the Endarian princess tap his life force again, drawing his attention from Carol Rafel. Her extended hand spewed forth a wall of flames that chewed through his charging minions. Their agonized shrieks echoed from the surrounding buildings, overtaking the other sounds of battle.

His warriors began shielding themselves behind the bodies of the dead that piled up in the street. Kragan called forth lightning as Carol erected a mystic shield of her own. Somehow she seemed to sense his attacks before he made them.

But one thing she didn't have at her disposal was an endless supply of warriors. Despite the price they paid, his vorgs were getting closer to the entrance.

Then the necrotic wielder gave a devious smile and extended both hands, one curled into a fist. Dozens of his vorgs slumped to the ground like limp sacks. Wails echoed from the tunnel behind the Endarian, growing louder with each passing moment.

Bodies only half-clothed in living flesh shambled past the princess to throw themselves on the vorg attackers. Kragan extended a new shield that blocked Carol's fire closer to its source, his warriors packed in behind the barrier. He felt the shards in his left fist frost over.

As fast as the necrotic wielder transferred life from his vorgs into the bones inside the catacombs, the sheer numbers Kragan was throwing at his opponents pushed them back. Step by step, Carol and the others retreated down the steps into the tomb. Kragan followed them, accompanied by his warriors.

Sorcery crackled off the walls, water flowed up through solid time stone only to be siphoned away through the walls. The living died, the dead rose, their agonized shrieks shaking loose stacks of bones and sending skulls bouncing through the hall.

The Endarian royal guards charged, shielded from Kragan's magic by the blind witch. But despite their superior skills, they found themselves swamped by the endless stream of attackers he pushed toward them.

Kragan saw Carol's group forced back into a large crypt and grinned.

There was nowhere else for them to run.

—⁂—

Carol backed into the imperial crypt, a sense of the inevitability of their defeat growing in her mind. With Arn showing her what was about to happen, she made a decision and linked both their minds to Kimber's. His six shards might outweigh their three, but Kragan faced three people who were capable of fighting as one. As she formed that link, the futures shifted.

As she had done in the royal vault in Paradiis, she merged their joint minds with Kragan's. But this time, Kim was part of the mental mix. Carol felt Kragan's sudden confusion as Arn stepped from one future to the next, searching for one where the wielder's powers failed him.

Then, in her mind, she heard Kim begin to wail.

—⁂—

With the king's guards battling to hold back the flood of vorgs, Kim felt herself sucked into Arn's visions. They spun by faster and faster. She felt herself die a thousand times, watched Arn and Carol do the same, saw Kragan gather the shards from each of their corpses and re-create Landrel's Trident. But her attention was drawn to an unadorned tomb in the corner of the imperial crypt.

She knelt over the simple slab that sealed it, reading the poorly chiseled inscription.

"In this pauper's grave rests the father of vorgs and the king of betrayers. May he forever slumber among his betters."

She slowly reached out to place her hand atop the words. The shard in her left hand pulsed with a deep thrumming sound, and agony hurled her back into the present. She channeled Kragan's life into herself, felt him do the same to her. But then she redirected some of her health into the nondescript tomb in the corner.

Pustules formed on her arms and legs, then spread across her body to burst open. This unexpected side effect of her use of necrotic magic shocked her. She shrieked and increased her channel to tap the health of Kragan and the warriors who surrounded him. Her sight dimmed, but she saw the wielder cringe, sweat popping out on his brow.

Carol sent forth hundreds of silvery darts. Kragan's mystic shielding wavered in and out of existence. Kim felt him shift more of his attention to combating her sister's assault, and she reached deep, dragging the health from Kragan in gobs that left him gasping. Tempted as she was to heal herself, she resisted, funneling that energy into Landrel's tomb.

A low growl escaped from Kragan's lips as he hammered at Carol, dropping her to her knees before him. Then Arn blurred into motion, sidestepping two vorgs and hurling himself forward.

Kim saw Kragan shift his attack to Arn. Kim drained more of Kragan's essence into the tomb. Arn ducked aside, but a bolt of force from the wielder struck his left shoulder, sending him tumbling to the floor. Then, to her horror, two vorgs, fangs bared, flung themselves down onto the prostrate assassin.

—⁂—

Arn foresaw Kragan's attack but, in the crush of the melee, was unable to avoid it. White-hot pain knifed through his shoulder as a fountain of blood sprayed his face and neck. As his injured arm popped from its socket upon hitting the ground, a groan escaped his throat. He managed to roll, thrusting Slaken between the snapping jaws of the first vorg to land atop him.

The vorg went limp, but the deadweight slowed Arn's reaction to the she-vorg that followed. Images of his death flashed before his eyes as the ripping fangs snapped toward his neck, but he chose a future where agony shoved death aside. He shifted his weight and placed his right forearm between his throat and the she-vorg's canines.

She ripped a hunk of bloody meat away, but he didn't release his grip on Slaken's ivory haft, driving it through the she-vorg's right eye and into her skull.

Another vision crystallized before his mind's eye. Ignoring the torment that racked his body, he shoved the corpses away and rolled to his knees an arm's length from the mage who'd murdered his parents. Tendrils of red-veined blackness crawled from Kragan's outstretched right hand, trying to burrow their way through the clear bubble that Carol had erected around herself.

Wounds crawled across the skin of Kragan's face only to heal and re-form on Kim. When Arn leapt forward, Kragan dropped the spell he'd cast toward Carol and thrust his hand toward the new threat. A silvery disk flashed from Carol's fingertips to cleave Kragan's half-closed fist from his wrist.

Kragan shrieked in pain and terror as Slaken flashed in the torchlight. Arn drove the blade down through the top of Kragan's head, burying the long knife to its hilt. Arn followed the body to the floor, his eyes staring directly into Kragan's sightless orbs. Unable to maintain his grasp on Slaken, Arn let his hand fall away.

Oblivious to the storm of magic that Carol and Kim were hurling into the vorgs around him, Arn watched his blood mingle with that of his enemy. After so many years, he'd fulfilled the vow he'd made as he stacked rocks on his parents' graves. He grinned down at the twitching corpse.

As an ebony haze squeezed his vision to a pinprick, Arn collapsed atop his nemesis. Carol's cries of despair followed him into the dark.

—◊—

Kim saw Carol launch a storm of shimmering bolts into the stunned vorgs who filled the skeletal hallway outside the royal crypt. They fell before her rage by the hundreds.

With the last of her energy, Kim funneled the health from one of Kragan's fleeing warriors into Arn, mending his wounds until he opened his eyes. Then she sank to the floor and leaned back against the ornate tomb in the chamber's center. She saw Arn rise, plucking his knife from Kragan's skull. Then Carol, her hands glowing with power, pursued the fleeing vorgs through the tunnel with Arn at her side.

King Kelond knelt beside Kim, offering her a water flask. The other high councillors moved out into the tunnel, looking toward the spot where Carol had disappeared. Kim took the flask, uncorked it, and drank deeply, savoring the relief as the cool liquid slid down her throat.

Something scraped, and a loud crash snapped her head around. A naked Endarian man stood up from within the pauper's tomb, his black locks cascading down his shoulders.

"Deep-spawn," Kelond said, pulling a long knife from his belt.

The other man flicked his hand, and the blade spun away to clatter off a wall.

The name slipped from Kim's lips in a breathy whisper.

"Landrel."

He glanced down at her as he strode past but did not speak or pause. Instead he walked out into the tunnel, knelt by Kragan's small corpse, and, with one swift tug, snapped the necklace from the dead wielder's neck.

Then he stood, walked past the startled councillors, and disappeared down the passage.

Kim struggled to her feet and stared out after him with a sinking feeling in her chest.

"By all the gods. What have I done?"

36

From where he stood, directing his general's actions from atop a rise, Hanibal could see Lektuvu's target through his far-glass. The enemy mage in black, whom Galad had called Draken, had risen ten paces into the air so that Kragan's warriors could see that he still lived. Lektuvu had done the same. She held up both hands, lightning shooting outward at Kragan's wielder and hitting the man's spherical shield.

More lightning arced down from the thunderheads, seemingly attracted to the charged sphere around the wielder in black. Lektuvu increased the pressure she exerted, calling forth more and more strikes from the electrical storm.

Hanibal's other four wielders joined the fray from where they stood. Hailstones the size of fists battered the glowing shield and all the nearby vorgs. A fireball streaked in, exploding with a detonation that shook the ground. Lightning webbed the sky, branching downward into the opposing forces. And the thunder rolled.

The mage in black shrugged aside the attacks directed at him. He raised both hands toward Rombus, Hanibal's heavyset, bald wielder in gray. When Draken clapped his hands together, two slabs of stone rose from the earth on either side of Rombus, slamming closed, drenching Hanibal in a stinking fountain of goo.

Draken slashed his right hand toward Hanibal, launching one of the huge stones toward the Talian king. The slab slammed into a shimmering wall Lektuvu erected less than one stride away from him.

Hanibal bellowed his rage at his wielder, who floated high overhead. "Kill Draken. Make it painful."

Lektuvu's jaw tightened and her eyes narrowed to slits. She extended her right hand, fingers curled into claws. The electrical energy around the distant sphere transformed into sparkling fingers of blue and white that curled around the black mage.

Hanibal adjusted the far-glass, watching desperation strain the man's features. When the protective bubble popped, electrical arcs burst the wielder's eyes. The man clutched at his face, his robe bursting into flames. When his body fell, a trail of smoke followed it to the ground.

An unnatural stillness fell upon the battlefield. Then, with a collective gasp, panic spread through the ranks of vorgs and brigands, all resistance to Hanibal's attacking army collapsing. The enemy legions broke into wild retreat.

Hanibal turned to his top commander.

"General Garland, give the order to re-form our lines. I want to be inside the city walls by sunset."

Hanibal lifted his far-glass once again, this time studying the ivory citadel, shocked at the sight that unfolded there.

What in the deep . . . ?

He blinked, wiped his eye, and looked again.

Vorgs poured over the walls, retreating from the city rather than entering it. Panic swept through the ranks of Kragan's forces gathered along the lake. Military discipline was breaking down all through the enemy lines, and Kragan's commanders could do nothing to stop it. The enemy army churned as if stirred by a giant spoon.

He lowered the glass. What had just happened inside the city?

—⁓—

Landrel strode through the catacombs, the six fragments of his shattered trident clutched in his left hand. He stopped before the corpse of a royal guardsman. Landrel stripped the body, discarded the armor, then slid into the uniform and boots. The fit was not perfect, but they would do.

He tied the snapped ends of the necklace together and slipped it over his head, tucking it inside his shirt. Then he resumed his walk.

As he neared the steps that led up out of the crypt, the number of dead multiplied. Vorgs lay among guards and the corpses of the temporarily risen dead. Even from behind, he recognized the two humans who stood beside a black dog atop the stairs, facing toward the street. How could he not?

Landrel had sketched Carol Rafel's image onto the scroll that had contained the prophecy that had brought all this to pass. Arn Tomas Ericson, the assassin also known as Blade, stood at her side, bloody knife in his right hand.

Then Arn turned toward him.

—⁓—

Arn sensed movement behind him and spun, Slaken held at the ready. Beside him he heard Zaislus's low growl and glimpsed the power that suddenly glowed in Carol's hands. Then the torchlight illuminated the familiar face that shocked Arn to his core.

"Landrel," he said. "That's . . . that's impossible."

The tall Endarian with the chiseled features shook his head.

"Improbable, but not impossible. And yes, I am as real as you are."

Landrel shifted his obsidian eyes to Carol.

"Carol, I assure you. There's no need to summon your magic. I intend no threat."

Arn didn't relax. But Carol took a deep breath and let the magic fade away.

"I think you owe us an explanation," she said.

Landrel lowered his head. "That is true. However, it's a long story. First we should dispense with any of Kragan's brigands who might remain within the city walls."

"We?" Arn asked.

"If you have no objection, I would find that most satisfactory."

Arn nodded, then leaned down to wipe Slaken's blade on a dead vorg's tunic. He straightened and sheathed the knife. He had always trusted his instincts, and this felt right.

"Fine. Let's do it."

—◊—

Carol was tired and felt as if a lead weight were pulling down her mood. With Zaislus guiding her forward, she headed for the palace, the focal point for Kragan's attack. Any survivors would gather there. When they reached the gardens, the dead lay scattered everywhere. Repulsed by the sight, she spotted Tudor standing with a dozen Forsworn, heads bowed, near one of the many fountains.

Someone nudged him, and he looked up to see her approach. Like the others, he was covered in blood. But the thing that stilled her heart was the sight of the trails that his tears had cut down his cheeks. Then she saw the three bodies, carefully laid side by side before the fountain.

"No."

Alan lay faceup between Kat and Quincy, his arms crossed upon his chest. Carol stumbled and would have fallen had not Arn been there to catch her. The Forsworn parted to let her and Zaislus through.

She fell to her knees, threw her arms around her little brother, buried her face in his neck, and wept. Some time later, when her racking sobs subsided, Arn knelt to put his arm around her.

"I didn't think he could die," she said, her throat thick with grief. "Even I came to believe that he truly was the Chosen."

"He is the Chosen," Tudor said. "The Dread Lord so named him when Alan held him down in defeat. I heard it. I watched it."

Carol wiped her eyes with the back of her hand and rose to her feet. Then she noticed something odd.

"Where's Alan's ax? Did he drop it?"

"He gave it to the Dread Lord," Tudor said.

"Willingly?"

"Yes. The Chosen said something about honoring his word. Then he released his grip on the ax, letting the Dread Lord take it. The look on his face stunned me. As if Alan had freed him from a mighty burden. Then he simply faded away. So did thousands of Kragan's warriors."

Tudor blinked several times.

"I rushed to the Chosen's side, but his injuries were fatal. And there was one thing I don't understand."

Carol swallowed hard before finding her voice. "What was that?"

"Just before our Chosen died, he grinned up at me. Before the mountain gods, I swear to you. He looked satisfied."

—⟆⟆—

Kim approached Carol alongside King Kelond and the entire Endarian High Council. Kim's eyes widened when she saw Landrel standing beside Arn. But then her gaze shifted down to Alan.

Kim raced forward and dropped to Alan's side, her hands moving to Alan's throat, searching for any sign of a pulse.

She spun toward Tudor, her eyes wild.

"Did you take any prisoners?" she asked.

"We have two for interrogation."

"Bring one of them to me, right here."

Kim felt Carol's hand on her shoulder and turned to see her sister shake her head.

"No."

"But I can bring him back."

"I know my brother. Alan wouldn't want that."

Kim didn't try to hide her desperation as she rose to face Carol.

"We must do something."

Carol stepped closer, taking Kim in her arms.

"We *will* do something. We'll give Alan a funeral that honors the way he lived and died. But we won't raise him from the dead."

Another of the Forsworn ran into the garden and halted before Tudor.

"The remnants of Kragan's horde have fled the city. The army of Tal is in pursuit. King Hanibal has entered the city. He awaits on the palace steps. He requests an audience with King Kelond. But first he wants to see Kimber."

Kim wiped at her eyes and took one more look at Alan, lying there between Quincy and Katrin. She dropped to her knees behind his head and took his bloody cheeks in her hands. Lowering herself, she rested her forehead against his. If she had not left his side, she could have saved him. Instead she had answered the call of the shard that now rested in her pocket.

Kim kissed her half brother's forehead.

Then she straightened her back, rose to her feet, and walked out of the garden.

—◊—

Arn watched Carol weep for Alan, sick to his very soul. He'd known Alan since the young lord had been a toddler, watching him grow into the man, the warrior, he'd become. Now he lay dead at the hands of his hero. All of this Kragan's doing.

But Landrel had played a hand in this as well. Arn glanced up at the Endarian master of the nine magics. Landrel had found the one future where Kim would raise him from the grave. And he'd made it happen. Now he stood here, looking serene but saddened.

Kim arrived with King Kelond and the other High Council members. She shot Landrel a glare, then saw Carol over Alan's body and rushed to kneel beside the corpse.

Kelond stopped beside Landrel.

"You're truly Landrel?"

Landrel met the king's gaze.

"Yes."

"We need to talk."

Landrel gestured toward the two distraught women.

"Yes, but now is not the time. See to your people and then send for me."

Arn saw the messenger arrive, listened to him speak to Tudor, and then watched Kim stride out of the garden toward the palace steps. King Kelond and the council members followed her.

Carol locked her gaze on Landrel, set her jaw, and approached him.

"You did this."

"I did not do any of this," Landrel said.

"You intervened to save Kragan when we had him at our mercy in Paradiis!"

"Is that what you think?"

"I saw what you did."

"But you do not understand what you saw. You had the upper hand on Kragan, but that would not have lasted. This," he said with a broad sweep of his hand, "was the only way for you and Arn to fulfill your destinies, and for your brother to fulfill his."

"And . . . for you to fulfill yours." Carol choked the words out.

"On any other path, Kragan would now be sitting atop the jade throne as a god."

"What now?" asked Arn.

"Now I make sure that my trident will not be reassembled."

"You mean to destroy the shards?"

"They cannot be destroyed. They can only be kept apart."

"You've already tried that," Carol said. "Separating them didn't work."

Landrel stroked his chin, considering what she'd said.

"The fragments' guardians were not strong enough to prevent them from being stolen. I may have found a solution."

"Like what?" Carol asked.

A fresh vision formed in Arn's mind. "You need three powerful guardians."

"I cut three fingers from the skeleton of the ancient master of time magic. I did the same with the corpses of the masters of mind and life magic. While they lived, no one could have defeated one of those wielders."

"Carol, Kim, and I each possess one."

"You see what I must do."

Carol looked back and forth between Arn and Landrel. "I don't."

"Each of you has a special talent for one of the three forms of magic. It was why the particular fragment found its way to you. But one is not sufficient."

Landrel reached up and pulled Kragan's necklace from around his neck.

"It is not for me to have any of these," he said. "The temptation they pose is something I will not abide."

For the second time, Landrel snapped the cord. He carefully removed the six shards that were attached and laid them on the ground. Studying them carefully, he grouped them in three sets of two. He plucked one grouping in his left palm and held them out to Arn.

"With these two shards, I create a new time master. Guard them well."

Arn swallowed, feeling the burden of the shard in the pouch fastened to his belt.

"I can barely control the one that I already have."

"It is the central finger. That one is the hardest to master. Take these and learn."

Arn reached out to accept the gift, surprised to see the tremor in his hand. But it didn't take long for him to tuck them into the pouch.

Landrel turned to Carol.

"Mind Mistress," he said, holding out two more.

Carol held her breath for several moments. Then Arn heard her release it. When she took the shards, she did so more adroitly than Arn.

Landrel looked out toward the spot where Kim had exited the garden. His eyes glimmered with the reflection of the scarlet sky.

"Will you give the last two to Kim?" Carol asked.

"When she is ready. Right now, she mourns her Endarian brother."

Carol touched Arn's mind. Together they watched Galad fall as clearly as if they had been standing beside him. Saw the Endarian prince melt into dust. Saw Hanibal holding Kim's trembling body to his breast as he stroked her hair.

"Yes," Arn said, taking Carol's hand in his and squeezing it. "Waiting would be best."

37

Endar Pass
YOR 416, Early Summer

Kim pulled herself together in King Hanibal's embrace. With her face still pressed tightly into his throat, she ran her right hand up onto his cheek, felt the dampness there, and leaned back to look into his shining eyes. He hadn't spoken a word since he had told her of Galad's heroic passing. He'd just held her close and let her burn through the emotional storm that his news had unleashed. She'd lost Galad and Alan on the same day.

Kim released herself from Hanibal and stepped back.

"I'm okay," she said. "Thank you for telling me and . . . for being here."

Hanibal merely gave a slight bow of acknowledgment.

"I know you need to speak with King Kelond," Kim said. "I have something to say to him as well."

They turned to see Kelond and the members of the High Council watching them from a respectful distance. Apparently they hadn't wanted to disturb the two by barging past them on the palace steps. Now Kelond came forward.

"King Hanibal," Kelond said. "I've been told that you've requested an audience with me. I'm anxious to hear what you have to say. But please, let us discuss these events in my audience chamber."

"Kimber will accompany me."

King Kelond glanced at Kim.

"She's performed admirably in defense of our kingdom. She is welcome."

"Should not Lorness Carol and Arn be included?" Kim asked.

"Indeed. I offered them as much. They said they would be along after they spoke with Landrel."

When Kelond said the ancient wielder's name, his lips curled into a worried frown. Kim shared his trepidation. She'd watched Landrel take the six shards of his trident from Kragan's corpse. If the resurrected wielder wanted to take back the other three to re-create his trident, there was going to be trouble.

Kim and Hanibal walked beside King Kelond with the dozen councillors following. Not one councillor had participated in the combat. That must have meant Kelond had forbidden engagement, quite a change from her mother's rule.

The thought of Elan under guard somewhere in the city stoked a fire in Kim's breast that she would soon release. It was good to know that King Hanibal would be at her side when she unleashed that fury. It would also be best if she let Hanibal conduct his business first. That would give Carol and Arn some time to put in an appearance.

When they opened the palace doors, Kim was shocked that the foyer had not been ransacked. Aside from one fallen tapestry, the place was in excellent condition. The absence of palace guards made the place feel as dead as all the royal infantry inside the catacombs.

When they reached the king's audience chamber, the space was much smaller than the throne room but larger than the High Council chamber and lit by numerous torches that burned in freestanding brackets. The ceiling and floor were of white time stone. The walls were covered in tapestries, depicting the scenery that surrounded the walled city. The scene on the south wall shoved a dagger into Kim's heart, depicting the once-lovely forest that had been Endar's pride and joy.

The white throne was much smaller than the jade throne. It sat facing twenty-three chairs that had been arranged in a half circle.

King Kelond seated himself upon the throne and motioned for the others to take seats. King Hanibal took the chair directly across from Kelond, and Kim sat on his right side. The high councillors arrayed themselves, leaving the two chairs to Kim's right empty for Carol and Arn.

"King Hanibal," Kelond said. "First, I wish to thank you for coming to the aid of the Endarian people. Without your timely arrival, I doubt that we could have prevailed."

"Prince Galad sacrificed himself to ensure that timeliness."

"Former Prince Galad."

Kim felt Hanibal squeeze her thigh, cutting off the words she wanted to spit at this poor excuse for a king.

Hanibal rose to his feet, his flaming locks draping his shoulders and framing his grim face.

"That was uncivil of you. I had hoped for better."

Kelond's eyes widened at Hanibal's threatening stance. The Endarian king glanced around, as if looking for his royal guards. A laugh almost escaped Kim's lips.

Hanibal continued.

"The former prince and princess are the only reason I arrived here. Princess Kimber just lost two brothers. I expect you to show her common courtesy."

The implied threat was clear for all present to see and hear.

At that moment Carol, Arn, and Zaislus walked into the room and halted. Arn's hand rested on Slaken's hilt, and Zaislus's lips curled back to reveal his long canines. Standing between Arn and her dog, Carol's hands glowed with a blue-white aura.

"Arn told me there might be trouble brewing here," Carol said, her white eyes shining in the torchlight. "Do you mind telling me what's going on?"

King Kelond shifted his eyes from Hanibal to Carol and then back again. Kim saw a mixture of chagrin and outrage on the faces of the high councillors. Kelond's expression shifted from one of anger to one of concern.

He held out his hands in a calming gesture and cleared his throat.

"King Hanibal, I'm sorry that my words and tone offended you. I also apologize to . . . Princess Kimber. Please, everyone, return to your seats."

For several heartbeats Hanibal remained standing. When he finally sat down, Arn and Carol moved to sit in the vacant chairs beside Kim. Zaislus sat at Carol's feet, his wolfish eyes locked on King Kelond.

"I don't need your apology," Kim said. "I need you to send word to bring my mother back to the palace and release her from arrest."

Kelond leaned back as if she had slapped him.

"I already offered to release her. She refused."

"I want you to release her unconditionally."

"You dare come into my court and make demands?"

"Think of it as granting me a reward for services rendered."

A murmur arose among the members of the High Council as angry whispers were exchanged. Fairly or not, it sounded as if most of the council members were keen to lay the blame for being forced to flee to the catacombs at the feet of their king.

King Kelond looked from face to face, judging the councillors' level of support, apparently not liking what he saw reflected there.

High Councillor Devan stood.

"Pardon my interruption, King Hanibal. But would you and the others please leave us? We have . . . rather urgent business to discuss."

Kelond shrank back on his throne.

When Hanibal stood, so did his entire party. As Kim walked out of the room, she shot Kelond one parting glance. She did not need Arn's prescience to see that His Highness was in trouble.

38

Kim watched the pink glow of dawn spread above the glacier-capped peaks to the east from atop the city wall. There weren't enough Endarian soldiers to fully man these battlements, but no living enemies remained within Endar Pass to threaten the city.

When she walked into one of the unmanned turrets, she found Landrel waiting for her. It shouldn't have surprised her. The man was a master time seer. Of course he'd known she would be walking this wall at dawn, one night having passed since the confrontation with Kelond.

"Good morning, Princess."

"Don't you mean 'former princess'?"

Landrel placed his hand on her shoulder. "Your title is yet to be determined."

The wielder was as maddeningly enigmatic as the scroll he had penned.

"What did you want to see me about?"

"These," Landrel said, holding out two shards of magic amplification, "are for you, Life Mistress."

Kim stared down into his upraised palm, thunderstruck. It took her several moments to find her speech.

"All I ask is that you protect them as long as you shall live."

Kim reached out, hesitated, and then gently plucked the shards from Landrel's hand. The magic thrummed through her, and she felt her nostrils flare.

"Exhilarating, isn't it?" Landrel said.

"Dangerously so."

"I'm sure you're up to the task," he said. "It's why I chose you."

"You said to protect these as long as I live. Doesn't that place them at risk when I die?"

Landrel smiled, his eyes kind.

"That's why I have come back. Then I will need to find your successor. Never fear, I will keep watch."

Landrel turned to look out through the eastern archway.

"Daybreak is upon us. It is time for my meeting with the High Council. Then I think the time for my departure will soon be upon me."

"Where will you go?"

He paused, leaning forward slightly in contemplation.

"Only time will tell."

—◇—

Landrel stepped into the council chambers and stopped as the lone royal guard closed the door behind him. Although he'd already experienced this in his visions, the sense of strife that hung in the air was palpable. Thirteen chairs had been arranged in a semicircle with an empty chair at its center. King Kelond, sitting facing Landrel, swept his hand toward the empty seat.

"Please be seated, Master Landrel," Kelond said.

He strode forward, moved the chair aside, and took its place on the floor.

"I prefer to remain standing."

The king frowned but said, "As you wish."

Landrel studied the faces of the assemblage, noting the tension in each one's features.

"Why have you returned to the world of the living?" Kelond asked.

"I stand before you because former princess Kimber saw fit to funnel the life of Kragan and some of his minions into my bones. Each of you sits here instead of rotting in the crypt because of Kimber's, Carol's, and Arn's magical efforts on your behalf. In fact, it was Kimber's and Galad's magics that summoned King Hanibal to Endar's aid. Dwell on that, High Councillors."

Again Landrel surveyed the assemblage, performing a count of the shades of their emotional auras, which ranged from furious magenta to the gentle greens of agreement.

"One who's been banished should *not* deign to lecture us," Kelond said.

But there was the barest hint of dread in his voice. The king sensed what Landrel already knew was about to happen.

Devan, the oldest of the councillors, rose to her feet. She walked forward to stand before the wielder.

"Time seer," she said, "this court deserves to hear your advice. How can we best restore Endar to its previous glory?"

"Councillor," King Kelond said, "return to your seat. I haven't granted you the floor."

The old woman spun with surprising grace. Her voice rang with outrage.

"You haven't granted me? This council has given you the kingship. What great and mighty things have you accomplished in that role? Is Endar better off today than when Queen Elan ruled? At your direction we chose to run away and try to hide within the catacombs when each and every one of us should have been fighting to hold the wall. Do not speak of granting me the floor. I have taken my spot and will not yield it until I have had my say."

Landrel saw eight of the thirteen heads nod in agreement. Kelond's lips moved, but he didn't speak. Devan stared the king into silence.

Once more, she turned to face Landrel. "Should we replace Kelond with Elan?"

A collective gasp whispered through the chamber.

"Given all that's happened, I don't think that would be your best choice of action."

From the corner of Landrel's eye, he saw the king and the few allies he retained on the council relax.

"What is your recommendation?" Devan asked.

"The answer to your question is self-evident. To what Endarian does everyone in this room, including myself, owe their lives? To whom does the kingdom of Endar owe its survival?"

As if drawn from their lips by Landrel's magic, a single name softly sounded.

"Princess Kimber."

"Do not listen to this traitorous mage," Kelond said, desperation thick on his tongue. "As your king, I command it."

Devan ignored him and turned to scan her fellow council members.

"As most senior among you, I call for an immediate tally. Would everyone on this council who thinks Kelond remains worthy of ruling our land please stand and be counted?"

Kelond rose, as did Sersos and two others, their faces livid.

Without pausing to allow them to object, Devan continued.

"Now, those of you who feel Kimber has earned the right to lead this kingdom, please stand and step forward."

Eight councillors stood and stepped toward Devan. Then she took her place in the midst of them and turned her back on Kelond, as if he had ceased to exist.

"Master Landrel," she said. "Would you relay the will of the High Council to Queen Kimber?"

A warmth blossomed within Landrel's breast. Knowing that something was going to happen was never as affecting as watching the events unfold.

"It will be my honor to do so."

Then the wielder turned and walked out through the door that the last of the Endarian royal guards opened before him.

—᠊ᢍ᠊—

It was midmorning when Arn found Kim sitting in the palace gardens.

"Good morning," he said.

"Today is better."

"So Landrel told you of the High Council's decision?"

She paused, a distant look in her eyes as she gazed at the sky.

"They have named me queen of Endar."

"And they released your mother. Did Landrel give you the last two shards?"

Kim reached into her pocket. She extended her right hand, palm up, to reveal the three ancient shards that had formed a single prong of Landrel's Trident.

"Think of it. He manipulated all of this through his prophecy. He brought us all together at this spot so that I would resurrect him. Does that worry you?"

"It would if he had not gifted us the shards. It's hard to see evil intent in that act."

"He proclaimed that we three are now the guardians," Kim said. "Then he departed. He didn't say where he will go."

Arn held out his hand and she took it, pulling herself back to her feet. Kim embraced Arn with such vigor that he felt his neck pop.

When she released him, he said, "I should share good news with you more often."

Kim's face clouded, sadness replacing the hope that had just graced it.

"Does Mother know about Galad?"

"No. The council thought that you should be the one to tell her."

Kim pursed her lips.

"We will consign Alan's body to the flames at sunset," Arn said.

"I wish I could place my brother's body beside that of my half brother, that we might honor their sacrifice together."

Arn placed a hand on her shoulder.

"Even though Galad's body is no more, we will honor them both."

"Where will the funeral take place?" Queen Kimber asked.

"The pyre is being erected on the lakeshore south of the bridge. King Hanibal has ordered the army of Tal to stand in formation throughout the ceremony to honor Alan."

"He is a good king."

Arn frowned, then slowly nodded.

"He has proven himself," he admitted. "And Carol has no desire to rule in the vale."

"Will the two of you remain there?"

"No. I think we'll return to Misty Hollow. It's a peaceful place. For a time we were happy there."

Kim leaned in and kissed him on the cheek.

"I'll go check on my mother now."

"Until sunset, then," Arn said.

"Until sunset."

Arn watched Kim turn away and walk toward the palace. She had been his friend and traveling companion since long before she became his sister-in-law and then a legendary mistress of life magic. And now queen.

He sighed. He was going to miss her deeply.

—⚒—

Carol stood beside Arn, hand in his, petting Zaislus's head with the other. Alan lay atop the twenty-foot-high pyramid of dried wood, face up toward the sky for all to see. He wore the bloody armor he had died in. King Hanibal stood beside Queen Kimber, who wore a lovely turquoise gown trimmed with glittering beads that reflected the orange sky. Twenty thousand Talian soldiers stood in formation on the west side of the pyre. The six thousand Endarian soldiers who'd survived the battle stood opposite Hanibal's force.

At the moment the sun sank below the horizon, six Endarian and six Talian soldiers put torch to tinder. The flames raced inward and upward, fanned by the evening breeze. The blaze crackled and popped as the flames chewed at Alan's corpse.

Carol wept unashamedly and saw that Kimber did as well. The inferno grew brighter, bathing the ivory bridge and city wall in orange. Carol lowered her eyes, unable to watch anymore.

Hanibal's startled exclamation was echoed by the nearest soldiers, and it drew Carol's gaze back to the conflagration. Something was wrong. The center of the tower of flame darkened into an obsidian portal as she watched. Alan sat up from his charred remains, his ethereal form semitransparent. Then he stood, facing the black passage through the center of the blaze.

The fire licked the edges of the tunnel and a lone figure emerged, a magnificent, shirtless warrior bearing a crescent-bladed ax.

Ty.

Carol's heart tried to climb from her chest.

Ty extended his hand, and Alan's body solidified. Carol's brother stepped forward to clasp forearms with his friend and mentor. The passage widened and brightened to reveal Quincy and Kat standing behind the Dread Lord. The tunnel through the blaze grew brighter still as the light of the fire bled through it.

Hundreds, then thousands, of warriors moved into the expanding light behind Quincy and Kat, the fire reflecting from their shaved heads. As one, they slapped their right fists to their chests. Alan returned their salute. From this angle, Carol saw a wide grin spread across her brother's face, a look of joy such as she hadn't seen for a long time.

Ty turned and ushered Alan forward. From the shadowy murk of the tunnel, Prince Galad stepped alongside Alan. Carol heard Kim's sharp intake of breath at the sight. Movement in the ranks behind her tore Carol's rapt gaze from the vortex within the bonfire to the eighteen Forsworn survivors who marched forward as one, with Tudor in the lead, following Alan into the land of the dead.

No flame touched these living warriors as they stepped through the portal. As the last of them crossed the threshold, the portal collapsed, as did the entire pyre, sending a fiery whirlwind spiraling into the twilight sky. The wind howled out of the southeast, stinging Carol's cheeks and scouring clean the spot where the pyre had stood. The flaming sticks and embers arced out over the lake and disappeared.

True to his legend, the Chosen of the Dread Lord had recruited a legion of the world's greatest warriors. They had pledged their lives to his service, despite believing that almost all of them were destined to fight alongside their Chosen in the land of the dead.

Carol felt Arn catch her and realized her knees had given way beneath her. The thousands of onlookers stood in stunned silence. But their military discipline held them in place.

Carol righted herself, caught her breath, and spoke three words.

"Goodbye, little brother."

Then she took Arn's hand, turned, and walked away, Zaislus at her side.

—◊—

The next morning dawned beneath a gray sky. Arn stood atop the city wall, staring across the water toward the desolate deadlands that this once-beautiful place had become. He had slipped from bed, leaving

Carol undisturbed. He had spent half the night holding his grieving wife until finally she'd slipped into a deep sleep.

His thoughts turned to what they'd just been through. Finally, after all these years, Arn had avenged his parents and helped Carol avenge the death of her father and brother. Strangely, it had not been the skills Arn had acquired in becoming the dreaded assassin known as Blade that had brought down Kragan. It had happened because Arn had embraced his latent ability as a time seer. Even that wouldn't have been enough without Carol's and Kim's magic.

Arn found himself clutching the pouch that contained the three arcane shards that would certainly change him. Right now, he had no desire to make use of them. He wanted to spend the coming weeks with the woman he loved, rediscovering her as they made the long journey to their solitary mountain home in Misty Hollow.

Arn intended to take every day of that trip one at a time.

—∭—

Carol opened her eyes to utter blackness. She would have thought that after all these months of blindness, she would have gotten used to the experience. Perhaps she never would.

Zaislus nuzzled her left hand, and she stroked his ear. But she didn't make the mental connection to her dog. Too many thoughts elbowed their way past each other on their way into her head.

When she had been twenty, living in her father's keep, she'd entertained dreams of becoming the leader of her people who would free them from the whims of a monarchy. She'd wanted to create a government where laws were passed according to the will of the governed. Somewhere along the way, Carol had given up on that goal.

It hadn't been when she married Arn, nor when her father died. She couldn't even blame the loss of her way upon her blinding. The realization that she would never lead her people had occurred when she returned to Areana's Vale after her monthslong journey to the Continent of Sadamad. The people of the vale wanted Hanibal as their king. Worse, most of them feared Carol.

In an odd way, it was fitting that Hanibal should be king. While Carol was of noble blood, Hanibal was not. So she had circuitously fulfilled her goal of eliminating noble privilege within the government of Tal, though she had not at all eradicated the power of the monarchy. Was there time and energy to eventually take up such a mission once again?

Carol had spent so much time trying to find and kill Kragan that, somehow, that seemingly impossible quest had become her purpose in life. Now that she and Kim had helped Arn kill the wielder who'd wanted to make of himself a god, she felt . . . what?

She thought about the three mummified fingers she now possessed. *Mind Mistress.* It had a nice ring to it.

Being a guardian with Arn and Kim sounded like a great, worthy purpose. In addition to protecting the artifacts, the trio could use their powers to secure the safety of the people of Areana's Vale, Tal, and Endar, should the need arise. In the meantime they would continue perfecting their talents.

Carol sat up, linked her mind with Zaislus, and got dressed. It was time to find her husband and get started on their new journey together.

She touched the pouch with its precious contents, smiled, and walked out of the palace. Zaislus sniffed, and Carol caught her lover's scent on the midmorning breeze. The call of the adventure that awaited them both pulled her to his side atop the wall.

Kim walked across the ivory bridge. Queen of Endar. King Hanibal met her midspan.

"Would you walk with me along the lakeshore?" he asked.

Kim regarded him, looking directly into his shining eyes. She had known when she'd cast the spell that had bound him to her that every use of magic had its cost.

"I would like that."

King Hanibal offered his elbow, and Queen Kimber slipped her left hand through it. A shiver ran through her body as her fingertips touched his skin. At the end of the bridge, they turned right, walking west along the beach. Kim had always loved the way the fine sand felt between her toes. Her silken shoes stole some of that magic, but Hanibal's presence served as a fine replacement.

"I haven't been able to get your image out of my head since that morning we spent together in Areana's Vale," he said.

She stopped and turned to face him. The hope she saw in his eyes was almost childlike. When she took both his hands in hers, his touch warmed her soul.

"Nor have you been far from my thoughts," she said.

The redheaded king dropped to one knee before her.

"I have no ring to offer you, Queen Kimber. But if you will have me as your husband, I vow to love you for as long as I shall live."

Kim stared down at him for several moments as she struggled to find the words to answer him. She saw worry creep into his eyes.

"I am sorry if I have overstepped," Hanibal said.

He tried to release her hands, but she held on tight, sinking to both knees before him.

"I wanted to answer you in a manner that you would always remember," Kim said, blinking back tears. "But you have robbed me of my breath."

She released his hands to place both her palms on his cheeks.

"Were I not queen of Endar, my answer would have been yes. But my responsibility to my people binds me here even as my soul binds my heart to you. Your duty calls you back to your people in Areana's Vale. It was much the same between my mother and my father, High

Lord Rafel. Though I have lost my mother's favor because of my use of forbidden magic, I still find inspiration in her history, in the path she has trod. To care for someone from afar, from another land, while doing my best to make Endar shine once more."

And with those words, the mighty Hanibal began to weep. When Kim's lips met his, she felt the warrior king drop to both knees and take her in his arms. How long they knelt there, locked in each other's embrace, she didn't know, didn't care. Time ceased to matter.

Together on the sand, their faces and tears intermingled.

—⟋⟍—

The morning of departure dawned beneath cloudy skies that painted the lake slate gray. Arn led Carol to the spot where Kimber stood hand in hand with Hanibal. Carol stepped forward to hug her half sister, not wanting to let her go. Arn took his turn embracing the newly crowned queen, noting the sadness in her eyes as he stepped away.

He understood that emotion. They all felt it. They'd now reached the end of the shared journey that had begun that night in Rafel's Keep when Arn had warned his adopted father of King Gilbert's assassination order. Of all their close friends who'd fought side by side for these last four years, only Arn, Carol, and Kim had survived.

The guardians.

"I will miss you, Sister," Carol said.

"As will I," Arn said.

"To part, after all of our travels. Who will I be without you two near?" Kim said.

"A hero to her people. A wonderful ruler," Carol said, beaming.

Arn saw Kim's eyes shift to Hanibal and then back to meet his, their longing all too evident.

"Will you not wait a few days and make the long march back to Areana's Vale with me?" Hanibal asked.

"I think Carol and I will make our own way to Misty Hollow," Arn said.

Kim looked from Arn to Carol, a hint of envy evident on her face.

"Take care, Kim," Carol said. "If ever you need us . . ."

"Fear not," Kim said. "I'll summon you with no hesitation."

Arn jiggled the belt-pouch at his side.

"You won't have to," he said. "If trouble comes your way, I'll know of it."

With nothing more left to say, Arn and Carol hefted their packs and, alongside Zaislus, took their first steps on the long trek that lay ahead. Arn looked at his wife and smiled, visions forming in his mind that had nothing to do with time-sight. Visions, finally, of peace.

ACKNOWLEDGMENTS

I would like to thank my developmental editor and good friend, Clarence Haynes, whose talent and effort have shaped the final manuscript into something I am proud to present to my readers. I also want to acknowledge the terrific team of editors, proofreaders, cover artists, graphic designers, and publishing experts at 47North, along with the talented producers at Brilliance Audio and the great audiobook actor who performed this novel, Scott Merriman. I also wish to thank Alan Werner for his help in shaping this ending to the Endarian Prophecy series. Finally, I send my love and appreciation to my lovely wife, Carol. She is my initial reader and gave me the best piece of advice I ever received when I was struggling to write my first novel. In her wonderful way, Carol told me, "Rick, just finish the damned book. You can edit it later." Fifteen published novels later, I can assure you that she gave me the key to writing success.

ABOUT THE AUTHOR

 Richard Phillips is the author of several science fiction and fantasy series, including The Rho Agenda (*The Second Ship*, *Immune*, and *Wormhole*); The Rho Agenda Inception (*Once Dead*, *Dead Wrong*, and *Dead Shift*); The Rho Agenda Assimilation (*The Kasari Nexus*, *The Altreian Enigma*, and *The Meridian Ascent*); and *Mark of Fire*, *Prophecy's Daughter*, *Curse of the Chosen*, *The Shattered Trident*, *The Time Seer*, and *Prophecy's End* in the epic Endarian Prophecy series. Born in Roswell, New Mexico, in 1956, Richard graduated from the United States Military Academy at West Point in 1979 and qualified as a US Army Ranger, serving as an officer in the army. He earned a master's degree in physics from the Naval Postgraduate School in 1989, completing his thesis work at Los Alamos National Laboratory. After working as a research associate at Lawrence Livermore National Laboratory, he returned to the army to complete his tour of duty. Richard lives with his wife, Carol, in Phoenix, Arizona. For more information, visit www.rhoagenda.me.